## EMILY MAKES A PACT

"You *won't* fail. Look at that star, Teddy—the one just over the youngest Princess. It's Vega of the Lyre. I've always loved it. It's my dearest among the stars. I want you to promise me," said Emily, "that whenever you see that star you'll remember that I am believing in you— *hard*."

"Will you promise *me* that whenever you look at that star you'll think of me?" said Teddy. "Or rather, let us promise each other that when-ever we see that star we'll *always* think of each other—*always*. Everywhere and as long as we live."

"I promise," said Emily, thrilled. She loved to have Teddy look at her like that.

# Emily's Quest
## L. M. Montgomery

This low-priced Bantam Book
has been completely reset in a type face
designed for easy reading, and was printed
from new plates. It contains the complete
text of the original hard-cover edition.

EMILY'S QUEST
A Bantam Book / published by arrangement with
McClelland & Stewart, Limited

PRINTING HISTORY
McClelland & Stewart edition published 1927
Bantam edition / August 1983

ISBN 0-553-23323-0

**BANTAM BOOKS**
TORONTO · NEW YORK · LONDON · SYDNEY

RL6, IL age 11 and up

EMILY'S QUEST

*A Bantam Book / published by arrangement with
Harper & Row, Publishers, Inc.*

PRINTING HISTORY
*J.B. Lippincott edition published August 1927
Bantam edition / August 1983*

*Bantam Books are published by Bantam Books, Inc. Its trade-
mark, consisting of the words "Bantam Books" and the por-
trayal of a rooster, is Registered in U.S. Patent and Trademark
Office and in other countries. Marca Registrada. Bantam
Books, Inc., 666 Fifth Avenue, New York, New York 10103.*

PRINTED IN CANADA

COVER PRINTED IN U.S.A.

U    0 9 8 7 6 5 4 3 2 1

To
Stella Campbell Keller
of the tribe of Joseph

# Chapter I

## I

"No more cambric tea" had Emily Byrd Starr written in her diary when she had come to New Moon from Shrewsbury, with her high school days behind her and immortality before her.

Which was a symbol. When Aunt Elizabeth Murray permitted Emily to drink real tea—as a matter of course and not as an occasional concession—she thereby tacitly consented to let Emily grow up. Emily had been considered grown-up by other people for sometime, especially by Cousin Andrew Murray and Friend Perry Miller, each of whom had asked her to marry him and been disdainfully refused for his pains. When Aunt Elizabeth found this out she knew it was no use to go on making Emily drink cambric tea. Though, even then, Emily had no real hope that she would ever be permitted to wear silk stockings. A silk petticoat might be tolerated, being a hidden thing, in spite of its seductive rustle, but silk stockings were immoral.

So Emily, of whom it was whispered somewhat mysteriously by people who knew her to people who didn't know her, "she *writes*," was accepted as one of the ladies of New Moon, where nothing had ever changed since her coming there seven years before and where the carved ornament on the sideboard still cast the same queer shadow of an Ethiopian silhouette on exactly the same place on the wall where she had noticed it delightedly on her first evening there. An old house that had lived its life long ago and so was very

1

quiet and wise and a little mysterious. Also a little austere, but very kind. Some of the Blair Water and Shrewsbury people thought it was a dull place and outlook for a young girl and said she had been very foolish to refuse Miss Royal's offer of "a position on a magazine" in New York. Throwing away such a good chance to make something of herself! But Emily, who had very clear-cut ideas of what she was going to make of herself, did not think life would be dull at New Moon or that she had lost her chance of Alpine climbing because she had elected to stay there.

She belonged by right divine to the Ancient and Noble Order of Story-tellers. Born thousands of years earlier she would have sat in the circle around the fires of the tribe and enchanted her listeners. Born in the foremost files of time she must reach her audience through many artificial mediums.

But the materials of story weaving are the same in all ages and all places. Births, deaths, marriages, scandals—these are the only really interesting things in the world. So she settled down very determinedly and happily to her pursuit of fame and fortune—and of something that was neither. For writing, to Emily Byrd Starr, was not primarily a matter of worldly lucre or laurel crown. It was something she *had* to do. A thing—an idea—whether of beauty or ugliness, tortured her until it was "written out." Humorous and dramatic by instinct, the comedy and tragedy of life enthralled her and demanded expression through her pen. A world of lost but immortal dreams, lying just beyond the drop-curtain of the real, called to her for embodiment and interpretation—called with a voice she could not—dared not—disobey.

She was filled with youth's joy in mere existence. Life was forever luring and beckoning her onward. She knew that a hard struggle was before her; she knew that she must constantly offend Blair Water neighbours who would want her to write obituaries for them and who, if she used an unfamiliar word, would say contemptuously that she was "talking big"; she knew there would be rejection slips galore; she knew there would be days when she would feel despairingly that she could not write and that it was of no use to try; days when the editorial phrase, "not necessarily a reflection on its merits," would get on her nerves to such an extent that she would feel like imitating Marie Bashkirtseff and hurling the taunting, ticking, remorseless sitting-room clock out of the window; days when everything she had done or tried to do would slump— become mediocre and despicable; days when she would be tempted to bitter disbelief in her fundamental conviction that there was as much truth in the poetry of life as in the prose; days when the echo of that "random word" of the gods, for which she so avidly listened, would only seem to taunt her with its suggestions of unattainable perfection and loveliness beyond the reach of mortal ear or pen.

She knew that Aunt Elizabeth tolerated but never approved her mania for scribbling. In her last two years in Shrewsbury High School Emily, to Aunt Elizabeth's almost incredulous amazement, had actually earned some money by her verses and stories. Hence the toleration. But no Murray had ever done such a thing before. And there was always that sense, which Dame Elizabeth Murray did not like, of being shut out of something. Aunt Elizabeth really resented the fact that Emily had another world, apart from the world of New Moon and Blair Water, a kingdom starry and illimitable, into which she could enter at will and into which not even the most determined and suspicious of aunts could follow her. I really think that if Emily's eyes had not so often seemed to be looking at something dreamy and lovely and secretive Aunt Elizabeth might have had more sympathy with her ambitions. None of us, not even self-sufficing Murrays of New Moon, like to be barred out.

## II

Those of you who have already followed Emily through her years of New Moon and Shrewsbury* must have a tolerable notion what she looked like. For those of you to whom she comes as a stranger let me draw a portrait of her as she seemed to the outward eye at the enchanted portal of seventeen, walking where the golden chrysanthemums lighted up an old autumnal, maritime garden. A place of peace, that garden of New Moon. An enchanted pleasaunce, full of rich, sensuous colours and wonderful spiritual shadows. Scents of pine and rose were in it; boom of bees, threnody of wind, murmurs of the blue Atlantic gulf; and always the soft sighing of the firs in Lofty John Sullivan's "bush" to the north of it. Emily loved every flower and shadow and sound in it, every beautiful old tree in and around it, especially her own intimate beloved trees—a cluster of wild cherries in the southwest corner, Three Princesses of Lombardy, a certain maiden-like wild plum on the brook path, the big spruce in the centre of the garden, a silver maple and a pine further on, an aspen in another corner always coquetting with gay little winds, and a whole row of stately white birches in Lofty John's bush.

Emily was always glad that she lived where there were many trees—old ancestral trees, planted and tended by hands long dead, bound up with everything of joy and sorrow that visited the lives in their shadows.

A slender, virginal young thing. Hair like black silk. Purplish-grey eyes, with violet shadows under them that always seemed darker and more alluring after Emily had sat up to some unholy and un-Elizabethan hour completing a story or working out the skeleton of a plot; scarlet lips with a Murray-like crease at the corners; ears with Puckish, slightly pointed tips. Perhaps it was the crease and the ears that made certain people think her something of a puss. An exquisite line

*See Emily of New Moon and Emily Climbs.

of chin and neck; a smile with a trick in it; such a slow-blossoming thing with a sudden radiance of fulfilment. And ankles that scandalous old Aunt Nancy Priest of Priest Pond commended. Faint stains of rose in her rounded cheeks that sometimes suddenly deepened to crimson. Very little could bring that transforming flush—a wind off the sea, a sudden glimpse of blue upland, a flame-red poppy, white sails going out of the harbour in the magic of morning, gulf-waters silver under the moon, a Wedgwood-blue columbine in the old orchard. Or a certain whistle in Lofty John's bush.

With all this—pretty? I cannot tell you. Emily was never mentioned when Blair Water beauties were being tabulated. But no one who looked upon her face ever forgot it. No one, meeting Emily the second time ever had to say "Er—your face seems familiar but—" Generations of lovely women were behind her. They had all given her something of personality. She had the grace of running water. Something, too, of its sparkle and limpidity. A thought swayed her like a strong wind. An emotion shook her as a tempest shakes a rose. She was one of those vital creatures of whom, when they do die, we say it seems impossible that they can be dead. Against the background of her practical, sensible clan she shone like a diamond flame. Many people liked her, many disliked her. No one was ever wholly indifferent to her.

Once, when Emily had been very small, living with her father down in the little old house at Maywood, where he had died, she had started out to seek the rainbow's end. Over long wet fields and hills she ran, hopeful, expectant. But as she ran the wonderful arch was faded—was dim—was gone. Emily was alone in an alien valley, not too sure in which direction lay home. For a moment her lips quivered, her eyes filled. Then she lifted her face and smiled gallantly at the empty sky.

"There will be other rainbows," she said.

Emily was a chaser of rainbows.

## III

Life at New Moon had changed. She must adjust herself to it. A certain loneliness must be reckoned with. Ilse Burnley, the madcap pal of seven faithful years, had gone to the School of Literature and Expression in Montreal. The two girls parted with the tears and vows of girlhood. Never to meet on quite the same ground again. For, disguise the fact as we will, when friends, even the closest—perhaps the more because of that very closeness— meet again after a separation there is always a chill, lesser or greater, of change. Neither finds the other *quite* the same. This is natural and inevitable. Human nature is ever growing or retrogressing—never stationary. But still, with all our philosophy, who of us can repress a little feeling of bewildered disappointment when we realise that our friend is not and never can be just the same as before—even though the change may be by way of improvement? Emily, with the strange intuition which supplied the place of experience, felt this as Ilse did not, and felt that in a sense she was bidding good-bye for ever to the Ilse of New Moon days and Shrewsbury years.

Perry Miller, too, former "hired boy" of New Moon, medalist of Shrewsbury High School, rejected but not quite hopeless suitor of Emily, butt of Ilse's rages, was gone. Perry was studying law in an office in Charlotte-town, with his eye fixed firmly on several glittering legal goals. No rainbow ends—no mythical pots of gold for Perry. He knew what *he* wanted would stay put and he was going after it. People were beginning to believe he would get it. After all, the gulf between the law clerk in Mr. Abel's office and the Supreme Court bench of Canada was no wider than the gulf between that same law clerk and the barefoot gamin of Stovepipe Town-by-the-Harbour.

There was more of the rainbow-seeker in Teddy Kent, of the Tansy Patch. He, too, was going. To the School of Design in Montreal. He, too, knew—had known for years—the delight and allurement and de-spair and anguish of the rainbow quest.

"Even if we never find it," he said to Emily, as they

lingered in the New Moon garden under the violet sky of a long, wondrous, northern twilight, on the last evening before he went away, "there's something in the search for it that's better than even the finding would be."

"But we *will* find it," said Emily, lifting her eyes to a star that glittered over the tip of one of the Three Princesses. Something in Teddy's use of "we" thrilled her with its implications. Emily was always very honest with herself and she never attempted to shut her eyes to the knowledge that Teddy Kent meant more to her than any one else in the world. Whereas she—what did she mean to him? Little? Much? Or nothing?

She was bareheaded and she had put a star-like cluster of tiny yellow 'mums in her hair. She had thought a good deal about her dress before she decided on her primrose silk. She thought she was looking very well, but what difference did that make if Teddy didn't notice it? He always took her so for granted, she thought a little rebelliously. Dean Priest, now, would have noticed it and paid her some subtle compliment about it.

"I don't know," said Teddy, morosely scowling at Emily's topaz-eyed grey cat, Daffy, who was fancying himself as a skulking tiger in the spirea thicket. "I don't know. Now that I'm really flying the Blue Peter I feel—flat. After all—perhaps I can never do anything worth while. A little knack of drawing—what does it amount to? Especially when you're lying awake at three o'clock at night?"

"Oh, I know that feeling," agreed Emily. "Last night I mulled over a story for hours and concluded despairingly that I could *never* write—that it was no use to try—that I couldn't do anything really worth while. I went to bed on that note and drenched my pillow with tears. Woke up at three and couldn't even cry. Tears seemed as foolish as laughter—or ambition. I was quite bankrupt in hope and belief. And then I got up in the chilly grey dawn and began a new story. Don't let a three-o'clock-at-night feeling fog your soul."

"Unfortunately there's a three o'clock every night," said Teddy. "At that ungodly hour I am always convinced that if you want things *too* much you're not likely ever to get them. And there are two things that I want tremendously. One, of course, is to be a great artist. I never supposed I was a coward, Emily, but I'm afraid now. If I don't make good! Everybody'll laugh at me. Mother will say she knew it. She hates to see me go really, you know. To go and fail! It would be better not to go."

"No, it wouldn't," said Emily passionately, wondering at the same time in the back of her head what was the *other* thing Teddy wanted so tremendously. "You must not be afraid. Father said I wasn't to be afraid of anything in that talk I had with him the night he died. And isn't it Emerson who said, 'Always do what you are afraid to do'?"

"I'll bet Emerson said that when he'd got through with being afraid of things. It's easy to be brave when you're taking off your harness."

"You know I believe in you, Teddy," said Emily softly.

"Yes, you do. You and Mr. Carpenter. You are the only ones who really do believe in me. Even Ilse thinks that Perry has by far the better chance of bringing home the bacon."

"But you are not going after bacon. You're going after rainbow gold."

"And if I fail to find it—and disappoint you—that will be worst of all."

"You *won't* fail. Look at that star, Teddy—the one just over the youngest Princess. It's Vega of the Lyre. I've always loved it. It's my dearest among the stars. Do you remember how, years ago when you and Ilse and I sat out in the orchard on the evenings when Cousin Jimmy was boiling pigs' potatoes, you used to spin us wonderful tales about that star—and of a life you had lived in it before you came to this world? There was no three o'clock in the morning in that star."

"What happy, carefree little shavers we were those times," said Teddy, in the reminiscent voice of a middle-aged, care-oppressed man wistfully recalling youthful irresponsibility.

"I want you to promise me," said Emily, "that whenever you see that star you'll remember that I am believing in you—*hard*."

"Will you promise *me* that whenever you look at that star you'll think of me?" said Teddy. "Or rather, let us promise each other that whenever we see that star we'll *always* think of each other—*always*. Everywhere and as long as we live."

"I promise," said Emily, thrilled. She loved to have Teddy look at her like that.

A romantic compact. Meaning what? Emily did not know. She only knew that Teddy was going away—that life seemed suddenly very blank and cold—that the wind from the gulf, sighing among the trees in Lofty John's bush was very sorrowful—that summer had gone and autumn had come. And that the pot of gold at the rainbow's end was on some very far-distant hill.

Why had she said that thing about the star? Why did dusk and fir-scent and the afterglow of autumnal sunsets make people say absurd things?

# Chapter II

## I

"NEW MOON.
"NOVEMBER 18, 19—

"To-day the December number of *Marchwood's* came with my verses *Flying Fold* in it. I consider the occasion worthy of mention in my diary because they were given a whole page to themselves and illustrated— the first time ever any poem of mine was so honoured. It is trashy enough in itself, I suppose—Mr. Carpenter only sniffed when I read it to him and refused to make any comment whatever on it. Mr. Carpenter never 'damns with faint praise' but he can damn with silence in a most smashing manner. But my poem *looked* so dignified that a careless reader might fancy there was something in it. Blessings on the good editor who was inspired to have it illustrated. He has bolstered up my self-respect considerably.

"But I did not care overmuch for the illustration itself. The artist did not catch my meaning at all. Teddy would have done better.

"Teddy is doing splendidly at the School of Design. And Vega shines brilliantly every night. I wonder if he really does always think of me when he sees it. Or if he ever does see it. Perhaps the electric lights of Montreal blot it out. He seems to see a good bit of Ilse. It's awfully nice for them to know each other in that big city of strangers."

## II

"NOVEMBER 26, 19—

"To-day was a glamorous November afternoon—summer-mild and autumn-sweet. I sat and read a long while in the pond burying-ground. Aunt Elizabeth thinks this is a most gruesome place to sit in and tells Aunt Laura that she is afraid there's a morbid streak in me. I can't see anything morbid about it. It's a beautiful spot where wild, sweet odours are always coming across Blair Water on the wandering winds. And so quiet and peaceful, with the old graves all about me— little green hillocks with small frosted ferns sprinkled over them. Men and women of my house are lying there. Men and women who had been victorious—men and women who had been defeated—and their victory and defeat are now one. I never can feel either much exalted or much depressed there. The sting and the tang alike go out of things. I like the old, old red sandstone slabs, especially the one for Mary Murray with its 'Here I Stay'—the inscription into which her husband put all the concealed venom of a lifetime. His grave is right beside hers and I feel sure they have forgiven each other long ago. And perhaps they come back sometimes in the dark o' the moon and look at the inscription and laugh at it. It is growing a little dim with tiny lichens. Cousin Jimmy has given up scraping them away. Some day they will overgrow it so that it will be nothing but a green-and-red-and-silver smear on the old red stone."

"DEC. 20, 19—

"Something nice happened to-day. I feel pleasantly exhilarated. *Madison's* took my story, *A Flaw in the Indictment!!!!* Yes, it deserves some exclamation-points after it to a certainty. If it were not for Mr. Carpenter I would write it in italics. Italics! Nay, I'd use capitals. It is very hard to get in there. Don't I know! Haven't I tried repeatedly and gained nothing for my pains but a harvest of 'we-regrets'- And at last it has opened its doors to me. To be in *Madison's* is a clear and unmistakable sign that you're getting somewhere on the Alpine path. The dear editor was kind enough to say it was a charming story.

"Nice man!

"He sent me a check for fifty dollars. I'll soon be able to begin to repay Aunt Ruth and Uncle Wallace what they spent on me in Shrewsbury. Aunt Elizabeth as usual looked at the check suspiciously but for the first time forebore to wonder if the bank would really cash it. Aunt Laura's beautiful blue eyes beamed with pride. Aunt Laura's eyes really do beam. She is one of the Victorians. Edwardian eyes glitter and sparkle and allure but they never beam. And somehow I do like beaming eyes—especially when they beam over my success.

"Cousin Jimmy says that *Madison's* is worth all the other Yankee magazines put together in *his opinion*.

"I wonder if Dean Priest will like *A Flaw in the Indictment*. And if he will say so. He *never* praises anything I write nowadays. And I feel such a craving to *compel* him to. I feel that his is the only commendation, apart from Mr. Carpenter's, that is worth anything.

"It's odd about Dean. In some mysterious way he seems to be growing younger. A few years ago I thought of him as quite old. Now he seems only middle-aged. If this keeps up he'll soon be a mere youth. I suppose the truth is that my mind is beginning to mature a bit and I'm catching up with him. Aunt Elizabeth doesn't like my friendship with him any more than she ever did. Aunt Elizabeth has a well-marked antipathy to any Priest. But I don't know what I'd do without Dean's friendship. It's the very salt of life."

"JANUARY 15, 19—
"To-day was stormy. I had a white night last night after four rejections of MSS. I had thought especially good. As Miss Royal predicted, I felt that I had been an

awful idiot not to have gone to New York with her when I had the chance. Oh, I don't wonder babies always cry when they wake up in the night. So often I want to do it, too. Everything presses on my soul then and no cloud has a silver lining. I was blue and disgruntled all the forenoon and looked forward to the coming of the mail as the one possible rescue from the doldrums. There is always such a fascinating expectancy and uncertainty about the mail. What would it bring me? A letter from Teddy—Teddy writes the most delightful letters. A nice thin envelope with a check? A fat one woefully eloquent of more rejected MSS? One of Ilse's fascinating scrawls? Nothing of the sort. Merely an irate epistle from Second-cousin-once-removed Beulah Grant of Derry Pond, who is furious because she thinks I 'put her' into my story *Fools of Habit*, which has just been copied into a widely circulated Canadian farm paper. She wrote me a bitterly reproachful letter which I received to-day. She thinks I 'might have spared an old friend who has always wished me well.' She is 'not accustomed to being ridiculed in the newspapers' and will I, in future, be so kind as to refrain from making her the butt of my supposed wit in the pulic press. Second-cousin-once-removed Beulah wields a facile pen of her own, when it comes to that, and while certain things in her letter hurt me other parts infuriated me. I never once even *thought* of Cousin Beulah when I wrote that story. And if I *had* thought of Cousin Beulah I most certainly wouldn't have put *her* in a story. She is too stupid and commonplace. And she isn't a bit like *Aunt Kate*, who is I flattered myself, a vivid, snappy, humorous old lady.

"But Cousin Beulah wrote to Aunt Elizabeth too, and we have had a family ruction. Aunt Elizabeth won't believe I am guiltless—she declares *Aunt Kate* is an exact picture of Cousin Beulah and she politely requests me—Aunt Elizabeth's polite requests are awesome things—*not* to caricature my relatives in my future productions.

"'It is not,' said Aunt Elizabeth in her stateliest manner, 'a thing *any* Murray should do—make money out of the peculiarities of her friends.'

"It was just another of Miss Royal's predictions fulfilled. Oh, was she as right about everything else? If she was—

"But the worst slam of all came from Cousin Jimmy, who had chuckled over *Fools of Habit*.

"'Never mind old Beulah, pussy,' he whispered. 'That was fine. You certainly did her up brown in *Aunt Kate*. I recognised her before I'd read a page. Knew her by her nose.' There you are! I unluckily happened to dower *Aunt Kate* with a 'long, drooping nose.' Nor can it be denied that Cousin Beulah's nose is long *and* drooping. People have been hanged on no clearer circumstantial evidence. It was of no use to wail despairingly that I had never even thought of Cousin Beulah. Cousin Jimmy just nodded and chuckled again.

"'Of course. Best to keep it quiet. Best to keep anything like that pretty quiet.'

"The worst sting in all this is, that if *Aunt Kate* is really like Cousin Beulah Grant then I failed egregiously in what I was trying to do.

"However, I feel much better now than when I began this entry. I've got quite a bit of resentment and rebellion and discouragement out of my system.

"That's the chief use of a diary, I believe."

### III

"FEB. 3, 19—

"This was a 'big day.' I had three acceptances. And one editor asked me to send him some stories. To be sure, I hate having an editor ask me to send a story, somehow. It's far worse than sending them unasked. The humiliation of having them returned after all is far deeper than when one just sends off a MS. to some dim impersonality behind an editorial desk a thousand miles away.

"And I have decided that I can't write a story 'to order.' 'Tis a diabolical task. I tried to lately. The editor of *Young People* asked me to write a story along certain lines. I wrote it. He sent it back, pointing out some faults and asking me to rewrite it. I tried to. I wrote and rewrote and altered and interlined until my MS. looked like a crazy patchwork of black and blue and red inks. Finally I lifted one of the covers of the kitchen stove and dumped in the original yarn and all my variations thereof.

"After this I'm just going to write what I want to. And the editors can be—canonised!

"There are northern lights and a misty new moon to-night."

## IV

"FEB. 16, 19—

"My story *What the Jest Was Worth* was in *The Home Monthly* to-day. But I was only one of 'others' on the cover. However, to balance that I have been listed by name as 'one of the well-known and popular contributors for the coming year' in *Girlhood Days*. Cousin Jimmy has read this editor's foreword over half a dozen times and I heard him murmuring *'well-known and popular'* as he split the kindlings. Then he went to the corner store and bought me a new Jimmy-book. Every time I pass a new milestone on the Alpine path Cousin Jimmy celebrates by giving me a new Jimmy-book. I never buy a notebook for myself. It would hurt his feelings. He always looks at the little pile of Jimmy-books on my writing table with awe and reverence, firmly believing that all sorts of wonderful literature is locked up in the hodge-podge of description and characters and 'bits' they contain.

"I always give Dean my stories to read. I can't help doing it, although he always brings them back with no comment, or, worse than no comment—faint praise. It has become a sort of obsession with me to *make* Dean admit I *can* write something worthwhile in its line. *That* would be triumph. But unless and until he does, everything will be dust and ashes. Because—he *knows*."

## V

"APRIL 2, 19—

"The spring has affected a certain youth of Shrewsbury who comes to New Moon occasionally. He is not a suitor of whom the House of Murray approves. Nor, which is more important, one of whom E. B. Starr approves. Aunt Elizabeth was very grim because I went to a concert with him. She was sitting up when I came home.

" 'You see I haven't eloped, Aunt Elizabeth,' I said. 'I promise you I won't. If I ever want to marry any one I'll tell you so and marry him in spite of your teeth.'

"I don't know whether Aunt Elizabeth went to bed with an easier mind or not. Mother eloped—thank goodness!—and Aunt Elizabeth is a firm believer in heredity."

## VI

"APRIL 15, 19—

"This evening I went away up the hill and prowled about the Disappointed House by moonlight. The Disappointed House was built thirty-seven years ago—partly built, at least—for a bride who never came to it. There it has been ever since, boarded up, unfinished, heartbroken, haunted by the timid, forsaken ghosts of things that should have happened but never did. I always feel so sorry for it. For its poor blind eyes that have never seen—that haven't even memories. No homelight ever shone out through them—only once, long ago, a gleam of firelight. It might have been such a nice little house, snuggled against that wooded hill, pulling little spruces all around it to cover it. A warm, friendly little house. Not like the new one at the

Corner that Tom Semple is putting up. *It* is a bad-tempered house. Vixenish, with little eyes and sharp elbows. It's odd how much personality a house can have even before it is ever lived in at all. Once long ago, when Teddy and I were children, we pried a board off the window and climbed in and made a fire in the fireplace. Then we sat there and planned out our lives. We meant to spend them together in that very house. I suppose Teddy has forgotten all about that childish nonsense. He writes often and his letters are full and jolly and Teddy-like. And he tells me all the little things I want to know about his life. But lately they have become rather impersonal, it seems to me. They might just as well have been written to Ilse as to me.

"Poor little Disappointed House. I suppose you will always be disappointed."

## VII

"MAY 1, 19—

"Spring again! Young poplars with golden, ethereal leaves. Leagues of rippling gulf beyond the silver-and-lilac sand-dunes.

"The winter has gone with a swiftness incredible, in spite of some terrible, black three-o'clocks and lonely, discouraged twilights. Dean will soon be home from Florida. But neither Teddy nor Ilse is coming home this summer. This gave me a white night or two recently. Ilse is going to the coast to visit an aunt—a mother's sister who never took any notice of her before. And Teddy has got the chance of illustrating a series of Northwest Mounted Police stories for a New York firm and must spend his holidays making sketches for it in the far North. Of course it's a splendid chance for him and I wouldn't be a bit sorry—if *he* seemed a bit sorry because he wasn't coming to Blair Water. But he didn't.

"Well, I suppose Blair Water and the old life here are to him as a tale that is told now.

"I didn't realise how much I had been building on Ilse and Teddy being here for the summer or how much the hope of it had helped me through a few bad times in the winter. When I let myself remember that not once this summer will I hear Teddy's signal whistle in Lofty John's bush—not once happen on him in our secret, beautiful haunts of lane and brookside—not once exchange a thrilling, significant glance in a crowd when something happened which had a special meaning for us, all the colour seems to die out of life, leaving it just a drab, faded thing of shreds and patches.

"Mrs. Kent met me at the post-office yesterday and stopped to speak—something she very rarely does. She hates me as much as ever.

"'I suppose you have heard that Teddy is not coming home this summer?'

"'Yes,' I said briefly.

"There was a certain odd, aching triumph in her eyes as she turned away—a triumph I understood. She is very unhappy because Teddy will not be home for *her* but she is exultant that he will not be home for *me*. This shows, she is almost sure, that he cares nothing about me.

"Well, I daresay she is right. Still, one can't be altogether gloomy in spring.

"And Andrew is engaged! To a girl of whom Aunt Addie entirely approves, 'I could not be more pleased with Andrew's choice if I had chosen her myself,' she said this afternoon to Aunt Elizabeth. *To* Aunt Elizabeth and *at* me. Aunt Elizabeth was coldly glad—or said she was. Aunt Laura cried a little—Aunt Laura always cries a bit when any one she knows is born or dead or married or engaged or come or gone or polling his first vote. She couldn't help feeling a little disappointed. Andrew would have been such a *safe* husband for me. Certainly there is no dynamite in Andrew."

# Chapter III

## I

At first nobody thought Mr. Carpenter's illness serious. He had had a good many attacks of rheumatism in recent years, laying him up for a few days. Then he could hobble back to work, as grim and sarcastic as ever, with a new edge to his tongue. In Mr. Carpenter's opinion teaching in Blair Water school was not what it had been. Nothing there now, he said, but rollicking, soulless young nonentities. Not a soul in the school who could pronounce February or Wednesday.

"I'm tired trying to make soup in a sieve," he said gruffly.

Teddy and Ilse and Perry and Emily were gone—the four pupils who had leavened the school with a saving inspiration. Perhaps Mr. Carpenter was a little tired of—everything. He was not very old, as years go, but he had burned up most of his constitution in a wild youth. The little, timid, faded slip of a woman who had been his wife had died unobtrusively in the preceding autumn. She had never seemed to matter much to Mr. Carpenter; but he had "gone down" rapidly after her funeral. The school children went in awe of his biting tongue and his more frequent spurts of temper. The trustees began to shake their heads and talk of a new teacher when the school year ended.

Mr. Carpenter's illness began as usual with an attack of rheumatism. Then there was heart trouble. Dr. Burnley, who went to see him despite his obstinate refusal to have a doctor, looked grave and talked mysteriously of

19

a lack of "the will to live." Aunt Louisa Drummond of Derry Pond came over to nurse him. Mr. Carpenter submitted to this with a resignation that was a bad omen—as if nothing mattered any more.

"Have your own way. She can potter round if it will ease your consciences. So long as she leaves me alone I don't care what she does. I *won't* be fed and I *won't* be coddled and I *won't* have the sheets changed. Can't bear her hair, though. Too straight and shiny. Tell her to do something to it. And why does her nose look as if it were always cold?"

Emily ran in every evening to sit awhile with him. She was the only person the old man cared to see. He did not talk a great deal, but he liked to open his eyes every few minutes and exchange a sly smile of understanding with her—as if the two of them were laughing together over some excellent joke of which only they could sample the flavour. Aunt Louisa did not know what to think of this commerce of grins and consequently disapproved of it. She was a kind-hearted creature, with much real motherliness in her thwarted maiden breast, but she was all at sea with these cheerful, Puckish, deathbed smiles of her patient. She thought he had much better be thinking of his immortal soul. He was not a member of the church, was he? He would not even let the minister come in to see him. But Emily Starr was welcomed whenever she came. Aunt Louisa had her own secret suspicion of the said Emily Starr. Didn't she write? Hadn't she put her own mother's second-cousin, body and bones, into one of her stories? Probably she was looking for "copy" in this old pagan's deathbed. *That* explained her interest in it, beyond a doubt. Aunt Louisa looked curiously at this ghoulish young creature. She hoped Emily wouldn't put *her* in a story.

For a long time Emily had refused to believe that it *was* Mr. Carpenter's deathbed. He *couldn't* be so ill as all that. He didn't suffer—he didn't complain. He would be all right as soon as warmer weather came. She told herself this so often that she made herself believe it. She could not let herself think of life in Blair Water without Mr. Carpenter.

One May evening Mr. Carpenter seemed much better. His eyes flashed with their old satiric fire, his voice rang with its old resonance; he joked poor Aunt Louisa—who never could understand his jokes but endured them with Christian patience. Sick people must be humoured. He told a funny story to Emily and laughed with her over it till the little low-raftered room rang. Aunt Louisa shook her head. There were some things she did not know, poor lady, but she did know her own humble, faithful little trade of unprofessional nursing; and she knew that this sudden rejuvenescence was no good sign. As the Scotch would say, he was "fey." Emily in her inexperience did not know this. She went home rejoicing that Mr. Carpenter had taken such a turn for the better. Soon he would be all right, back at school, thundering at his pupils, striding absently along the road reading some dog-eared classic, criticising her manuscripts with all his old trenchant humour. Emily was glad. Mr. Carpenter was a friend she could not afford to lose.

## II

Aunt Elizabeth wakened her at two. She had been sent for. Mr. Carpenter was asking for her.

"Is he—worse?" asked Emily, slipping out of her high black bed with its carved posts.

"Dying," said Aunt Elizabeth briefly. "Dr. Burnley says he can't last till morning."

Something in Emily's face touched Aunt Elizabeth.

"Isn't it better for him, Emily?" she said with an unusual gentleness. "He is old and tired. His wife has gone—they will not give him the school another year. His old age would be very lonely. Death is his best friend."

"I am thinking of myself," choked Emily.

She went down to Mr. Carpenter's house, through the dark, beautiful spring night. Aunt Louisa was crying but Emily did not cry. Mr. Carpenter opened his eyes and smiled at her—the same old, sly smile.

"No tears," he murmured. "I forbid tears at my deathbed. Let Louisa Drummond do the crying out in the kitchen. She might as well earn her money that way as another. There's nothing more she can do for me."

"Is there anything *I* can do?" asked Emily.

"Just sit here where I can see you till I'm gone, that's all. One doesn't like to go out—alone. Never liked the thought of dying alone. How many old she-weasels are out in the kitchen waiting for me to die?"

"There are only Aunt Louisa and Aunt Elizabeth," said Emily, unable to repress a smile.

"Don't mind my not—talking much. I've been talking—all my life. Through now. No breath—left. But if I think of anything—like you to be here."

Mr. Carpenter closed his eyes and relapsed into silence. Emily sat quietly, her head a soft blur of darkness against the window that was beginning to whiten with dawn. The ghostly hands of a fitful wind played with her hair. The perfume of June lilies stole in from the bed under the open window—a haunting odour, sweeter than music, like all the lost perfumes of old, unutterably dear years. Far off, two beautiful, slender, black firs, of exactly the same height, came out against the silver dawn-lit sky like the twin spires of some Gothic cathedral rising out of a bank of silver mist. Just between them hung a dim old moon, as beautiful as the evening crescent. Their beauty was a comfort and stimulant to Emily under the stress of this strange vigil. Whatever passed—whatever came—beauty like this was eternal.

Now and then Aunt Louisa came in and looked at the old man. Mr. Carpenter seemed unconscious of these visitations but always when she went out he opened his eyes and winked at Emily. Emily found

herself winking back, somewhat to her own horror—
for she had sufficient Murray in her to be slightly
scandalised over deathbed winks. Fancy what Aunt
Elizabeth would say.

"Good little sport," muttered Mr. Carpenter after the
second exchange of winks. "Glad—you're there."

At three o'clock he grew rather restless. Aunt Louisa
came in again.

"He can't die till the tide goes out, you know," she
explained to Emily in a solemn whisper.

"Get out of this with your superstitious blather,"
said Mr. Carpenter loudly and clearly. "I'll die when
I'm d—n well ready, tide or no tide."

Horrified, Aunt Louisa excused him to Emily on the
ground that he was wandering in his mind and slipped
out.

"Excuse my common way, won't you?" said Mr.
Carpenter. "I *had* to shock her out. Couldn't have that
elderly female person—round watching me die. Given
her—a good yarn to tell—the rest of her—life. Awful—
warning. And yet—she's a good soul. So good—she
bores me. No evil in her. Somehow—one needs—a
spice—of evil—in every personality. It's the—pinch of—
salt—that brings out—the flavour."

Another silence. Then he added gravely,

"Trouble is—the Cook—makes the pinch—too large—
in most cases. Inexperienced Cook—wiser after—a few
eternities."

Emily thought he really was "wandering" now but
he smiled at her.

"Glad you're here—little pal. Don't mind being—here—
do you?"

"No," said Emily.

"When a Murray says—no—she means it."

After another silence Mr. Carpenter began again, this
time more to himself, as it seemed, than any one else.

"Going out—out beyond the dawn. Past the morning
star. Used to think I'd be frightened. Not frightened.
Funny. Think how much I'm going to know—in just a

few more minutes, Emily. Wiser than anybody else living. Always wanted to know—to *know*. Never liked guesses. Done with curiosity—about life. Just curious now—about death. I'll know the truth, Emily—just a few more minutes and I'll know the—truth. No more guessing. And if—it's as I think—I'll be—young again. You can't know what—it means. You—who *are* young—can't have—the least idea—what it means—to be young—*again*."

His voice sank into restless muttering for a time, then rose clearly,

"Emily, promise me—that you'll never write—to please anybody—but yourself."

Emily hesitated a moment. Just what did such a promise mean?

"Promise," whispered Mr. Carpenter insistently.

Emily promised.

"That's right," said Mr. Carpenter with a sigh of relief. "Keep that—and you'll be—all right. No use trying to please everybody. No use trying to please—critics. Live under your own hat. Don't be—led away—by those howls about realism. Remember—pine woods are just as real as—pigsties—and a darn sight pleasanter to be in. You'll get there—sometime—you have the root—of the matter—in you. And don't—tell the world—everything. That's what's the—matter—with our—literature. Lost the charm of mystery—and reserve. There's something else I wanted to say—some caution—I can't—seem to remember—"

"Don't try," said Emily gently. "Don't tire yourself."

"Not—tired. Feel quite through—with being tired. I'm dying—I'm a failure—poor as a rat. But after all, Emily—I've had a—darned interesting time."

Mr. Carpenter shut his eyes and looked so death-like that Emily made an involuntary movement of alarm. He lifted a bleached hand.

"No—don't call her. Don't call that weeping lady back. Just yourself, little Emily of New Moon. Clever little girl, Emily. What was it—I wanted to say to her?"

A moment or two later he opened his eyes and said in a loud clear voice, "Open the door—open the door. Death must not be kept waiting."

Emily ran to the little door and set it wide. A strong wind off the grey sea rushed in. Aunt Louisa ran in from the kitchen.

"The tide has turned—he's going out with it—he's gone."

Not quite. As Emily bent over him the keen, shaggy-browed eyes opened for the last time. Mr. Carpenter essayed a wink but could not compass it.

"I've—thought of it," he whispered. "Beware—of—italics."

Was there a little impish chuckle at the end of the words? Aunt Louisa always declared there was. Graceless old Mr. Carpenter had died laughing—saying something about Italians. Of course he was delirious. But Aunt Louisa always felt it had been a very unedifying deathbed. She was thankful that few such had come in her experience.

### III

Emily went blindly home and wept for her old friend in the room of her dreams. What a gallant old soul he was—going out into the shadow—or into the sunlight? —with a laugh and a jest. Whatever his faults there had never been anything of the coward about old Mr. Carpenter. Her world, she knew, would be a colder place now that he was gone. It seemed many years since she had left New Moon in the darkness. She felt some inward monition that told her she had come to a certain parting of the ways of life. Mr. Carpenter's death would not make any external difference for her. Nevertheless, it was as a milestone to which in after years she could look back and say,

"After I passed that point everything was different."

All her life she had grown, as it seemed, by these fits and starts. Going on quietly and changelessly for months and years; then all at once suddenly realising that she had left some "low-vaulted past" and emerged into some "new temple" of the soul more spacious than all that had gone before. Though always, at first, with a chill of change and a sense of loss.

# Chapter IV

## I

The year after Mr. Carpenter's death passed quietly for Emily—quietly, pleasantly—perhaps, though she tried to stifle the thought, a little monotonously. No Ilse—no Teddy—no Mr. Carpenter. Perry only very occasionally. But of course in the summer there was Dean. No girl with Dean Priest for a friend could be altogether lonely. They had always been such good friends, ever since the day, long ago, when she had fallen over the rocky bank of Malvern Bay and been rescued by Dean.* It did not matter in the least that he limped slightly and had a crooked shoulder, or that the dreamy brilliance of his green eyes sometimes gave his face an uncanny look. On the whole, there was no one in all the world she *liked* quite so well as Dean. When she thought this she always italicised the "*liked*." There were some things Mr. Carpenter had not known.

Aunt Elizabeth never quite approved of Dean. But then Aunt Elizabeth had no great love for any Priest. There seemed to be a temperamental incompatibility between the Murrays and the Priests that was never bridged over, even by the occassional marriage between the clans.

"Priests, indeed," Aunt Elizabeth was wont to say contemptuously, relegating the whole clan, root and branch, to limbo with one wave of her thin, unbeautiful Murray hand. "Priests, indeed!"

*See *Emily of New Moon.*

27

"Murray is Murray and Priest is Priest and never the twain shall meet," Emily shamelessly, mischievously misquoted Kipling once when Dean had asked in pretended despair why none of her aunts liked him.

"Your old Great-aunt Nancy over there at Priest Pond detests me," he said, with the little whimsical smile that sometimes gave him the look of an amused gnome. "And the Ladies Laura and Elizabeth treat me with the frosty politeness reserved by the Murrays for their dearest foes. Oh, I think I know why."

Emily flushed. She, too, was beginning to have an unwelcome suspicion why Aunts Elizabeth and Laura were even more frostily polite to Dean than of yore. She did not want to have it; she thrust it fiercely out and locked the door of thought upon it whenever it intruded there. But the thing whined on her doorstep and would not be banished. Dean, like everything and everybody else, seemed to have changed overnight. And what did the change imply—hint? Emily refused to answer this question. The only answer that suggested itself was too absurd. And too unwelcome.

Was Dean Priest changing from friend to lover? Nonsense. Arrant nonsense. Disagreeable nonsense. For she did not want him as a lover and she did want him madly as a friend. She *couldn't* lose his friendship. It was too dear, delightful, stimulating, wonderful. Why did such devilish things ever happen? When Emily reached this point in her disconnected musings she always stopped and retraced her mental steps fiercely, terrified to realise that she was almost on the point of admitting that "the something devilish" had already happened or was in process of happening.

In one way it was almost a relief to her when Dean said casually one November evening:

"I suppose I must soon be thinking of my annual migration."

"Where are you going this year?" asked Emily.

"Japan. I've never been there. Don't want to go now particularly. But what's the use of staying? Would you want to talk to me in the sitting-room all winter with the aunts in hearing?"

"No," said Emily between a laugh and a shiver. She recalled one fiendish autumn evening of streaming rain and howling wind when they couldn't walk in the garden but had to sit in the room where Aunt Elizabeth was knitting and Aunt Laura crocheting by the table. It had been awful. And again why? Why couldn't they talk as freely and whimsically and intimately then as they did in the garden? The answer to this at least was not to be expressed in any terms of sex. Was it because they talked of so many things Aunt Elizabeth could not understand and so disapproved of? Perhaps. But whatever the cause Dean might as well have been at the other side of the world for all the real conversation that was possible.

"So I might as well go," said Dean, waiting for this exquisite, tall, white girl in an old garden to say she would miss him horribly. She had said it every one of his flitting autumns for many years. But she did not say it this time. She found she dared not.

Again, why?

Dean was looking at her with eyes that could be tender or sorrowful or passionate, as he willed, and which now seemed to be a mixture of all three expressions. He *must* hear her say she would miss him. His true reason for going away this winter was to make her realise how much she missed him—make her feel that she could not live without him.

"Will you miss me, Emily?"

"That goes without saying," answered Emily lightly—too lightly. Other years she had been very frank and serious about it. Dean was not altogether regretful for the change. But he could guess nothing of the attitude of mind behind it. She must have changed because she felt something—suspected something, of what he had striven for years to hide and suppress as rank madness.

What then? Did this new lightness indicate that she didn't want to make a too important thing of admitting she would miss him? Or was it only the instinctive defence of a woman against something that implied or evoked too much?

"It will be so dreadful here this winter without you and Teddy and Ilse that I will not let myself think of it at all," went on Emily. "Last winter was bad. And this—I know somehow—will be worse. But I'll have my work."

"Oh, yes, your work," agreed Dean with a little, tolerant, half-amused inflection in his voice that always came now when he spoke of her "work," as if it tickled him hugely that she should call her pretty scribblings "work." Well, one must humour the charming child. He could not have said so more plainly in words. His implications cut across Emily's sensitive soul like a whiplash. And all at once her work and her ambitions became—momentarily at least—as childish and unimportant as he considered them. She could not hold her own conviction against him. He must know. He was so clever—so well-educated. He *must* know. That was the agony of it. She could not ignore his opinion. Emily knew deep down in her heart that she would never be able wholly to believe in herself until Dean Priest admitted that she could do something honestly worth while in its way. And if he never admitted it—

"I shall carry pictures of you wherever I go, Star," Dean was saying. Star was his old nickname for her—not a pun on her name but because he said she reminded him of a star. "I shall see you sitting in your room by that old lookout window, spinning your pretty cobwebs—pacing up and down in this old garden—wandering in the Yesterday Road—looking out to sea. Whenever I shall recall a bit of Blair Water loveliness I shall see you in it. After all, all other beauty is only a background for a beautiful woman."

"Her pretty cobwebs—" ah, there it was. That was

all Emily heard. She did not even realise that he was telling her he thought *her* a beautiful woman.

"Do you think what I write is nothing but cobwebs, Dean?" she asked chokingly.

Dean looked surprised, doing it very well.

"Star, what else is it? What do you think it is yourself? I'm glad you can amuse yourself by writing. It's a splendid thing to have a little hobby of the kind. And if you can pick up a few shekels by it—well, that's all very well too in this kind of a world. But I'd hate to have you dream of being a Brontë or an Austen—and wake to find you'd wasted your youth on a dream."

"I don't fancy myself a Brontë or an Austen," said Emily. "But you didn't talk like that long ago, Dean. You used to think then I *could* do something some day."

"We don't bruise the pretty visions of a child," said Dean. "But it's foolish to carry childish dreams over into maturity. Better face facts. You write charming things of their kind, Emily. Be content with that and don't waste your best years yearning for the unattainable or striving to reach some height far beyond your grasp."

## II

Dean was not looking at Emily. He was leaning on the old sundial and scowling down at it with the air of a man who was forcing himself to say a disagreeable thing because he felt it was his duty.

"I *won't* be just a mere scribbler of pretty stories," cried Emily rebelliously. He looked into her face. She was as tall as he was—a trifle taller, though he would not admit it.

"You do not need to be anything but what you are," he said in a low vibrant tone. "A woman such as this old New Moon has never seen before. You can do more with those eyes—that smile—than you can ever do with your pen."

"You sound like Great-aunt Nancy Priest," said Emily cruelly and contemptuously.

But had he not been cruel and contemptuous to her? Three o'clock that night found her wide-eyed and anguished. She had lain through sleepless hours face to face with two hateful convictions. One was that she could never do anything worth doing with her pen. The other was that she was going to lose Dean's friendship. For friendship was all she could give him and it would not satisfy him. She must hurt him. And oh, how could she hurt Dean whom life had used so cruelly? She had said "no" to Andrew Murray and laughed a refusal to Perry Miller without a qualm. But this was an utterly different thing.

Emily sat up in bed in the darkness and moaned in a despair that was none the less real and painful because of the indisputable fact that thirty years later she might be wondering what on earth she had been moaning about.

"I wish there were no such things as lovers and lovemaking in the world," she said with savage intensity, honestly believing she meant it.

### III

Like everybody, in daylight Emily found things much less tragic and more endurable than in the darkness. A nice fat cheque and a kind letter of appreciation with it restored a good deal of her self-respect and ambition. Very likely, too, she had imagined implications into Dean's words and looks that he never meant. She was not going to be a silly goose, fancying that every man, young or old, who liked to talk to her, or even to pay her compliments in shadowy, moonlit gardens, was in love with her. Dean was old enough to be her father.

Dean's unsentimental parting when he went away confirmed her in this comforting assurance and left her free to miss him without any reservations. Miss him she did abominably. The rain in autumn fields that year was a very sorrowful thing and so were the grey ghost-fogs coming slowly in from the gulf. Emily was glad when snow and sparkle came. She was very busy, writing such long hours, often far into the night, that Aunt Laura began to worry over her health and Aunt Elizabeth once or twice remarked protestingly that the price of coal-oil had gone up. As Emily paid for her own coal-oil this hint had no effect on her. She was very keen about making enough money to repay Uncle Wallace and Aunt Ruth what they had spent on her high school years. Aunt Elizabeth thought this was a praiseworthy ambition. The Murrays were an independent folk. It was a clan by-word that the Murrays had a boat of their own at the Flood. No promiscuous Ark for *them*.

Of course there were still many rejections—which Cousin Jimmy carried home from the post-office speechless with indignation. But the percentage of acceptances rose steadily. Every new magazine conquered meant a step upward on her Alpine path. She knew she was steadily gaining the mastery over her art. Even the "love talk" that had bothered her so much in the old days came easily now. Had Teddy Kent's eyes taught her so much? If she had taken time to think she might have been very lonely. There were some bad hours. Especially after a letter had come from Ilse full of all her gay doings in Montreal, her triumphs in the School of Oratory and her pretty new gowns. In the long twilights when she looked shiveringly from the windows of the old farmhouse and thought how very white and cold and solitary were the snow fields on the hill, how darkly remote and tragic the Three Princesses, she lost confidence in her star. She wanted summer; fields of daisies; seas misty with moonrise or purple with sunset; companionship; Teddy. In such moments she always knew she wanted Teddy.

Teddy seemed far way. They still corresponded faithfully, but the correspondence was not what it was. Suddenly in the autumn Teddy's letters had grown slightly colder and more formal. At this first hint of frost the temperature of Emily's dropped noticeably.

## IV

But she had hours of rapture and insight that shed a glory backward and forward. Hours when she felt the creative faculty within her, burning like a never-dying flame. Rare, sublime moments when she felt as a god, perfectly happy and undesirous. And there was always her dream-world into which she could escape from monotony and loneliness, and taste strange, sweet happiness unmarred by any cloud or shadow. Sometimes she slipped mentally back into childhood and had delightful adventures she would have been ashamed to tell her adult world.

She liked to prowl about a good deal by herself, especially in twilight or moonlight alone with the stars and the trees, rarest of companions.

"I can't be contented indoors on a moonlight night. I have to be up and away," she told Aunt Elizabeth, who did not approve of prowling. Aunt Elizabeth never lost her uneasy consciousness that Emily's mother had eloped. And anyhow, prowling was odd. None of the other Blair Water girls prowled.

There were walks over the hills in the owl's light when the stars rose—one after another, the great constellations of myth and legend. There were frosty moonrises that hurt her with their beauty; spires of pointed firs against firey sunsets; spruce copses dim with mystery; pacings to and fro on the To-morrow Road. Not the To-morrow Road of June, blossom-misted, tender in young green. Nor yet the To-morrow Road of October, spendid in crimson and gold. But the To-morrow Road of a still, snowy winter twilight—a white, mysterious, silent place full of wizardry. Emily loved it better than all her other dear spots. The spirit delight of that dream-haunted solitude never cloyed— its remote charm never palled.

If only there had been a friend to talk things over with! One night she awakened and found herself in tears, with a late moon shining bluely and coldly on her through the frosted window-panes. She had dreamed that Teddy had whistled to her from Lofty John's bush—the old, dear, signal whistle of childhood days; and she had run so eagerly across the garden to the bush. But she could not find Teddy.

"Emily Byrd Starr, if I catch you crying again over a dream!" she said passionately.

# Chapter V

## I

Only three dynamic things happened that year to vary the noiseless tenor of Emily's way. In the autumn she had a love-affair—as Aunt Laura Victorianly phrased it. Rev. James Wallace, the new, well-meaning, lady-like young minister at Derry Pond, began making excuses for visiting Blair Water Manse quite often and from there drifted over to New Moon. Soon everybody in Blair Water and Derry Pond knew that Emily Starr had a ministerial beau. Gossip was very rife. It was a foregone conclusion that Emily would jump at him. A minister! Heads were shaken over it. She would never make a suitable minister's wife. Never in the world. But wasn't it always that way? A minister picking on the very last girl he should have.

At New Moon opinion was divided. Aunt Laura, who owned to a Dr. Fell feeling about Mr. Wallace, hoped Emily wouldn't "take" him. Aunt Elizabeth, in her secret soul, was not overfond of him either, but she was dazzled by the idea of a minister. And such a safe lover. A minister would never think of eloping. She thought Emily would be a very lucky girl if she could "get" him.

When it became sadly evident that Mr. Wallace's calls at New Moon had ceased, Aunt Elizabeth gloomily asked Emily the reason and was horrified to hear that the ungrateful minx had told Mr. Wallace she could not marry him.

"Why?" demanded Aunt Elizabeth in icy disapproval.

"His ears, Aunt Elizabeth, his ears," said Emily flippantly. "I really couldn't risk having my children inherit ears like that."

The indelicacy of such a reply staggered Aunt Elizabeth—which was probably why Emily had made it. She knew Aunt Elizabeth would be afraid to refer to the subject again.

The Rev. James Wallace thought it was "his duty" to go West the next spring. And that was that.

## II

Then there was the episode of the local theatricals in Shrewsbury which were written up with vitriolic abuse in one of the Charlottetown papers. Shrewsbury people blamed Emily Byrd Starr for doing it. Who else, they demanded, could or would have written with such diabolical cleverness and sarcasm? Everyone knew that Emily Byrd Starr had never forgiven Shrewsbury people for believing those yarns about her in the old John House affair. This was her method of revenge. Wasn't that like the Murrays? Carrying a secret grudge for years, until a suitable chance for revenge presented itself. Emily protested her innocence in vain. It was never discovered who had written the report and as long as she lived it kept coming up against her.

But in one way it worked out to her advantage. She was invited to all the social doings in Shrewsbury after that. People were afraid to leave her out lest she "write them up." She could not get to everything—Shrewsbury was seven miles from Blair Water. But she got to Mrs. Tom Nickle's dinner dance and thought for six weeks that it had changed the current of her whole existence.

Emily-in-the-glass looked very well that night. She had got the dress she had longed for for years—spent the whole price of a story on it, to her aunt's horror. Shot silk—blue in one light, silver in another, with mists of lace. She remembered that Teddy had said that when she got that dress he would paint her as an Ice-maiden in it."

Her righthand neighbour was a man who kept making "funny speeches" all through the meal and kept her wondering for what good purpose God had ever fashioned him.

But her lefthand neighbor! He talked little but he looked! Emily decided that she liked a man whose eyes said more than his lips. But he told her she looked like "the moonbeam of a blue summer night" in that gown. I think it was the phrase that finished Emily—shot her clean through the heart—like the unfortunate little duck of the nursery rhyme. Emily was helpless before the charm of a well-turned phrase. Before the evening was over Emily, for the first time in her life, had fallen wildly and romantically into the wildest and most romantic kind of love—"the love the poets dreamed of," as she wrote in her diary. The young man—I believe his beautiful and romantic name was Aylmer Vincent—was quite as madly in love as she. He literally haunted New Moon. He wooed beautifully. His way of saying "dear lady" charmed her. When he told her that "a beautiful hand was one of the chief charms of a beautiful woman" and looked adoringly at hers Emily kissed her hands when she went to her room that night because *his* eyes had caressed them. When he called her raptly "a creature of mist and flame" she misted and flamed about dim old New Moon until Aunt Elizabeth unthinkingly quenched her by asking her to fry up a batch of doughnuts for Cousin Jimmy. When he told her she was like an opal—milk-white outside but with a heart of fire and crimson, she wondered if life would always be like this.

"And to think I once imagined I cared for Teddy Kent," she thought in amazement at herself.

She neglected her writing and asked Aunt Elizabeth if she could have the old blue box in the attic for a hope chest. Aunt Elizabeth graciously acceded. The record of the new suitor had been investigated and found impeccable. Good family—good social position—good business. All the omens were auspicious.

## III

And then a truly terrible thing happened.

Emily fell out of love just as suddenly as she had fallen into it. One day she was, and the next she wasn't. That was all there was to it.

She was aghast. She couldn't believe it. She tried to pretend the old enchantment still existed. She tried to thrill and dream and blush. Nary thrill, nary blush. Her dark-eyed lover—*why* had it never struck her before that his eyes were exactly like a cow's—bored her. Ay, bored her. She yawned one evening in the very midst of one of his fine speeches. There was nothing to add to that.

She was so ashamed that she was almost ill over it. Blair people thought she had been jilted and pitied her. The aunts who knew better were disappointed and disapproving.

"Fickle—fickle—like all the Starrs," said Aunt Elizabeth bitterly.

Emily had no spunk to defend herself. She supposed she deserved it all. Perhaps she was fickle. She must be fickle. When such a glorious conflagration fizzed out so speedily and utterly into ashes. Not a spark of it left. Not even a romantic memory. Emily viciously inked out the passage in her diary about "the love the poets dreamed of."

She was really very unhappy about it for a long while. Had she no depth at all? Was she such a superficial creature that even love with her was like the seeds that fell into the shadow soil in the immortal parable? She knew other girls had these silly, tempestuous, ephemeral affairs but she would never have supposed she would have one—*could* have one. To be swept off her feet like that by a handsome face and mellifluous voice and great dark eyes and a trick of pretty speeches!

In brief Emily felt that she had made an absolute fool of herself and the Murray pride could not stick it.

To make it worse the young man married a Shrewsbury girl in six months. Not that Emily cared whom he married or how soon. But it meant that *his* romantic ardours were but things of superficiality, too, and lent a deeper tinge of humiliation to the silly affair. Andrew had been so easily consoled also. Perry Miller was not wasting in despair. Teddy had forgotten her. Was she really incapable of inspiring a deep and lasting passion in a man? To be sure, there was Dean. But even Dean could go away winter after winter and leave her to be wooed and won by a chance-met suitor.

"Am I fundamentally superficial?" poor Emily demanded of herself with terrible intensity.

She took up her pen again with a secret gladness. But for a considerable time the love-making in her stories was quite cynical and misanthropic in its flavour.

# Chapter VI

## I

Teddy Kent and Ilse Burnley came home in the summer for a brief vacation. Teddy had won an Art Scholarship which meant two years in Paris and was to sail for Europe in two weeks. He had written the news to Emily in an offhand way and she had responded with the congratulations of a friend and sister. There was no reference in either letter to rainbow gold or Vega of the Lyre. Yet Emily looked forward to his coming with a wistful, ashamed hope that would not be denied. Perhaps—dared she hope it?—when they met again face to face, in their old haunted woods and trysts—this coldness that had grown up so inexplicably between them would vanish as a sea-fog vanishes when the sun rose over the gulf. No doubt Teddy had had his imitation love affairs as she had hers. But when he came—when they looked again into each other's eyes—when she heard his signal whistle in Lofty John's bush—

But she never heard it. On the evening of the day when she knew Teddy was expected home she walked in the garden among brocaded moths, wearing a new gown of "powder-blue" chiffon and listened for it. Every robin call brought the blood to her cheek and made her heart beat wildly. Then came Aunt Laura through the dew and dusk.

"Teddy and Ilse are here," she said.

Emily went in to the stately, stiff, dignified parlour of New Moon, pale, queenly, aloof. Ilse hurled herself upon her with all her old, tempestuous affection, but Teddy shook hands with a cool detachment that almost equalled her own. Teddy? Oh, dear, no. Frederick Kent, R.A.-to-be. What was there left of the old Teddy in this slim, elegant young man with his sophisticated air and cool, impersonal eyes, and general implication of having put off forever all childish things—including foolish old visions and insignificant little country girls he had played with in his infancy?

In which conclusion Emily was horribly unjust to Teddy. But she was not in a mood to be just to anybody. Nobody is who has made a fool of herself. And Emily felt that that was just about what she had done—again. Mooning romantically about in a twilight garden, specially wearing powder-blue, waiting for a lover's signal from a beau who had forgotten all about her—or only remembered her as an old schoolmate on whom he had called very properly and kindly and conscientiously come to call. Well, thank heaven, Teddy did not know how absurd she had been. She would take excellent care that he should never suspect it. Who could be more friendly and remote than a Murray of New Moon? Emily's manner, she flattered herself, was admirable. As gracious and impersonal as to an entire stranger. Renewed congratulations on his wonderful success, coupled with an absolute lack of all real interest in it. Carefully phrased, polite questions about *his* work on her side; carefully phrased polite questions about *her* work on his side. She had seen some of *his* pictures in the magazines. He had read some of *her* stories. So it went, with a wider gulf opening between them at every moment. Never had Emily felt herself so far away from Teddy. She recognised with a feeling that was almost terror how completely he had changed in those two years of absence. It would in truth have been a ghastly interview had it not been for Ilse, who chattered with all her old breeziness and tang, planning out a two weeks of gay doings while she was home, asking hundreds of questions; the same lovable old madcap of laughter and jest and dressed with all her old gorgeous violations of accepted canons of taste. In an extraordinary dress—a thing of greenish-yellow. She had a big pink peony at her waist and another at her shoulder. She wore a bright green hat with a wreath of pink flowers on it. Great hoops of pearl swung in her ears. It as a weird costume. No one but Ilse could have worn it successfully. And she looked like the incarnation of a thousand tropic springs in it—exotic, provocative, beautiful. So beautiful! Emily realised her friend's beauty afresh with a pang not of envy, but of bitter humiliation. Beside Ilse's golden sheen of hair and brilliance of amber eyes and red-rose loveliness of cheeks she must look pale and dark and insignificant. Of course Teddy was in love with Ilse. He had gone to see her first—had been with her while Emily waited for him in the garden. Well, it made no real difference. Why should it? She would be just as friendly as ever. And was. Friendly with a vengeance. But when Teddy and Ilse had gone—together—laughing and teasing each other through the old To-morrow Road Emily went up to her room and locked the door. Nobody saw her again until the next morning.

## II

The gay two weeks of Ilse's planning followed. Picnics, dances and jamborees galore. Shrewsbury society decided that a rising young artist was somebody to be taken notice of and took notice accordingly. It was a veritable whirl of gaiety and Emily whirled about in it with the others. No step lighter in the dance, no voice quicker in the jest, and all the time feeling like the miserable spirit in a ghost story she had once read who had a live coal in its breast instead of a heart. All the time, feeling, too, far down under surface pride and hidden pain, that sense of completion and fulfilment which always came to her when Teddy was near her. But she took good care never to be alone with Teddy, who certainly could not be accused of any attempt to inveigle her into twosomes. His name was freely coupled with Ilse's and they took so composedly the teasing they encountered, that the impression gained ground that "things were pretty well understood between them." Emily thought Ilse might have told her if it were so. But Ilse, though she told many a tale of lovers forlorn whose agonies seemed to lie very lightly on her conscience, never mentioned Teddy's name, which Emily thought had a torturing significance of its own. She inquired after Perry Miller, wanting to know, if he were as big an oaf as ever and laughing over Emily's indignant defence.

"He will be Premier some day no doubt," agreed Ilse scornfully. "He'll work like the devil and never miss anything by lack of asking for it, but won't you always smell the herring-barrels of Stovepipe Town?"

Perry came to see Ilse, bragged a bit too much over his progress and got so snubbed and manhandled that he did not come again. Altogether the two weeks seemed a nightmare to Emily, who thought she was unreservedly thankful when the time came for Teddy to go. He was going on a sailing vessel to Halifax, wanting to make some nautical sketches for a magazine, and an hour before flood-tide, while the *Mira Lee* swung at anchor by the wharf at Stovepipe Town, he came to say good-bye. He did not bring Ilse with him—no doubt, thought Emily, because Ilse was visiting in Charlottetown; but Dean Priest was there, so there was no dreaded solitude *à deux*. Dean was creeping back into his own, after the two weeks' junketings from which he had been barred out. Dean would not go to dances and clam-bakes, but he was always hovering in the background, as everybody concerned felt. He stood with Emily in the garden and there was a certain air of victory and possession about him that did not escape Teddy's eye. Dean, who never made the mistake of thinking gaiety was happiness, had seen more than others of the little drama that had been played out in Blair Water during those two weeks and the dropping of the curtain left him a satisfied man. The old, shadowy, childish affair between Teddy Kent of the Tansy Patch and Emily of New Moon, was finally ended. Whatever its significance or lack of significance had been, Dean no longer counted Teddy among his rivals.

Emily and Teddy parted with the hearty handshake and mutual good wishes of old schoolmates who do indeed wish each other well but have no very vital interest in the matter.

"Prosper and be hanged to you," as some old Murray had been wont to say.

Teddy got himself away very gracefully. He had the gift of making an artistic exit, but he did not once look back. Emily turned immediately to Dean and resumed the discussion which Teddy's coming had interrupted. Her lashes hid her eyes very securely. Dean, with his uncanny ability to read her thoughts, should not—must not guess—what? What was there to guess? Nothing—absolutely nothing. Yet Emily kept her lashes down.

When Dean, who had some other engagement that evening, went away half an hour later she paced sedately up and down among the gold of primroses for a little while, the very incarnation, in all seeming, of maiden meditation fancy free.

"Spinning out a plot, no doubt," thought Cousin Jimmy proudly, as he glimpsed her from the kitchen window. "It beats me how she does it."

### III

Perhaps Emily was spinning out a plot. But as the shadows deepened she slipped out of the garden, through the dreamy peace of the old columbine orchard— along the Yesterday Road—over the green pasture field— past the Blair Water—up the hill beyond—past the Disappointed House—through the thick fir wood. There, in a clump of silver birches, one had an unbroken view of the harbour, flaming in lilac and rose-colour. Emily reached it a little breathlessly—she had almost run at the last. Would she be too late? Oh, what if she should be too late!

The *Mira Lee* was sailing out of the harbour, a dream vessel in the glamour of sunset, past purple headlands and distant, fairylike, misty coasts. Emily stood and watched her till she had crossed the bar into the gulf beyond. Stood and watched her until she had faded from sight in the blue dimness of the falling night, conscious only of a terrible hunger to see Teddy once more—just once more. To say good-bye as it should have been said.

Teddy was gone. To another world. There was no rainbow in sight. And what was Vega of the Lyre but a whirling, flaming, incredibly distant sun?

She slipped down among the grasses at her feet and lay there sobbing in the cold moonshine that had suddenly taken the place of the friendly twilight.

Mingled with her sharp agony was incredulity. This thing could not have happened. Teddy could not have gone away with only that soulless, chilly, polite good-bye. After all their years of comradeship, if nothing else. Oh, how could she ever get herself past three o'clock this night?

"I am a hopeless fool," she whispered savagely. "He has forgotten. I am nothing to him. And I deserve it. Didn't I forget him in those crazy weeks when I was imagining myself in love with Aylmer Vincent? Of course somebody has told him all about that. I've lost my chance of real happiness through that absurd affair. Where is my pride? To cry like this over a man who has forgotten me. But—but—it's so nice to cry after having had to laugh for these hideous weeks."

## IV

Emily flung herself into work feverishly after Teddy had gone. Through long summer days and nights she wrote, while the purple stains deepened under her eyes and the rose stains faded out of her cheeks. Aunt Elizabeth thought she was killing herself and for the first time was reconciled to her intimacy with Jarback Priest, since he dragged Emily away from her desk in the evenings at least for walks and talks in the fresh air. That summer Emily paid off the last of her indebtedness to Uncle Wallace and Aunt Ruth with her "pot-boilers."

But there was more than pot-boiling a-doing. In her first anguish of loneliness, as she lay awake at three o'clock, Emily had remembered a certain wild winter night when she and Ilse and Perry and Teddy had been "stormed in" in the old John House on the Derry Pond Road;* remembered all the scandal and suffering that had arisen therefrom; and remembered also that night of rapt delight "thinking out" a story that had flashed into her mind at a certain gay, significant speech of Teddy's. At least, she had thought it significant then. Well, *that* was all over. But wasn't the story somewhere? She had written the outline of that alluring, fanciful tale in a Jimmy-book the next day. Emily sprang out of bed in the still summer moonlight, lighted one of the famous candles of New Moon, and rummaged through a pile of old Jimmy-books. Yes, here it was. *A Seller of Dreams*. Emily squatted down on her haunches and read it through. It was *good*. Again it seized hold of her imagination and called forth all her creative impulse. She would write it out—she would begin that very moment. Flinging a dressing-gown over her white shoulders to protect them from the keen gulf air she sat down before her open window and began to write. Everything else was forgotten—for a time at least—in the subtle, all-embracing joy of creation. Teddy was nothing but a dim memory—love was a blown-out candle. Nothing mattered but her story. The characters came to life under her hand and swarmed through her consciousness, vivid, alluring, compelling. Wit, tears, and laughter trickled from her pen. She lived and

*See *Emily Climbs.*

breathed in another world and came back to New Moon only at dawn to find her lamp burned out, and her table littered with manuscript—the first four chapters of her book. Her book! What magic and delight and awe and incredulity in the thought.

For weeks Emily seemed to live really only when she was writing it. Dean found her strangely rapt and remote, absent and impersonal. Her conversation was as dull as it was possible for Emily's conversation to be, and while her body sat or walked beside him her soul was—where? In some region where he could not follow, at all events. It had escaped him.

## V

Emily finished her book in six weeks—finished it at dawn one morning. She flung down her pen and went to her window, lifting her pale, weary, triumphant little face to the skies of morning.

Music was dripping through the leafy silence in Lofty John's bush. Beyond were dawn-rosy meadows and the garden of New Moon lying in an enchanted calm. The wind's dance over the hills seemed some dear response to the music and rhythm in her being. Hills, sea, shadows, all called to her with a thousand elfin voices of understanding and acclaim. The old gulf was singing. Exquisite tears were in her eyes. She had written it—oh, how happy she was! This moment atoned for everything.

Finished—complete! There it lay—*A Seller of Dreams*— her first book. Not a great book—oh, no, but *hers*—her very own. Something to which she had given birth, which would never have existed had she not brought it into being. And it was *good*. She knew it was—felt it was. A fiery, delicate tale, instinct with romance, pathos, humour. The rapture of creation still illuminated it. She turned the pages over, reading a bit here and there—wondering if she could really have written *that*. She was right under the rainbow's end. Could she not touch the magic, prismatic thing? Already her fingers were clasping the pot of gold.

Aunt Elizabeth walked in with her usual calm disregard of any useless formality such as knocking.

"Emily," she said severly, "have you been sitting up all night *again*?"

Emily came back to earth with that abominable mental jolt which can only be truly described as a thud—a "sickening thud" at that. Very sickening. She stood like a convicted schoolgirl. And *A Seller of Dreams* became instantly a mere heap of scribbled paper.

"I—I didn't realise how time was passing, Aunt Elizabeth," she stammered.

"You are old enough to have better sense," said Aunt Elizabeth. "I don't mind your writing—now. You seem to be able to earn a living by it in a very ladylike way. But you will wreck your health if you keep this sort of thing up. Have you forgotten that your mother died of consumption? At any rate, don't forget that you must pick those beans to-day. It's high time they were picked."

Emily gathered up her manuscript with all her careless rapture gone. Creation was over; remained now the sordid business of getting her book published. Emily typewrote it on the little third-hand machine Perry had picked up for her at an auction sale—a machine that wrote only half of any capital letter and wouldn't print the "m's" at all. She put the capitals and the "m's" in afterwards with a pen and sent the MS. away to a publishing firm. The publishing firm sent it back with a type-written screed stating that "their readers had found some merit in the story but not enough to warrant an acceptance."

This "damning with faint praise" flattened Emily out as not even a printed slip could have done. Talk about three o'clock that night! No, it is an act of mercy not to talk about it—or about many successive three o'clocks.

"Ambition!" wrote Emily bitterly in her diary. "I could laugh! Where is my ambition now? What is it like to be ambitious? To feel that life is before you, a fair, unwritten white page where you may inscribe your name in letters of success? To feel that you have the wish and power to win your crown? To feel that the coming years are crowding to meet you and lay their largess at your feet? I *once* knew what it was to feel so."

All of which goes to show how very young Emily still was. But agony is none the less real because in later years when we have learned that everything passes, we wonder what we agonized about. She had a bad three weeks of it. Then she recovered enough to send her story out again. This time the publisher wrote to her that he might consider the book if she would make certain changes in it. It was too "quiet." She must "pep it up." And the ending must be changed entirely. It would never do.

Emily tore his letter savagely into bits. Mutilate and degrade her story? Never! The very suggestion was an insult.

When a third publisher sent it back with a printed slip Emily's belief in it died. She tucked it away and took up her pen grimly.

"Well, I can write short stories at least. I must continue to do that."

Nevertheless, the book haunted her. After a few weeks she took it out and reread it—coolly, critically, free alike from the delusive glamour of her first rapture and from the equally delusive depression of rejection slips. And still it seemed to her good. Not quite the wonder-tale she had fancied it, perhaps; but still a good piece of work. What then? No writer, so she had been told, was ever capable of judging his own work correctly. If only Mr. Carpenter were alive! He would tell her the truth. Emily made a sudden terrible resolution. She would show it to Dean. She would ask for his calm, unprejudiced opinion and abide by it. It would be hard. It was always hard to show her stories to any one, most of all to Dean, who knew so much and had read everything in the world. But she must *know*. And she knew Dean would tell her the truth, good or bad. He thought nothing of her stories. But *this* was different. Would he not see something worth while in this? If not—

## VI

"Dean, I want your candid opinion about this story. Will you read it carefully and tell me exactly what you think of it? I don't want flattery—or false encouragement—I want the truth—the naked truth."

"Are you sure of that?" asked Dean dryly. "Very few people can endure seeing the naked truth. It has to have a rag or two to make it presentable."

"I *do* want the truth," said Emily stubbornly. "This book has been"—she choked a little over the confession, "refused three times. If you find any good in it I'll keep on trying to find a publisher for it. If you condemn it I'll burn it."

Dean looked inscrutably at the little packet she held out to him. So *this* was what had wrapped her away from him all summer—absorbed her—possessed her. The one black drop in his veins—that Priest jealousy of being first—suddenly made its poison felt.

He looked into her cold, sweet face and starry eyes, grey-purple as a lake at dawn, and hated whatever was in the packet, but he carried it home and brought it back three nights later. Emily met him in the garden, pale and tense.

"Well," she said.

Dean looked at her, guilty. How ivory white and exquisite she was in the chill dusk!

"'Faithful are the wounds of a friend.' I should be less than your friend if I told you falsehoods about this, Emily."

"So—it's no good."

"It's a pretty little story, Emily. Pretty and flimsy and ephemeral as a rose-tinted cloud. Cobwebs—only cobwebs. The whole conception is too far-fetched. Fairy tales are out of the fashion. And this one of yours makes overmuch of a demand on the credulity of the reader. And your characters are only puppets. How could you write a real story? You've never *lived*."

Emily clenched her hands and bit her lips. She dared not trust her voice to say a single word. She had not felt like this since the night Ellen Greene had told her her father must die. Her heart, that had beaten so tumultuously a few minutes ago, was like lead, heavy and cold. She turned and walked away from him. He limped softly after her and touched her shoulder.

"Forgive me, Star. Isn't it better to know the truth? Stop reaching for the moon. You'll never get it. Why try to write, anyway? Everything has already been written."

"Some day,' said Emily, compelling herself to speak steadily, "I may be able to thank you for this. To-night I hate you."

"Is that just?" asked Dean quietly.

"No, of course it isn't just," said Emily wildly. "Can you expect me to be just when you've just killed me? Oh, I know I asked for it—I know it's good for me. Horrible things always are good for you, I suppose. After you've been killed a few times you don't mind it. But the first time one does—squirm. Go away, Dean. Don't come back for a week at least. The funeral will be over then."

"Don't you believe I know what this means to you, Star?" asked Dean pityingly.

"You can't—altogether. Oh, I know you're sympathetic. I don't want sympathy. I only want time to bury myself decently."

Dean, knowing it would be better to go, went. Emily watched him out of sight. Then she took up the little dog-eared, discredited manuscript he had laid on the stone bench and went up to her room. She looked it over by her window in the fading light. Sentence after sentence leaped out at her—witty, poignant, beautiful. No, that was only her fond, foolish, material delusion. There was nothing of that sort in the book. Dean had said so. And her book people. How she loved them.

How real they seemed to her. It was terrible to think of destroying them. But they were *not* real. Only "puppets." Puppets would not mind being burned. She glanced up at the starlit sky of the autumn night. Vega of the Lyre shone bluely down upon her. Oh, life was an ugly, cruel, wasteful thing!

Emily crossed over to her little fireplace and laid *A Seller of Dreams* in the grate. She struck a match, knelt down and held it to a corner with a hand that did not tremble. The flame seized on the loose sheets eagerly, murderously. Emily clasped her hands over her heart and watched it with dilated eyes, remembering the time she had burned her old "account book" rather than let Aunt Elizabeth see it. In a few moments the manuscript was a mass of writhing fires—in a few more seconds it was a heap of crinkled ashes, with here and there an accusing ghost-word coming out whitely on a blackened fragment, as if to reproach her.

Repentance seized upon her. Oh, why had she done it? Why had she burned her book? Suppose it was no good. Still, it was hers. It was wicked to have burned it. She had destroyed something incalculably precious to her. What did the mothers of old feel when their children had passed through the fire to Moloch—when the sacrificial impulse and excitement had gone? Emily thought she knew.

Nothing of her book, her dear book that had seemed so wonderful to her, but ashes—a little, pitiful heap of black ashes. Could it be so? Where had gone all the wit and laughter and charm that had seemed to glimmer in its pages—all the dear folks who had lived in them—all the secret delight she had woven into them as moonlight is woven among pines? Nothing left but ashes. Emily sprang up in such an anguish to regret that she could not endure it. She must get out—away—anywhere. Her little room, generally so dear and beloved and cosy, seemed like a prison. Out—somewhere—into the cold, free autumn night with its grey ghost-mists—away from walls and boundaries—away from that little heap of dark flakes in the grate—away from the reproachful ghosts of her murdered book folks. She flung open the door of the room and rushed blindly to the stair.

## VII

Aunt Laura never to the day of her death forgave herself for leaving that mending-basket at the head of the stair. She had never done such a thing in her life before. She had been carrying it up to her room when Elizabeth called peremptorily from the kitchen asking where something was. Laura set her basket down on the top step and ran to get it. She was away only a moment. But that moment was enough for predestination and Emily. The tear-blinded girl stumbled over the basket and fell—headlong down the long steep staircase of New Moon. There was a moment of fear—a moment of wonderment—she felt plunged into deadly cold—she felt plunged into burning heat—she felt a soaring upward—a falling into unseen depth—a fierce stab of agony in her foot—then nothing more. When Laura and Elizabeth came running in there was only a crumpled silken heap lying at the foot of the stairs with balls and stockings all around it and Aunt Laura's scissors bent and twisted under the foot they had so cruelly pierced.

# Chapter VII

## I

From October to April Emily Starr lay in bed or on the sitting-room lounge watching the interminable windy drift of clouds over the long white hills or the passionless beauty of winter trees around quiet fields of snow, and wondering if she would ever walk again— or walk only as a pitiable cripple. There was some obscure injury to her back upon which the doctors could not agree. One said it was negligible and would right itself in time. Two others shook their heads and were afraid. But all were agreed about the foot. The scissors had made two cruel wounds—one by the ankle, one on the sole of the foot. Blood-poisoning set in. For days Emily hovered between life and death, then between the scarcely less terrible alternative of death and amputation. Aunt Elizabeth prevented that. When all the doctors agreed that it was the only way to save Emily's life she said grimly that it was not the Lord's will, as understood by the Murrays, that people's limbs should be cut off. Nor could she be removed from this position. Laura's tears and Cousin Jimmy's pleadings and Dr. Burnley's execrations and Dean Priest's agreements budged her not a jot. Emily's foot should not be cut off. Nor was it. When she recovered unmaimed Aunt Elizabeth was triumphant and Dr. Burnley confounded.

The danger of amputation was over, but the danger of lasting and bad lameness remained. Emily faced that all winter.

"If I only *knew* one way or the other," she said to Dean. "If I *knew,* I could make up my mind to bear it—perhaps. But to lie here—wondering—wondering if I'll ever be well."

"You will be well," said Dean savagely.

Emily did not know what she would have done without Dean that winter. He had given up his invariable winter trip and stayed in Blair Water that he might be near her. He spent the days with her, reading, talking, encouraging, sitting in the silence of perfect companionship. When he was with her Emily felt that she might even be able to face a lifetime of lameness. But in the long nights when everything was blotted out by pain she could not face it. Even when there was no pain her nights were often sleepless and very terrible when the wind wailed drearily about the old New Moon eaves or chased flying phantoms of snow over the hills. When she slept she dreamed, and in her dreams she was forever climbing stairs and could never get to the top of them, lured upward by an odd little whistle—two higher notes and a low one—that ever retreated as she climbed. It was better to lie awake than to have that terrible, recurrent dream. Oh, those bitter nights! Once Emily had not thought that the Bible verse declaring that there would be no night in heaven contained an attrative promise. No night? No soft twilight enkindled with stars? No white sacrament of moonlight? No mystery of velvet shadow and darkness? No ever-amazing miracle of dawn? Night was as beautiful as day and heaven would not be perfect without it.

But now in these dreary weeks of pain and dread she shared the hope of the Patmian seer. Night was a dreadful thing.

People said Emily Starr was very brave and patient and uncomplaining. But she did not seem so to herself. They did not know of the agonies of rebellion and despair and cowardice behind her outward calmness of

Murray pride and reserve. Even Dean did not know—though perhaps he suspected.

She smiled gallantly when smiling was indicated, but she never laughed. Not even Dean could make her laugh, though he tried with all the powers of wit and humour at his command.

"My days of laughter are done," Emily said to herself. And her days of creation as well. She could never write again. The "flash" never came. No rainbow spanned the gloom of that terrible winter. People came to see her continuously. She wished they would stay away. Especially Uncle Wallace and Aunt Ruth, who were sure she would never walk again and said so every time they came. Yet they were not so bad as the callers who were cheerfully certain she would be all right in time and did not believe a word of it themselves. She had never had any intimate friends except Dean and Ilse and Teddy. Ilse wrote weekly letters in which she rather too obviously tried to cheer Emily up. Teddy wrote once when he heard of her accident. The letter was very kind and tactful and sincerely sympathetic. Emily thought it was the letter any indifferent friendly acquaintance might have written and she did not answer it though he had asked her to let him know how she was getting on. No more letters came. There was nobody but Dean. He had never failed her—never would fail her. More and more as the interminable days of storm and gloom passed she turned to him. In that winter of pain she seemed to herself to grow so old and wise that they met on equal ground at last. Without him life was a bleak, grey desert devoid of colour or music. When he came the desert would—for a time at least—blossom like the rose of joy and a thousand flowerets of fancy and hope and illusion would fling their garlands over it.

## II

When spring came Emily got well—got well so suddenly and quickly that even the most optimistic of the three doctors was amazed. True, for a few weeks she had to limp around on a crutch, but the time came when she could do without it—could walk alone in the garden and look out on the beautiful world with eyes that could not be satisfied with seeing. Oh, how good life was again! How good the green sod felt beneath her feet! She had left pain and fear behind her like a cast-off garment and felt gladness—no, not gladness exactly, but the possibility of being glad once more sometime.

It was worth while to have been ill to realise the savour of returning health and well-being on a morning like this, when a sea-wind was blowing up over the long, green fields. There was nothing on earth like a sea-wind. Life might, in some ways, be a thing of shreds and tatters, everything might be changed or gone; but pansies and sunset clouds were still fair. She felt again her old joy in mere existence.

" 'Truly the light is sweet and a pleasant thing it is for the eye to behold the sun,' " she quoted dreamily.

Old laughter came back. On the first day that Emily's laughter was heard again in New Moon Laura Murray, whose hair had turned from ash to snow that winter, went to her room and knelt down by her bed to thank God. And while she knelt there Emily was talking about God to Dean in the garden on one of the most beautiful spring twilights imaginable, with a little, growing moon in the midst of it.

"There have been times this past winter when I felt God hated me. But now again I feel sure He loves me," she said softly.

"So sure?" questioned Dean dryly. "I think God is interested in us but He doesn't love us. He likes to watch us to see what we'll do. Perhaps it amuses Him to see us squirm."

"What a horrible conception of God!" said Emily with a shudder. "You don't really believe that about Him, Dean."

"Why not?"

"Because He would be worse than a devil then—a God who thought only about his own amusement, without even the devil's justification of hating us."

"Who tortured you all winter with bodily pain and mental anguish?" asked Dean.

"Not God. And He—sent me *you*," said Emily steadily. She did not look at him; she lifted her face to the Three Princesses in their Maytime beauty—a white-rose face now, pale from its winter's pain. Beside her the big spirea, which was the pride of Cousin Jimmy's heart, banked up in its June-time snow, making a beautiful background for her. "Dean, how can I ever thank you for what you've done for me—been to me—since last October? I can never put it in words. But I want you to know how I feel about it."

"I've done nothing except snatch at happiness. Do you know what happiness it was to me to do something for you, Star—help you in some way—to see you turning to me in your pain for something that only I could give—something I had learned in my own years of loneliness? And to let myself dream something that couldn't come true—that I knew ought not to come true—"

Emily trembled and shivered slightly. Yet why hesitate—why put off that which she had fully made up her mind to do?

"Are you so sure, Dean," she said in a low tone, "that your dream—can't come true?"

# Chapter VIII

## I

There was a tremendous sensation in the Murray clan when Emily announced that she was going to marry Dean Priest. At New Moon the situation was very tense for a time. Aunt Laura cried and Cousin Jimmy went about shaking his head and Aunt Elizabeth was exceedingly grim. Yet in the end they made up their minds to accept it. What else could they do? By this time even Aunt Elizabeth realised that when Emily said she was going to do a thing she would do it.

"You would have made a worse fuss if I had told you I was going to marry Perry of Stovepipe Town," said Emily when she had heard all Aunt Elizabeth had to say.

"Of course that is true enough," admitted Aunt Elizabeth when Emily had gone out. "And, after all, Dean is well-off—and the Priests are a good family."

"But so—so *Priestly*," sighed Laura. "And Dean is far, far too old for Emily. Besides, his great-great grandfather went insane."

"Dean won't go insane."

"His children might."

"Laura," said Elizabeth rebukingly, and dropped the subject.

"Are you very sure you love him, Emily?" Aunt Laura asked that evening.

"Yes—in a way," said Emily.

Aunt Laura threw out her hands and spoke with a sudden passion utterly foreign to her.

"But there's only one way of loving."

"Oh, no, dearest of Victorian aunties," answered Emily gaily. "There are a dozen different ways. *You* know I've tried one or two ways already. And they failed me. Don't worry about Dean and me. We understand each other perfectly."

"I only want you to be happy, dear."

"And I will be happy—I am happy. I'm not a romantic little dreamer any longer. Last winter took that all out of me. I'm going to marry a man whose companionship satisfies me absolutely and he's quite satisfied with what I can give him—real affection and comradeship. I am sure that is the best foundation for a happy marriage. Besides, Dean *needs* me. I can make him happy. He has never been happy. Oh, it is delightful to feel that you hold happiness in your hand and can hold it out, like a pearl beyond price, to one who longs for it."

"You're too young," reiterated Aunt Laura.

"It's only my body that's young. My soul is a hundred years old. Last winter made me feel so old and wise. *You* know."

"Yes, I know." But Laura also knew that this very feeling old and wise merely proved Emily's youth. People who *are* old and wise never feel either. And all this talk of aged souls didn't do away with the fact that Emily, slim, radiant, with eyes of mystery, was not yet twenty, while Dean Priest was forty-two. In fifteen years—but Laura would not think of it.

And, after all, Dean would not take her away. There *had* been happy marriages with just as much disparity of age.

## II

Nobody, it must be admitted, seemed to regard the match with favour. Emily had a rather abominable time of it for a few weeks. Dr. Burnley raged about the affair and insulted Dean. Aunt Ruth came over and made a scene.

"He's an infidel, Emily."

"He isn't!" said Emily indignantly.

"Well, he doesn't believe what *we* believe," declared Aunt Ruth as if that ought to settle the matter for any true Murray.

Aunt Addie, who had never forgiven Emily for refusing her son, even though Andrew was now happily and suitably, *most* suitably, married, was very hard to bear. She contrived to make Emily feel a most condescending pity. She had lost Andrew, so must console herself with lame Jarback Priest. Of course Aunt Addie did not put it in so many blunt words but she might as well have. Emily understood her implications perfectly.

"Of course, he's richer than a *young* man could be," conceded Aunt Addie.

"And interesting," said Emily. "Most young men are *such* bores. They haven't lived long enough to learn that they are not the wonders to the world they are to their mothers."

So honours were about even *there*.

The Priests did not like it any too well either. Perhaps because they did not care to see a rich uncle's possessions thus slipping through the fingers of hope. They said Emily Starr was just marrying Dean for his money, and the Murrays took care that she should hear they had said it. Emily felt that the Priests were continually and maliciously discussing her behind her back.

"I'll never feel at home in your clan," she told Dean rebelliously.

"Nobody will ask you to. You and I, Star, are going to live unto ourselves. We are not going to walk or talk or think or breathe according to any clan standard, be it Priest or Murray. If the Priests disapprove of you as a wife for me the Murrays still more emphatically disapprove of me as a husband for you. Never mind. Of course the Priests find it hard to believe that you are marrying me because you care anything for me. How could you? I find it hard to believe myself."

"But you *do* believe it, Dean? Truly I care more for you than any one in the world. Of course—I told you—I don't love you like a silly, romantic girl."

"Do you love any one else?" asked Dean quietly. It was the first time he had ventured to ask the question.

"No. Of course—you know—I've had one or two broken-backed love affairs—silly schoolgirl fancies. That is all years behind me. Last winter seems like a lifetime— dividing me by centuries from those old follies. I'm all yours, Dean."

Dean lifted the hand he held and kissed it. He had never yet touched her lips.

"I can make you happy, Star. I know it. Old—lame as I am, I can make you happy. I've been waiting for you all my life, my star. That's what you've always seemed to me, Emily. An exquisite, unreachable star. Now I have you—hold you—wear you on my heart. And you will love me yet—some day you will give me more than affection."

The passion in his voice startled Emily a little. It seemed in some way to demand more of her than she had to give. And Ilse, who had graduated from the School of Oratory and had come home for a week before going on a summer concert tour, struck another note of warning that disturbed faintly for a time.

"In some ways, honey, Dean is just the man for you. He's clever and fascinating and not so horribly conscious of his own importance as most of the Priests. But you'll belong to him body and soul. Dean can't bear any one to have any interest outside of him. He must possess exclusively. If you don't mind that—"

"I don't think I do."

"Your writing—"

"Oh, I'm done with *that*. I seem to have no interest in it since my illness. I saw—then—how little it really mattered—how many more important things there were—"

"As long as you feel like that you'll be happy with Dean. Heigh-ho." Ilse sighed and pulled the blood-red rose that was pinned to her waist to pieces. "It makes me feel fearfully old and wise to be talking like this of your getting married, Emily. It seems so—absurd in some ways. Yesterday we were schoolgirls. To-day you're engaged. To-morrow—you'll be a grandmother."

"Aren't you—isn't there anybody in your own life, Ilse?"

"Listen to the fox that lost her tail. No, thank you. Besides—one might as well be frank. I feel an awful mood of honest confession on me. There's never been anybody for me but Perry Miller. And you've got your claws in him."

Perry Miller. Emily could not believe her ears.

"Ilse Burnley! You've always laughed at him—raged at him—"

"Of course I did. I liked him so much that it made me furious to see him making a fool of himself. I wanted to be proud of him and he always made me ashamed of him. Oh, there were times when he made me mad enough to bite the leg off a chair. If I hadn't cared, do you suppose it would have mattered what kind of a donkey he was? I can't get over it—the 'Burnley softness,' I suppose. We never change. Oh, I'd have jumped at him—would yet—herring-barrels, Stovepipe Town and all. There you have it. But never mind. Life is very decent without him."

"Perhaps—some day—"

"Don't dream it. Emily, I won't have you setting about making matches for me. Perry never gave me two thoughts—never will. I'm not going to think of him. What's that old verse we laughed over once that last year in high school—thinking it was all nonsense?

"'Since ever the world was spinning
And till the world shall end
You've your man in the beginning
Or you have him in the end,
But to have him from start to finish

And neither to borrow nor lend
Is what all the girls are wanting
And none of the gods can send.'

"Well, next year I'll graduate. For years after that a career. Oh, I daresay I'll marry some day."

"Teddy?" said Emily, before she could prevent herself. She could have bitten her tongue off the moment the word escaped it.

Ilse gave her a long, keen look, which Emily parried successfully with all the Murray pride—too successfully, perhaps.

"No, not Teddy. Teddy never thought about me. I doubt if he thinks of any one but himself. Teddy's a duck but he's selfish, Emily, he really is."

"No, no," indignantly. She could not listen to this.

"Well, we won't quarrel over it. What difference does it make if he is? He's gone out of our lives anyway. The cat can have him. He's going to climb to the top—they thought him a wow in Montreal. He'll make a wonderful portrait painter—if he can only cure himself of his old trick of putting *you* into all the faces he paints."

"Nonsense. He doesn't—"

"He *does*. I've raged at him about it times without number. Of course he denies it. I really think he's quite unconscious of it himself. It's the hang-over from some old unconscious emotion, I suppose—to use the jargon of modern phychologists. Never mind. As I said, I mean to marry sometime. When I'm tired of a career. It's very jolly *now*—but some day. I'll make a sensible wedding o't, just as you're doing, with a heart of gold and a pocket of silver. Isn't it funny to be talking of marrying some man you've never even seen? What is he doing at this very moment? Shaving—swearing—breaking his heart over some other girl? Still, he's to marry *me*. Oh, we'll be happy enough, too. And we'll visit each other, you and I—and compare our children—call your first girl Ilse, won't you, friend of my heart—

and—and what a devilish thing it is to be a woman, isn't it, Emily!"

Old Kelly, the tin peddler, who had been Emily's friend of many years, had to have his say about it, too. One could not suppress Old Kelly.

"Gurrl dear, is it true that ve do be after going to marry Jarback Praste?"

"Quite true." Emily knew it was of no use to expect Old Kelly to call Dean anything but Jarback. But she always winced.

Old Kelly crabbed his face.

"Ye're too young at the business of living to be marrying any one—laste of all a Praste."

"Haven't you been twitting me for years with my slowness in getting a beau?" asked Emily slyly.

"Gurrl dear, a joke is a joke. But this is beyond joking. Don't be pig-headed now, there's a jewel. Stop a bit and think it over. There do be some knots mighty aisy to tie but the untying is a cat of a different brade. I've always been warning ye against marrying a Praste. 'Twas a foolish thing—I might av known it. I should've towld ye to marry one."

"Dean isn't like the other Priests, Mr. Kelly. I'm going to be very happy."

Old Kelly shook his bushy, reddish grey head incredulously.

"Then you'll be the first Praste woman that ever was, not aven laving out the ould Lady at the Grange. But *she* liked a fight every day. It'll be the death av you."

"Dean and I won't fight—at least not every day." Emily was having some fun to herself. Old Kelly's gloomy predictions did not worry her. She took rather an impish delight in egging him on.

"Not if ye give him his own way. He'll sulk if ye don't. All the Prastes sulk if they don't get it. And he'll be that jealous—ye'll never dare spake to another man. Oh, the Prastes rule their wives. Old Aaron Praste made his wife go down on her knees whenever she had a little favour to ask. Me feyther saw it wid his own eyes."

"Mr. Kelly, do you really suppose *any* man could make *me* do that?"

Old Kelly's eyes twinkled in spite of himself.

"The Murray knee jints do be a bit stiff for that," he acknowledged. "But there's other things. Do ye be after knowing that his Uncle Jim never spoke when he could grunt and always said 'Ye fool' to his wife when she conterdicted him."

"But perhaps she *was* a fool, Mr. Kelly."

"Mebbe. But was it polite? I lave it to ye. And his father threw the dinner dishes at his wife whin she made him mad. 'Tis a fact, I'm telling you. Though the old divil *was* amusing when he was pleased."

"That sort of thing always skips a generation," said Emily. "And if not—I can dodge."

"Gurrl dear, there do be worse things than having a dish or two flung at ye. Ye *kin* dodge them. But there's things ye can't dodge. Tell me now, do ye know"—Old Kelly lowered his voice ominously—"that 'tis said the Prastes do often get tired av bein' married to the wan woman."

Emily was guilty of giving Mr. Kelly one of the smiles Aunt Elizabeth had always disapproved of.

"Do you really think Dean will get tired of me? I'm not beautiful, dear Mr. Kelly, but I am very interesting."

Old Kelly gathered up his lines with the air of a man who surrenders at discretion.

"Well, gurrl dear, ye do be having a good mouth for kissing, anyway. I see ye're set on it. But I do be thinking the Lord intended ye for something different. Anyway, here's hoping we'll all make a good end. But he knows too much, that Jarback Praste, he's after knowing far too much."

Old Kelly drove off, waiting till he was decently out of earshot to mutter:

"Don't it bate hell? And him as odd-looking as a cross-eyed cat!"

Emily stood still for a few minutes looking after Old Kelly's retreting chariot. He had found the one joint in her armour and the thrust had struck home. A little chill crept over her as if a wind from the grave had blown across her spirit. All at once an old, old story whispered long ago by Great-aunt Nancy to Caroline Priest flashed into her recollection. Dean, so it was said, had seen the Black Mass celebrated.

Emily shook the recollection from her. *That* was all nonsense—silly, malicious, envious gossip of stay-at-homes. But Dean *did* know too much. He had eyes that had seen too much. In a way that had been part of the distinct fascination he had always had for Emily. But now it frightened her. Had she not always felt—did she not still feel—that he always seemed to be laughing at the world from some mysterious standpoint of inner knowledge—a knowledge she did not share—could not share—did not, to come down to the bare bones of it, want to share? He had lost some intangible, all-real zest of faith and idealism. It was there deep in her heart—an inescapable conviction, thrust it out of sight as she might. For a moment she felt with Ilse that it was a decidedly devilish thing to be a woman.

"It serves me right for bandying words with Old Jock Kelly on such a subject," she thought angrily.

Consent was never given in set terms to Emily's engagement. But the thing came to be tacitly accepted. Dean was well-to-do. The Priests had all the necessary traditions, including that of a grandmother who had danced with the Prince of Wales at the famous ball in Charlottetown. After all, there would be a certain relief in seeing Emily safely married.

"He won't take her far away from us," said Aunt Laura, who could have reconciled herself to almost anything for that. How could they lose the one bright, gay thing in that faded house?

"Tell Emily," wrote old Aunt Nancy, "that twins run in the Priest family."

But Aunt Elizabeth did not tell her.

Dr. Burnley, who had made the most fuss, gave in when he heard that Elizabeth was overhauling the chest of quilts in the attic of New Moon and that Laura was hemstitching table linen.

"Those whom Elizabeth Murray has joined together let no man put asunder," he said resignedly.

Aunt Laura cupped Emily's face in her gentle hands and looked deep into her eyes. "God bless you, Emily, dear child."

"Very mid-Victorian," commented Emily to Dean. "But I liked it."

# Chapter IX

## I

On one point Aunt Elizabeth was adamant. Emily should not be married until she was twenty. Dean, who had dreamed of an autumn wedding and a winter spent in a dreamy Japanese garden beyond the western sea, gave in with a bad grace. Emily, too, would have preferred an earlier bridal. In the back of her mind, where she would not even glance at it, was the feeling that the sooner it was over and made irrevocable, the better.

Yet she was happy, as she told herself very often and very sincerely. Perhaps there *were* dark moments when a disquieting thought stared her in the face—it was but a crippled, broken-winged happiness—not the wild, free-flying happiness she had dreamed of. But that, she reminded herself, was lost to her forever.

One day Dean appeared before her with a flush of boyish excitement on his face.

"Emily, I've been and gone and done something. Will you approve? Oh, Lord, what will I do if you don't approve?"

"What is it you've done?"

"I've bought a house."

"A house!"

"A house! I, Dean Priest, am a landed proprietor—owning a house, a garden and a spruce lot five acres in extent. I, who this morning hadn't a square inch of earth to call my own. I, who all my life have been hungry to own a bit of land."

"*What* house have you bought, Dean?"

"Fred Clifford's house—at least the house he has always owned by a legal quibble. Really *our* house—appointed—foreordained for us since the foundation of the world."

"The Disappointed House?"

"Oh, yes, that was your old name for it. But it isn't going to be Disappointed any longer. That is—if—Emily, *do* you approve of what I've done?"

"Approve? You're simply a darling, Dean. I've always loved that house. It's one of those houses you love the minute you see them. Some houses are like that, you know—full of magic. And others have nothing at all of it in them. I've always longed to see that house fulfilled. Oh—and somebody told me you were going to buy that big horrible house at Shrewsbury. I was afraid to ask if it were true."

"Emily, take back those words. You knew it wasn't true. You knew me better. Of course, all the Priests wanted me to buy that house. My dear sister was almost in tears because I wouldn't. It was to be had at a bargain—and it was *such* an elegant house."

"It *is* elegant—with all the word implies," agreed Emily. "But it's an impossible house—not because of its size or its elegance but just because of its impossibility."

"E-zackly. Any proper woman would feel the same. I'm so glad you're pleased, Emily. I had to buy Fred's house yesterday in Charlottetown—without waiting to consult you—another man was on the point of buying it, so I wired Fred instantly. Of course, if you hadn't liked it I'd have sold it again. But I *felt* you would. We'll make such a home of it, dear. I want a home. I've had many habitations but no homes. I'll have it finished and fixed up as beautifully as possible for you, Star—my Star who is fit to shine in the palaces of kings."

"Let's go right up and look at it," said Emily. "I want to tell it what is coming to it. I want to tell it it is going to *live* at last."

"We'll go up and look at it and *in* it. I've got the key.

Got it from Fred's sister. Emily, I feel as if I'd reached up and plucked the moon."

"Oh, *I've* picked a lapful of stars," cried Emily gaily.

## II

They went up to the Disappointed House—through the old orchard full of columbines and along the To-morrow Road, across a pasture field, up a little slope of golden fern, and over an old meandering fence with its longers bleached to a silvery grey, with clusters of wild everlastings and blue asters in its corners, then up the little winding, capricious path on the long fir hill, which was so narrow they had to walk singly and where the air always seemed so full of nice whispering sounds.

When they came to its end there was a sloping field before them, dotted with little, pointed firs, windy, grassy, lovable. And on top of it, surrounded by hill glamour and upland wizardry, with great sunset clouds heaped up over it, the house—*their* house.

A house with the mystery of woods behind it and around it, except on the south side where the land fell away in a long hill looking down on the Blair Water, that was like a bowl of dull gold now, and across it to meadows of starry rest beyond and the Derry Pond Hills that were as blue and romantic as the famous Alsatian Mountains. Between the house and the view, but not hiding it, was a row of wonderful Lombardy poplars.

They climed the hill to the gate of a little enclosed garden—a garden far older than the house which had been built on the site of a little log cabin of pioneer days.

"That's a view I can live with," said Dean exultingly. "Oh, 'tis a dear place this. The hill is haunted by squirrels, Emily. And there are rabbits about. Don't you love squirrels and rabbits? And there are any number of shy violets hereabouts in spring, too. There is a little mossy hollow behind those young firs that is full of violets in May—violets,

> 'Sweeter than lids of Emily's eyes
> Or Emily's breath.'

Emily's a nicer name than Cytherea or Juno, *I* think. I want you to notice especially that little gate over yonder. It isn't really needed. It opens only into that froggy marsh beyond the wood. But isn't it a gate? I love a gate like that—a reasonless gate. It's full of promise. There *may* be something wonderful beyond. A gate is always a mystery, anyhow—it lures—it is a symbol. And listen to that bell ringing somewhere in the twilight across the harbour. A bell in twilight always has a magic sound—as if it came from somewhere 'far far in fairyland.' There are roses in that far corner—old-fashioned roses like sweet old songs set to flowering. Roses white enough to lie in your white bosom, my sweet, roses red enough to star that soft dark cloud of your hair. Emily, do you know I'm a little drunk to-night —on the wine of life. Don't wonder if I say crazy things."

Emily was very happy. The old, sweet garden seemed to be talking to her as a friend in the drowsy, winking light. She surrendered herself utterly to the charm of the place. She looked at the Disappointed House adoringly. Such a dear *thoughtful* little house. Not an old house—she liked it for that—an old house knew too much—was haunted by too many feet that had walked over its threshold—too many anguished or impassioned eyes that had looked out of its windows. This house was ignorant and innocent like herself. Longing for happiness. It should have it. She and Dean would drive out the ghosts of things that never happened. How sweet it would be to have a home of her very own.

"That house wants us as badly as we want it," she said.

"I love you when your tones soften and mute like

that, Star," said Dean. "Don't ever talk so to any other man, Emily."

Emily threw him a glance of coquetry that very nearly made him kiss her. He had never kissed her yet. Some subtle prescience always told him she was not yet ready to be kissed. He might have dared it there and then, in that hour of glamour that had transmuted everything into terms of romance and charm—he might even have won her wholly then. But he hesitated—and the magic moment passed. From somewhere down the dim road behind the spruces came laughter. Harmless, innocent laughter of children. but it broke some faintly woven spell.

"Let us go in and see our house," said Dean. He led the way across the wild-grown gasses to the door that opened into the living-room. The key turned stiffly in the rusted lock. Dean took Emily's hand and drew her in.

"Over your own threshold, sweet—"

He lifted his flashlight and threw a circle of shifting light around the unfinished room, with its bare, staring, lathed walls, its sealed windows, its gaping doorways, its empty fireplace—no, not quite empty. Emily saw a little heap of white ashes in it—the ashes of the fire she and Teddy had kindled years ago that adventurous summer evening of childhood—the fire by which they had sat and planned out their lives together. She turned to the door with a little shiver.

"Dean, it looks too ghostly and forlorn. I think I'd rather explore it by daylight. The ghosts of things that never happened are worse than the ghosts of things that did."

### III

It was Dean's suggestion that they spend the summer finishing and furnishing their house—doing everything possible themselves and fixing it up exactly as they wanted it.

"Then we can be married in the spring—spend the summer listening to temple bells tinkling over eastern sands—watch Philae by moonlight—hear the Nile moaning by Memphis—come back in the autumn, turn the key of our own door—be at home."

Emily thought the program delightful. Her aunts were dubious about it—it didn't seem quite proper and respectable really—people would talk terribly. And Aunt Laura was worried over some old superstition that it wasn't lucky to furnish a house *before* a wedding. Dean and Emily didn't care whether it was respectable and lucky or not. They went ahead and did it.

Naturally they were overwhelmed with advice from every one in the Priest and Murray clans—and took none of it. For one thing, they wouldn't paint the Disappointed House—just shingled it and left the shingles to turn woodsy grey, much to Aunt Elizabeth's horror.

"It's only Stovepipe Town houses that aren't painted," she said.

They replaced the old, unused, temporary board steps, left by the carpenters thirty years before, with broad red sandstones from the shore. Dean had casement windows put in with diamond-shaped panes which Aunt Elizabeth warned Emily would be terrible things to keep clean. And he added a dear little window over the front door with a little roof over it like a shaggy eyebrow and in the living-room they had a French window from which you could step right out into the fir wood.

And Dean had jewels of closets and cupboards put in everywhere.

"I'm not such a fool as to imagine that a girl can keep on loving a man who doesn't provide her with proper cupboards," he declared.

Aunt Elizabeth approved of the cupboards but thought they were clean daft in regard to the wallpapers. Especially the living-room paper. They should have had something cheerful there—flowers or gold stripes; or even, as a vast concession to modernity, some of those "landscape papers" that were coming in. But Emily insisted on papering it with a shadowy grey paper with snowy pine branches over it. Aunt Elizabeth declared she would as soon live in the woods as in such a room. But Emily in this respect, as in all others concerning her own dear house, was "as pig-headed as ever," so exasperated Aunt Elizabeth averred, quite unconscious that a Murray was borrowing one of Old Kelly's expressions.

But Aunt Elizabeth was really very good. She dug up, out of long undisturbed boxes and chests, china and silver belonging to her stepmother—the things Juliet Murray would have had if she had married in orthodox fashion a husband approved of her clan—and gave them to Emily. There were some lovely things among them—especially a priceless pink lustre jug and a delightful old dinner set of real willow-ware—Emily's grandmother's own wedding set. Not a piece was missing. And it had shallow thin cups and deep saucers and scalloped plates and round, fat, pobby tureens. Emily filled the built-in cabinet in the living-room with it and gloated over it. There were other things she loved too; a little gilt-framed oval mirror with a black cat on top of it, a mirror that had so often reflected beautiful women that it lent a certain charm to every face; and an old clock with a pointed top and two tiny gilded spires on each side, a clock that gave warning ten minutes before it struck, a gentlemanly clock never taking people unawares. Dean would it up but would not start it.

"When we come home—when I bring you in here as bride and queen, you shall start it going," he said.

It turned out, too, that the Chippendale sideboard and the claw-footed mahogany table at New Moon were Emily's. And Dean had no end of quaint, delightful things picked up all over the world—a sofa covered with striped silk that had been in the Salon of a Marquise of the Old Régime, a lantern of wrought-iron lace from an old Venetian palace to hang in the living-room, a Shiraz rug, a prayer-rug from Damascus, brass andirons from Italy, jades and ivories from China, lacquer bowls from Japan, a delightful little green owl in Japanese china, a painted Chinese perfume-bottle of agate which he had found in some weird place in Mongolia, with the perfume of the east—which is never the perfume of the west—clinging to it, a Chinese teapot with dreadful golden dragons coiling over it—five-clawed dragons whereby the initiated knew that it was of the Imperial cabinets. It was part of the loot of the Summer Palace in the Boxer Rebellion, Dean told Emily, but he would not tell her how it had come into his possession.

"Not yet. Some day. There's a story about almost everything I've put in this house."

## IV

They had a great day putting the furniture in the living-room. They tried it in a dozen different places and were not satisfied until they had found the absolutely right one. Sometimes they could not agree about it and then they would sit on the floor and argue it out. And if they couldn't settle it they got Daffy to pull straws with his teeth and decide it that way. Daffy was always around. Saucy Sal had died of old age and Daffy was getting stiff and cranky and snored dreadfully when he was sleeping, but Emily adored him and would not go to the Disappointed House without him. He always slipped up the hill path beside her like a grey shadow dappled with dark.

"You love that old cat more than you do me, Emily," Dean once said—jestingly yet with an undernote of earnest.

"I *have* to love him," defended Emily. "He's growing old. *You* have all the years before us. And I must always have a cat about. A house isn't a home without the ineffable contentment of a cat with its tail folded about its feet. A cat gives mystery, charm, suggestion. And you must have a dog.

"I've never cared to have a dog since Tweed died. But perhaps I'll get one—an altogether different kind of a one. We'll need a dog to keep your cats in order. Oh, isn't it nice to feel that a place belongs to you?"

"It's nicer to feel that you belong to a place," said Emily, looking about her affectionately.

"Our house and we are going to be good friends," agreed Dean.

## V

They hung their pictures one day. Emily brought her favourites up, including the Lady Giovanna and Mona Lisa. These two were hung in the corner between the windows.

"Where your writing desk will be," said Dean. "And Mona Lisa will whisper to you the ageless secret of her smile and you shall put it in a story."

"I thought you didn't want me to write any more stories," said Emily. "You've never seemed to like the fact of my writing."

"That was when I was afraid it would take you away from me. Now, it doesn't matter. I want you to do just as pleases you."

Emily felt indifferent. She had never cared to take up her pen since her illness. As the days passed she felt a growing distaste to the thought of ever taking it up. To think of it meant to think of the book she had burned; and *that* hurt beyond bearing. She had ceased to listen for her "random word"—she was an exile from her old starry kingdom.

"I'm going to hang old Elizabeth Bas by the fireplace," said Dean. " 'Engraving from a portrait by Rembrandt.' Isn't she a delightful old woman, Star, in her white cap and tremendous white ruff collar? And did you ever see such a shrewd, humorous, complacent, slightly contemptuous old face?"

"I don't think I should want to have an argument with Elizabeth," reflected Emily. "One feels that she is keeping her hands folded under compulsion and might box your ears if you disagreed with her."

"She has been dust for over a century," said Dean dreamily. "Yet here she is living on this cheap reprint of Rembrandt's canvas. You are expecting her to speak to you. And I feel, as you do, that she wouldn't put up with any nonsense."

"But likely she has a sweetmeat stored away in some pocket of her gown for you. That fine, rosy, wholesome old woman. *She* ruled her family—not a doubt of it. Her husband did as she told him—but never knew it."

"*Had* she a husband?" said Dean doubtfully. "There's no wedding-ring on her finger."

"Then she must have been a most delightful old maid," averred Emily.

"What a difference between her smile and Mona Lisa's," said Dean, looking from one to the other. "Elizabeth is tolerating things—with just a hint of a sly, meditative cat about her. But Mona Lisa's face has that everlasting lure and provocation that drives men mad and writes scarlet pages on dim historical records. La Gioconda would be a more stimulating sweetheart. But Elizabeth would be nicer for an aunt."

Dean hung a little old miniature of his mother up over the mantelpiece. Emily had never seen it before. Dean Priest's mother had been a beautiful woman.

"But why does she look so sad?"

"Because she was married to a Priest," said Dean.

"Will I look sad?" teased Emily.

"Not if it rests with me," said Dean.

But did it? Sometimes that question forced itself on Emily, but she would not answer it. She was very happy two-thirds of that summer—which she told herself was a high average. But in the other third were hours of which she never spoke to any one—hours in which her soul felt caught in a trap—hours when the great, green emerald winking on her finger seemed like a fetter. And once she even took it off just to feel free for a little while—a temporary escape for which she was sorry and ashamed the next day, when she was quite sane and normal again, contented with her lot and more interested than ever in her little grey house, which meant so much to her—"more to me than Dean does," she said to herself once in a three-o'clock moment of stark, despairing honesty; and then refused to believe it next morning.

## VI

Old Great-aunt Nancy of Priest Pond died that summer, very suddenly. "I'm tired of living. I think I'll stop," she said one day—and stopped. None of the Murrays benefited by her will; everything she had was left to Caroline Priest; but Emily got the gazing-ball and the brass chessy-cat knocker and the gold ear-rings—and the picture Teddy had done of her in water-colours years ago. Emily put the chessy-cat on the front porch door of the Disappointed House and hung the great silvery gazing-ball from the Venetian lantern and wore the quaint old ear-rings to many rather delightful pomps and vanities. But she put the picture away in a box in the New Moon attic—a box that held certain sweet—old, foolish letters full of dreams and plans.

## VII

They had glorious minutes of fun when they stopped to rest occasionally. There was a robin's nest in the fir at the north corner which they watched and protected from Daffy.

"Think of the music penned in this fragile, pale blue wall," said Dean, touching an egg one day. "Not the music of the moon perhaps, but an earthlier, homelier music, full of wholesome sweetness and the joy of living. This egg will some day be a robin, Star, to whistle us blithely home in the afterlight."

They made friends with an old rabbit that often came hopping out of the woods into the garden. They had a game as to who could count the most squirrels in the daytime and the most bats in the evening. For they did not always go home as soon as it got too dark to work. Sometimes they sat out on their sandstone steps listening to the melancholy loveliness of night-wind on the sea and watching the twilight creep up from the old valley and the shadows waver and flicker under the fir-trees and the Blair Water turning to a great grey pool tremulous with early stars. Daff sat beside them, watching everything with his great moonlight eyes, and Emily pulled his ears now and then.

"One understands a cat a little better now. At all other times he is inscrutable, but in the time of dusk and dew we can catch a glimpse of the tantalising secret of his personality."

"One catches a glimpse of all kinds of secrets now," said Dean. "On a night like this I always think of the 'hills where spices grow.' That line of the old hymn Mother used to sing has always intrigued me—though I can't 'fly like a youthful hart or roe.' Emily, I can see that you are getting your mouth in the proper shape to talk about the colour we'll paint the woodshed. Don't you do it. No one should talk paint when she's expecting a moonrise. There'll be a wonderful one presently— I've arranged for it. But if we *must* talk of furniture let's plan for a few things we haven't got yet and *must* have—a canoe for our boating trips along the Milky Way, for instance—a loom for the weaving of dreams and a jar of pixy-brew for festal hours. And can't we arrange to have the spring of Ponce de Leon over in that corner? Or would you prefer a fount of Castaly? As for your trousseau, have what you like in it but there *must* be a gown of grey twilight with an evening star for your hair. Also trimmed with moonlight and a scarf of sunset cloud."

Oh, she liked Dean. *How* she liked him. If she could only love him!

One evening she slipped up alone to see her little house by moonlight. What a dear place it was. She saw herself there in the future—flitting through the little rooms—laughing under the firs—sitting hand in hand with Teddy at the fireplace—Emily came to herself with a shock. With Dean, of course, with Dean. A mere trick of the memory.

## VIII

There came a September evening when everything was done—even to the horseshoe over the door to keep the witches out—even to the candles Emily had struck all about the living-room—a little, jolly, yellow candle—a full, red pugnacious candle—a dreamy, pale blue candle—a graceless candle with aces of hearts and diamonds all over it—a slim, dandyish candle.

And the result was good. There was a sense of harmony in the house. The things in it did not have to become acquainted but were good friends from the very start. They did not shriek at each other. There was not a noisy room in the house.

"There's absolutely nothing more we can do," sighed Emily. "We can't even *pretend* there's anything more to do."

"I suppose not," agreed Dean regretfully. Then he looked at the fireplace where kindlings and pine wood were laid.

"Yes, there is," he cried. "How could we have forgotten it? We've got to see if the chimney will draw properly. I'm going to light that fire."

Emily sat down on the settee in the corner and when the fire began to burn Dean came and sat beside her. Daffy lay stretched out at their feet, his little striped flanks moving peacefully up and down.

Up blazed the merry flames. They shimmered over the old piano—they played irreverent hide-and-seek with Elizabeth Bas' adorable old face—they danced on the glass doors of the cupboard where the willow-ware dishes were; they darted through the kitchen door and the row of brown and blue bowls Emily had ranged on the dresser winked back at them.

"This is home," said Dean softly. "It's lovelier than I've ever dreamed of its being. This is how we'll sit on autumn evenings all our lives, shutting out the cold misty nights that come in from the sea—just you and I alone with the firelight and the sweetness. But sometimes we'll let a friend come in and share it—sip of our joy and drink of our laughter. We'll just sit here and think about it all—till the fire burns out."

The fire crackled and snapped. Daffy purred. The moon shone down through the dance of the fir-boughs straight on them through the windows. And Emily was thinking—could not help thinking—of the time she and Teddy had sat there. The odd part was that she did not think of him longingly or lovingly. She just thought of him. Would she, she asked herself, in mingled exasperation and dread, find herself thinking of Teddy when she was standing up to be married to Dean?

When the fire had died down into white ashes Dean got up.

"It was worth while to have lived long dreary years for this—and to live them again, if need be, looking back to it," he said, holding out his hand. He drew her nearer. What ghost came between the lips that might have met? Emily turned away with a sigh.

"Our happy summer is over, Dean."

"Our *first* happy summer," corrected Dean. But his voice suddenly sounded a little tired.

# Chapter X

## I

They locked the door of the Disappointed House one November evening and Dean gave the key to Emily.

"Keep it till spring," he said, looking out over the quiet, cold, grey fields across which a chilly wind was blowing. "We won't come back here till then."

In the stormy winter that followed, the cross-lots path to the little house was so heaped with drifts that Emily never went near it. But she thought about it often and happily, waiting amid its snows for spring and life and fulfilment. That winter was, on the whole, a happy time. Dean did not go away and made himself so charming to the older ladies of New Moon that they almost forgave him for being Jarback Priest. To be sure, Aunt Elizabeth never could understand more than half of his remarks and Aunt Laura put down to his debit account the change in Emily. For she was changed. Cousin Jimmy and Aunt Laura knew that, though no one else seemed to notice it. Often there was an odd restlessness in her eyes. And something was missing from her laughter. It was not so quick—so spontaneous as of old. She was a woman before her time, thought Aunt Laura with a sigh. Was that dreadful fall down the New Moon stairs the only cause? *Was* Emily happy? Laura dared not ask. *Did* she love Dean Priest whom she was going to marry in June? Laura did not know; but she *did* know that love is something that cannot be generated by an intellectual rule o' thumb.

Also that a girl who is as happy as an engaged girl should be does not spend so many hours when she should be sleeping pacing up and down her room. This was not to be explained away on the ground that Emily was thinking out stories. Emily had given up writing. In vain Miss Royal wrote pleading and scolding letters from New York. In vain Cousin Jimmy slyly laid a new Jimmy-book at intervals on her desk. In vain Laura timidly hinted that it was a pity not to keep on when you had made such a good start. Even Aunt Elizabeth's contemptuous assertion that she had always known Emily would get tired of it—"the Starr fickleness, you see"—failed to sting Emily back to her pen. She could not write—she would never try to write again.

"I've paid my debts and I've enough in the bank to get what Dean calls my wedding doo-dabs. And you've crocheted two filet spreads for me," she told Aunt Laura a little wearily and bitterly. "So what does it matter?"

"Was it—your fall that took away your—your ambition?" faltered poor Aunt Laura, voicing what had been her haunting dread all winter.

Emily smiled and kissed her.

"No, darling. That had nothing to do with it. Why worry over a simple, natural thing? Here I am, going to be married, with a prospective house and husband to think about. Doesn't that explain why I've ceased to care about—other things?"

It should have, but that evening Emily went out of the house after sunset. Her soul was pining for freedom and she went out to slip its leash for a little while. It had been an April day, warm in the sun, cold in the shadow. You felt the coldness even amid the sunlight warmth. The evening was chill. The sky was overcast with wrinkled, grey clouds, save along the west where a strip of yellow sky gleamed palely and in it, sad and fair, a new moon setting behind a dark hill. No living creature but herself seemed abroad and the cold shadows settling down over the withered fields lent to the landscape of too-early spring an aspect inexpressibly dreary and mournful. It made Emily feel hopeless, as if the best of life already lay in the past. Externals always had a great influence upon her—too great perhaps. Yet she was glad it was a dour evening. Anything else would have insulted her mood. She heard the sea shuddering beyond the dunes. An old verse from one of Roberts' poems came into her head:

"Grey rocks and greyer sea
And surf along the shore,
And in my heart a name
My lips shall speak no more."

Nonsense! Weak, silly, sentimental nonsense. No more of it!

## II

But that letter from Ilse that day. Teddy was coming home. He was to sail on the *Flavian*. He was going to be home most of the summer.

"If it could have been all over—before he came," muttered Emily.

Always to be afraid of to-morrow? Content—even happy with to-day—but always afraid of to-morrow. Was this to be her life? And *why* that fear of to-morrow?

She had brought the key of the Disappointed House with her. She had not been in it since November and she wanted to see it—beautiful, waiting, desirable. *Her* home. In its charm and sanity vague, horrible fears and doubts would vanish. The soul of that happy last summer would come back to her. She paused at the garden gate to look lovingly at it—the dear little house nestled under the old trees that sighed softly as they had sighed to her childhood visions. Below, Blair Water was grey and sullen. She loved Blair Water in all its changes—its sparkle of summer, its silver of dusk, its miracle of moonlight, its dimpled rings of rain. And she loved it now, dark and brooding. There was somehow a piercing sadness in that sullen, waiting landscape all around her—as if—the odd fancy crossed her mind—as if it were *afraid* of spring. How this idea of fear haunted her! She looked up beyond the spires of the Lombardies on the hill. And in a sudden pale rift between the clouds a star shone down on her—Vega of the Lyre.

With a shiver Emily hurriedly unlocked the door and stepped in. The house seemed to be vacant—waiting for her. She fumbled through the darkness to the matches she knew were on the mantelpiece and lighted the tall, pale-green taper beside the clock. The beautiful room glimmered out at her in the flickering light—just as they had left it that last evening. There was Elizabeth Bas, who could never have known the meaning of fear—Mona Lisa, who mocked at it. But the Lady Giovanna, who never turned her saintly profile to look squarely at you. Had she ever known it—this subtle, secret fear that one could never put in words?—that would be so ridiculous if one could put it in words? Dean Priest's sad lovely mother. Yes, she had known fear; it looked out of her pictured eyes now in that dim, furtive light.

Emily shut the door and sat down in the armchair beneath Elizabeth Bas' picture. She could hear the dead, dry leaves of a dead summer rustling eerily on the beach just outside the window. And the wind—rising—rising—rising. But she liked it. "The wind is free—not a prisoner like me." She crushed the unbidden thought down sternly. She would *not* think such things. Her fetters were of her own forging. She had put them on willingly, even desirously. Nothing to do but wear them gracefully.

How the sea moaned down there below the fields! But here in the little house what a silence there was! Something strange and uncanny about the silence. It seemed to hold some profound meaning. She would not have dared to speak lest *something* should answer her. Yet fear suddenly left her. She felt dreamy—happy—far away from life and reality. The walls of the shadowy room seemed slowly to fade from her vision. The pictures withdrew themselves. There seemed to be nothing before her but Great-aunt Nancy's gazing-ball hung from the old iron lantern—a big, silvery, gleaming globe. In it she saw the reflected room, like a shining doll's-house, with herself sitting in the old, low chair and the taper on the mantelpiece like a tiny, impish star. Emily looked at it as she leaned back in her chair—looked at it till she saw nothing but that tiny point of light in a great misty universe.

## III

Did she sleep? Dream? Who knows? Emily herself never knew. Twice before in her life—once in delirium*—once in sleep† she had drawn aside the veil of sense and time and seen beyond. Emily never liked to remember those experiences. She forgot them deliberately. She had not recalled them for years. A dream—a fancy fever-bred. But this?

A small cloud seemed to shape itself within the gazing-ball. It dispersed—faded. But the reflected doll's-house in the ball was gone. Emily saw an entirely different scene—a long lofty room filled with streams of hurrying people—and among them a face she knew.

The gazing-ball was gone—the room in the Disappointed House was gone. She was no longer sitting in her chair looking on. She was *in* that strange, great room—she was among those throngs of people—she was standing by the man who was waiting impatiently before a ticket-window. As he turned his face and their eyes met she saw that it was Teddy—she saw the amazed recognition in his eyes. And she knew, indis-

*See *Emily of New Moon*.
†See *Emily Climbs*.

putably, that he was in some terrible danger—and that *she* must save him.

"Teddy. *Come*."

It seemed to her that she caught his hand and pulled him away from the window. Then she was drifting back from him—back—back—and he was following—running after her—heedless of the people he ran into—following—following—she was back on the chair—outside of the gazing-ball—in it she still saw the station-room shrunk again to play-size—and that one figure running—still running—the cloud again—filling the ball—whitening—wavering—thinning—clearing. Emily was lying back in her chair staring fixedly into Aunt Nancy's gazing-ball, where the living-room was reflected calmly and silverly, with a dead-white spot that was her face and one solitary taper-light twinkling like an impish star.

## IV

Emily, feeling as if she had died and come back to life, got herself out of the Disappointed House somehow, and locked the door. The clouds had cleared away and the world was dim and unreal in starlight. Hardly realising what she was doing she turned her face seaward through the spruce wood—down the long, windy, pasture-field—over the dunes to the sandshore—along it like a haunted, driven creature in a weird, uncanny half-lit kingdom. The sea afar out was like grey satin half hidden in a creeping fog but it washed against the sands as she passed in little swishing, mocking ripples. She was shut in between the misty sea and the high, dark sand-dunes. If she could only go on so forever—never have to turn back and confront the unanswerable question the night had put to her.

She *knew*, beyond any doubt or cavil or mockery, that she had seen Teddy—had saved, or tried to save him, from some unknown peril. And she knew, just as simply and just as surely that she loved him—had always loved him, with a love that lay at the very foundation of her being.

And in two months' time she was to be married to Dean Priest.

What could she do? To marry him now was unthinkable. She could not live such a lie. But to break his heart—snatch from him all the happiness possible to his thwarted life—that, too, was unthinkable.

Yes, as Ilse had said, it *was* a very devilish thing to be a woman.

"Particularly," said Emily, filled with bitter self-contempt, "a woman who seemingly doesn't know her own mind for a month at a time. I was so sure last summer that Teddy no longer meant anything to me—so sure that I really cared enough for Dean to marry him. And now to-night—and that horrible power or gift or curse coming again when I thought I had outgrown it—left it behind forever."

Emily walked on that eerie sandshore half the night and slipped guiltily and stealthily into New Moon in the wee sma's to fling herself on her bed and fall at last into the absolute slumber of exhaustion.

## V

A very ghastly time followed. Fortunately Dean was away, having gone to Montreal on business. It was during his absence that the world was horrified by the tragedy of the *Flavian's* fatal collision with an iceberg. The headlines struck Emily in the face like a blow. Teddy was to have sailed on the *Flavian*— Had he—had he? Who could tell her? Perhaps his mother—his queer, solitary mother who hated her with a hatred that Emily always felt like a tangible thing between them. Hitherto Emily would have shrunk unspeakably from seeking Mrs. Kent. Now nothing mattered except finding out if Teddy were on the *Flavian*. She hurried to the Tansy Patch. Mrs. Kent came to the door—unaltered in all the years since Emily had first known her—frail, furtive, with her bitter mouth and that disfiguring red scar across her paleness. Her face changed as it always did when she saw Emily. Hostility and fear contended in her dark, melancholy eyes.

"Did Teddy sail on the *Flavian*?" demanded Emily without circumlocution.

Mrs. Kent smiled—an unfriendly little smile.

"Does it matter to you?" she said.

"Yes." Emily was very blunt. The "Murray look" was on her face—the look few people could encounter undefeatedly. "If you know—tell me."

Mrs. Kent told her, unwillingly, hating her, shaking like a little dead leaf quivering with a semblance of life in a cruel wind.

"He did not. I had a cable from him to-day. At the last moment he was prevented from sailing."

"Thank you." Emily turned away, but not before Mrs. Kent had seen the joy and triumph that had leaped into her shadowy eyes. She sprang forward and caught Emily's arm.

"It is nothing to you," she cried wildly. "Nothing to you whether he is safe or not. You are going to marry another man. How dare you come here—demanding to know of my son—as if you had a right?"

Emily looked down at her pityingly, understandingly. This poor creature whose jealousy, coiled in her soul like a snake, had made life a vale of torment for her.

"No right perhaps—except the right of loving him," she said.

Mrs. Kent struck her hands together wildly.

"You—you dare to say that—you who are to marry another man?"

"I am not going to marry another man," Emily found herself saying. It was quite true. For days she had not known what to do—now quite unmistakably she knew what she must do. Dreadful as it would be, still something that must be done. Everything was suddenly clear and bitter and inevitable before her.

"I cannot marry another man, Mrs. Kent, because I

love Teddy. But he does not love me. I know that quite
well. So you need not hate me any longer."

She turned and went swiftly away from the Tansy
Patch. Where was her pride, she wondered—the pride
of "the proud Murrays"—that she could so calmly
acknowledge an unsought, unwanted love. But pride
just then had no place in her.

# Chapter XI

## I

When the letter came from Teddy—the first letter for so long—Emily's hand trembled so that she could hardly open it.

"I must tell you of the strange thing that has happened," he wrote. "Perhaps you know it already. And perhaps you know nothing and will think me quite mad. I don't know what to think of it myself. I know only what I saw—or thought I saw.

"I was waiting to buy my ticket for the boat-train to Liverpool—I was to sail on the *Flavian*. Suddenly I felt a touch on my arm—I turned and saw *you*. I swear it. You said, 'Teddy—come.' I was so amazed I could not think or speak. I could only follow you. You were running—no, *not* running. I don't know how you went—I only knew that you were retreating. How rotten this all sounds. *Was* I crazy? And all at once you weren't there—though we were by now away from the crowd in an open space where nothing could have prevented me from seeing you. Yet I looked everywhere—and came to my senses to realise that the boat-train had gone and I had lost my passage on the *Flavian*. I was furious—ashamed—until the news came. Then—I felt my scalp crinkle.

"Emily—you're not in England? It can't be possible you are in England. But then—what was it I saw in that station?

"Anyhow, I suppose it saved my life. If I had gone on the *Flavian*—well, I didn't. Thanks to—what?

93

"I'll be home soon. Will sail on the *Moravian*—if you don't prevent me again. Emily, I heard a queer story of you long ago—something about Ilse's mother. I've almost forgotten. Take care. They don't burn witches nowadays, of course—but still—"

No, they didn't burn witches. But still—Emily felt that she could have more easily faced the stake than what was before her.

## II

Emily went up the hill path to keep tryst with Dean at the Disappointed House. She had had a note from him that day, written on his return from Montreal, asking her to meet him there at dusk. He was waiting for her on the doorstep—eagerly, happily. The robins were whistling softly in the fir copse and the evening was fragrant with the tang of balsam. But the air all about them was filled with the strangest, saddest, most unforgettable sound in nature—the soft, ceaseless wash on a distant shore on a still evening of the breakers of a spent storm. A sound rarely heard and always to be remembered. It is even more mournful than the rain-wind of night—the heartbreak and despair of all creation is in it. Dean took a quick step forward to meet her— then stopped abruptly. Her face—her eyes—what had happened to Emily in his absence? *This* was not Emily —this strange, white, remote girl of the pale twilight.

"Emily—what is it?" asked Dean—knowing before she told him.

Emily looked at him. If you had to deal a mortal blow why try to lighten it?

"I can't marry you after all, Dean," she said. "I don't love you."

That was all she could say. No excuses—no self-defence. There was none she could make. But it was shocking to see all the happiness wiped out of a human face like that.

There was a little pause—a pause that seemed an

eternity with that unbearable sorrow of the sea throbbing through it. Then Dean said still quietly:

"I knew you didn't love me. Yet you were—content to marry me—before this. What has made it impossible?"

It was his right to know. Emily stumbled through her silly, incredible tale.

"You see," she concluded miserably, "when—I can call like that to him across space—I belong to him. He doesn't love me—he never will—but I belong to him. . . . Oh, Dean, don't look so. I *had* to tell you this—but if you wish it—I *will* marry you—only I felt you must know the whole truth—when I knew it myself."

"Oh, a Murray of New Moon always keeps her word." Dean's face twisted mockingly. "You will marry me—if I want you to. But I don't want it—now. I see how impossible it is just as clearly as you do. I will not marry a woman whose heart is another man's."

"Can you ever forgive me, Dean?"

"What is there to forgive? I can't help loving you and you can't help loving him. We must let it go at that. Even the gods can't unscramble eggs. I should have known that only youth could call to youth—and I was never young. If I ever had been, even though I am old now, I might have held you."

He dropped his poor grey face in his hands. Emily found herself thinking what a nice, pleasant, friendly thing death would be.

But when Dean looked up again his face had changed. It had the old, mocking, cynical look.

"Don't look so tragic, Emily. A broken engagement is a very slight thing nowadays. And it's an ill wind that blows nobody good. Your aunts will thank whatever gods there be and my own clan will think that I have escaped as a bird out of the snare of the fowler. Still—I rather wish that old Highland Scotch grandmother who passed that dangerous chromosome down to you had taken her second sight to the grave with her."

Emily put her hands against the little porch column

and laid her head against them. Dean's face changed again as he looked at her. His voice when he spoke was very gentle—though cold and pale. All the brilliance and colour and warmth had gone from it.

"Emily, I give your life back to you. It has been mine, remember, since I saved you that day on Malvern rocks. It's your own again. And we must say good-bye at last—in spite of our old compact. Say it briefly—'all farewells should be sudden when forever.'"

Emily turned and caught at his arm.

"Oh, not good-bye, Dean—not good-bye. Can't we be friends still? I can't live without your friendship."

Dean took her face in his hands—Emily's cold face that he had once dreamed might flush against his kiss—and looked gravely and tenderly into it.

"We can't be friends again, dear."

"Oh, you will forget—you will not always care—"

"A man must die to forget you, I think. No, Star, we cannot be friends. You will not have my love and it has driven everything else out. I am going away. When I am old—really old—I will come back and we will be friends again, perhaps."

"I can never forgive myself."

"Again I ask what for? I do not reproach you—I even thank you for this year. It has been a royal gift to me. Nothing can ever take it from me. After all, I would not give that last perfect summer of mine for a generation of other men's happiness. My Star—my Star!"

Emily looked at him, the kiss she had never given him in her eyes. What a lonely place the world would be when Dean was gone—the world that had all at once grown very old. And would she ever be able to forget his eyes with that terrible expression of pain in them?

If he had gone then she would never have been quite free—always fettered by those piteous eyes and the thought of the wrong she had done him. Perhaps Dean realised this, for there was a hint of some malign triumph in his parting smile as he turned away. He walked

down the path—he paused with his hand on the gate—
he turned and came back.

### III

"Emily, I've something to confess, too. May as well
get it off my conscience. A lie—an ugly thing. I won
you by a lie, I think. Perhaps that is why I couldn't
keep you."

"A lie?"

"You remember that book of yours? You asked me to
tell you the truth about what I thought of it? I didn't. I
lied. It is a good piece of work—very good. Oh, some
faults in it of course—a bit emotional—a bit overstrained.
You still need pruning—restraint. But it is good. It is
out of the ordinary both in conception and develop-
ment. It has charm and your characters *do* live. Natural, human, delightful. There, you know what I think
of it now."

Emily stared at him, a hot flush suddenly staining
the pallor of her tortured little face.

"Good? And I burned it," she said in a whisper.

Dean started.

"You—burned it!"

"Yes. And I can never write it again. Why—why did
you lie to me? *You?*"

"Because I hated the book. You were more interested
in it than in me. You *would* have found a publisher
eventually—and it would have been successful. You
would have been lost to me. How ugly some motives
look when you put them into words. And you burned
it? It seems very idle to say I'm bitterly sorry for all
this. Idle to ask your forgiveness."

Emily pulled herself together. Something had happened—she was really free—free from remorse, shame,
regret. Her own woman once more. The balance hung
level between them.

"I must not hold a grudge against Dean for this—like

old Hugh Murray," she thought confusedly. Aloud—
"But I do—I do forgive it, Dean."

"Thank you." He looked up at the little grey house
behind her. "So this is still to be the Disappointed
House. Verily, there is a doom on it. Houses, like
people, can't escape their doom, it seems."

Emily averted her gaze from the little house she had
loved—still loved. It would never be hers now. It was
still to be haunted by the ghosts of things that never
happened.

"Dean—here is the key."

Dean shook his head. "Keep it till I ask for it. What
use would it be to me? The house can be sold, I
suppose—though that seems like sacrilege."

There was still something more. Emily held out her
left hand with averted face. Dean must take off the
emerald he had put on. She felt it drawn from her
finger, leaving a little cold band where it had warmed
against her flesh, like a spectral circlet. It had often
seemed to her like a fetter, but she felt sick with regret
when she realised it was gone—forever. For with it
went something that had made life beautiful for years—
Dean's wonderful friendship and companionship. To
miss that—forever. She had not known how bitter a
thing freedom could be.

When Dean had limped out of sight Emily went
home. There was nothing else to do. With her mocking
triumph that Dean had at last admitted she could
write.

## IV

If Emily's engagement to Dean had made a commo-
tion in the clans the breaking of it brewed a still wilder
teapot tempest. The Priests were exultant and indignant at one and the same time, but the inconsistent
Murrays were furious. Aunt Elizabeth had steadily
disapproved of the engagement, but she disapproved
still more strongly of its breaking. What would people

think? And many things were said about "the Starr fickleness."

"Did you," demanded Uncle Wallace sarcastically, "expect that girl to remain in the same mind from one day to another?"

All the Murrays said things, according to their separate flavour, but for some reason Andrew's dictum rankled with the keenest venom in Emily's bruised spirit. Andrew had picked up a word somewhere—he said Emily was "temperamental." Half the Murrays did not know just what it meant but they pounced on it eagerly. Emily was "temperamental"—just that. It explained everything—henceforth it clung to her like a burr. If she wrote a poem—if she didn't like carrot pudding when everybody else in the clan did—if she wore her hair low when every one else was wearing it high—if she liked a solitary ramble over moonlit hills—if she looked some mornings as if she had not slept—if she took a notion to study the stars through a field-glass—if it was whispered that she had been seen dancing alone by moonlight among the coils of a New Moon hayfield—if tears came into her eyes at the mere glimpse of some beauty—if she loved a twilight tryst in the "old orchard" better than a dance in Shrewsbury—it was all because she was temperamental. Emily felt herself alone in a hostile world. Nobody, not even Aunt Laura, understood. Even Ilse wrote rather an odd letter, every sentence of which contradicted some other sentence and left Emily with a nasty, confused feeling that Ilse loved her as much as ever but thought her "temperamental" too. Could Ilse, by any chance, have suspected the fact that, as soon as Perry Miller heard that "everything was off" between Dean Priest and Emily Starr, he had come out to New Moon and again asked Emily to promise to marry him? Emily had made short work of him, after a fashion which made Perry vow disgustedly that he was done with the proud monkey. But then he had vowed that so many times before.

# Chapter XII

## I

"MAY 4, 19—

"One o'clock is a somewhat unearthly hour to be writing in a journal. The truth is, I've been undergoing a white night. I can't sleep and I'm tired of lying in the dark fancying things—unpleasant things—so I've lighted my candle and hunted up my old diary to 'write it out.'

"I've never written in this journal since the night I burned my book and fell downstairs—and died. Coming back to life to find everything changed and all things made new. And unfamiliar and dreadful. It seems a lifetime ago. As I turn over the pages and glance at those gay, light-hearted entries I wonder if they were really written by me, Emily Byrd Starr.

"Night is beautiful when you are happy—comforting when you are in grief—terrible when you are lonely and unhappy. And to-night I have been horribly lonely. Misery overwhelmed me. I seem never to be able to stop half-way in any emotion and when loneliness does seize hold on me it takes possession of me body and soul and wrings me in its blank pain until all strength and courage go out of me. To-night I am lonely—lonely. Love will not come to me—friendship is lost to me—most of all, as I verily feel, I cannot write. I have tried repeatedly and failed. The old creative fire seems to have burned out into ashes and I cannot rekindle it. All the evening I tried to write a story—a wooden thing in which wooden puppets moved when

I jerked the strings. I finally tore it into a thousand pieces and felt that I did God service.

"These past weeks have been bitter ones. Dean has gone—where I know not. He has never written—never will, I suppose. Not to be getting letters from Dean when he is away seems strange and unnatural.

"And yet it is terribly sweet to be free once more.

"Ilse writes me that she is to be home for July and August. Also that Teddy will be, too. Perhaps this latter fact partly accounts for my white night. I want to run away before he comes.

"I have never answered the letter he wrote me after the sinking of the *Flavian*. I could not. I could not write of *that*. And if when he comes he speaks of it—I shall not be able to bear it. Will he guess that it is because I love him that I was able to set at naught the limitations of time and space to save him? I am ready to die of shame at thought of it. And at thought of what I said to Mrs. Kent. Yet somehow I have never been able to wish *that* unsaid. There was a strange relief in the stark honesty of it. I am not afraid she will ever tell him what I said. She would never have him know I cared if she could prevent it.

"But I'd like to know how I am to get through the summer.

"There are times when I hate life. Other times again when I love it fiercely with an agonised realisation of how beautiful it is—or might be—if—

"Before Dean went away he boarded up all the windows of the Disappointed House. I never go where I can see it. But I *do* see it for all that. Waiting there on its hill—waiting—dumb—blind. I have never taken my things out of it—which Aunt Elizabeth thinks a sure indication of insanity. And I don't think Dean did either. Nothing has been touched. Mona Lisa is still mocking in the gloom and Elizabeth Bas is tolerantly contemptuous of temperamental idiots and the Lady Giovanna understands it all. My dear little house! And it is never to be a home. I feel as I felt that evening years ago when I followed the rainbow—and lost it. 'There will be other rainbows' I said then. But will there be?"

## II

"MAY 15, 19—

"This has been a lyric spring day—and a miracle has happened. It happened at dawn—when I was leaning out of my window, listening to a little, whispering, tricksy wind o' morning blowing out of Lofty John's bush. Suddenly—the flash came—again—after these long months of absence—my old, inexpressible glimpse of eternity. And all at once I knew I could write. I rushed to my desk and seized my pen. All the hours of early morning I wrote; and when I heard Cousin Jimmy going downstairs I flung down my pen and bowed my head over my desk in utter thankfulness that I could work again.

" 'Get leave to work—
In this world 'tis the best you get at all,
For God in cursing gives us better gifts
Than men in benediction.'

"So wrote Elizabeth Barret Browning—and truly. It is hard to understand why work should be called a curse—until one remembers what bitterness forced or uncongenial labour is. But the work for which we are fitted—which we feel we are sent into the world to do—what a blessing it is and what fulness of joy it holds. I felt this to-day as the old fever burned in my finger-tips and my pen once more seemed a friend.

" 'Leave to work'—one would think any one could obtain so much. But sometimes anguish and heart-break forbid us the leave. And then we realise what we have lost and know that it is better to be cursed by God than forgotten by Him. If He had punished Adam and

Eve by sending them out to *idleness*, indeed they would have been outcast and accursed. Not all the dreams of Eden 'whence the four great rivers flow' could have been as sweet as those I am dreaming to-night, because the power to work has come back to me.

"Oh, God, as long as I live give me 'leave to work.' Thus pray I. Leave and courage."

### III

"MAY 25, 19—

"Dear sunshine, what a potent medicine you are. All day I revelled in the loveliness of the wonderful white bridal world. And to-night I washed my soul free from dust in the aerial bath of a spring twilight. I chose the old hill road over the Delectable Mountain for its solitude and wandered happily along, pausing every few moments to think out fully some thought or fancy that came to me like a winged spirit. Then I prowled about the hill fields till long after dark, studying the stars with my field-glass. When I came in I felt as if I had been millions of miles away in the blue ether and all my old familiar surroundings seemed momentarily forgotten and strange.

"But there was one star at which I did not look. Vega of the Lyre."

### IV

"MAY 30, 19—

"This evening, just when I was in the middle of a story Aunt Elizabeth said she wanted me to weed the onion-bed. So I had to lay down my pen and go out to the kitchen garden. But one can weed onions and think wonderful things at the same time, glory be. It is one of the blessings that we don't always have to put our souls into what our hands may be doing, praise the gods—for otherwise who would have any soul left? So

I weeded the onion-bed and roamed the Milky Way in imagination."

## V

"JUNE 10, 19—

"Cousin Jimmy and I felt like murderers last night. We were. Baby-killers at that!

"It is one of the springs when there is a crop of maple-trees. Every key that fell from a maple this year seems to have grown. All over the lawn and garden and old orchard tiny maple-trees have sprung up by the hundreds. And of course they have to be rooted out. It would never do to let them grow. So we pulled them up all day yesterday and felt so mean and guilty over it. The dear, tiny, baby things. They have a right to grow—a right to keep on growing into great, majestic, splendid trees. Who are we to deny it to them? I caught Cousin Jimmy in tears over the brutal necessity.

" 'I sometimes think,' he whispered, 'that it's wrong to prevent anything from growing. *I* never grew up—not in my head.'

"And last night I had a horrible dream of being pursued by thousands of indignant young maple-tree ghosts. They crowded around me—tripped me up—thrashed me with their boughs—smothered me with their leaves. And I woke gasping for breath and nearly frightened to death, but with a splendid idea for a story in my head—*The Vengeance of the Tree.*"

## VI

"JUNE 15, 19—

"I picked strawberries on the banks of Blair Water this afternoon among the windy, sweet-smelling grasses. I love picking strawberries. The occupation has in it something of perpetual youth. The gods might have picked strawberries on high Olympus without injuring their dignity. A queen—or a poet—might stoop to it; a beggar has the privilege.

"And to-night I've been sitting here in my dear old room, with my dear books and dear pictures and dear little window of the kinky panes, dreaming in the soft, odorous summer twilight, while the robins are calling to each other in Lofty John's bush and the poplars are talking eerily of old, forgotten things.

"After all, it's not a bad old world—and the folks in it are not half bad either. Even Emily Byrd Starr is decent in spots. Not altogether the false, fickle, ungrateful perversity she thinks she is in the wee sma's—not altogether the friendless, forgotten maiden she imagines she is on white nights—not altogether the failure she supposes bitterly when three MSS. are rejected in succession. And *not* altogether the coward she feels herself to be when she thinks of Frederick Kent's coming to Blair Water in July."

# Chapter XIII

## I

Emily was reading by the window of her room when she heard it—reading Alice Meynell's strange poem, "Letter From A Girl To Her Own Old Age," and thrilling mystically to its strange prophecies. Outside dusk falling over the old New Moon garden; and clear through the dusk came the two high notes and the long low one of Teddy's old whistle in Lofty John's bush—the old, old call by which he had so often summoned her in the twilights of long ago.

Emily's book fell unheeded to the floor. She stood up, mist-pale, her eyes dilating into darkness. Was Teddy there? He had not been expected till the next week, though Ilse was coming that night. Could she have been mistaken? Could she have fancied it? Some chance robin call—

It came again. She knew as she had known at first that it was Teddy's whistle. There was no sound like it in the world. And it had been so long since she had heard it. He was there—waiting for her—calling for her. Should she go? She laughed under her breath. Go? She had no choice. She must go. Pride could not hold her back—bitter remembrance of the night she had waited for his call and it had not come could not halt her hurrying footsteps. Fear—shame—all were forgotten in the mad ecstasy of the moment. Without giving herself time to reflect that she was a Murray—only snatching a moment to look in the glass and assure herself that her ivory crêpe dress was very becoming—

how lucky it was that she had happened to put on that dress!—she flew down the stairs and through the garden. He was standing under the dark glamour of the old firs where the path ran through Lofty John's bush—bare-headed, smiling.

"Teddy."

"Emily."

Her hands were in his—her eyes were shining into his. Youth had come back—all that had once made magic made it again. Together once more after all those long weary years of alienation and separation. There was no longer any shyness—any stiffness—any sense or fear of change. They might have been children together again. But childhood had never known this wild, insurgent sweetness—this unconsidered surrender. Oh, she was his. By a word—a look—an intonation, he was still her master. What matter if, in some calmer mood, she might not quite like it—to be helpless—dominated like this? What matter if to-morrow she might wish she had not run so quickly, so eagerly, so unhesitatingly to meet him? To-night nothing mattered except that Teddy had come back.

Yet, outwardly, they did not meet as lovers—only as old, dear friends. There was so much to talk of—so much to be silent over as they paced up and down the garden walks, while the stars laughed through the dark at them—hinting—hinting—

Only one thing was not spoken of between them—the thing Emily had dreaded. Teddy made no reference to the mystery of that vision in the London station. It was as if it had never been. Yet Emily felt that it had drawn them together again after long misunderstanding. It was well not to speak of it—it was one of those mystic things—one of the gods' secrets—that must not be spoken of. Best forgotten now that its work was done. And yet—so unreasonable are we mortals!—Emily felt a ridiculous disappointment that he didn't speak of it. She didn't want him to speak of it. But if it had meant anything to him must he not have spoken of it?

"It's good to be here again," Teddy was saying. "Nothing seems changed here. Time has stood still in this Garden of Eden. Look, Emily, how bright Vega of the Lyre is. Our star. Have you forgotten it?"

Forgotten? How she had wished she *could* forget.

"They wrote me you were going to marry Dean," said Teddy abruptly.

"I meant to—but I couldn't," said Emily.

"Why not?" asked Teddy as if he had a perfect right to ask it.

"Because I didn't love him," answered Emily, conceding his right.

Laughter—golden, delicious laughter that made you suddenly want to laugh too. Laughter was so *safe*—one could laugh without betraying anything. Ilse had come— Ilse was running down the walk. Ilse in a yellow silk gown the colour of her hair and a golden-brown hat the colour of her eyes, giving you the sensation that a gorgeous golden rose was at large in the garden.

Emily almost welcomed her. The moment had grown too vital. Some things were terrible if put into words. She drew away from Teddy almost primly—a Murray of New Moon once more.

"Darlings," said Ilse, throwing an arm around each of them. "Isn't it divine—all here together again? Oh, how much I love you! Let's forget we are old and grown-up and wise and unhappy and be mad, crazy, happy kids again for just one blissful summer."

## II

A wonderful month followed. A month of indescribable roses, exquisite hazes, silver perfection of moonlight, unforgettable amethystine dusks, march of rains, bugle-call of winds, blossoms of purple and star-dust, mystery, music, magic. A month of laughter and dance and joy, of enchantment infinite. Yet a month of restrained, hidden realisation. Nothing was ever said. She and Teddy were seldom ever alone together. But one felt—

knew. Emily fairly sparkled with happiness. All the old restlessness that had worried Aunt Laura had gone from her eyes. Life was good. Friendship—love—joy of sense and joy of spirit—sorrow—loveliness—achievement— failure—longing—all were part of life and therefore interesting and desirable.

Every morning when she awakened the new day seemed to her like some good fairy who would bring her some beautiful gift of joy. Ambition was, for the time at least, forgotten. Success—power—fame. Let those who cared for them pay the price and take them. But love is not bought and sold. It is a gift.

Even the memory of her burned book ceased to ache. What did one book more or less matter in this great universe of life and passion? How pale and shadowy was any pictured life beside this throbbing, scintillant existence! Who cared for laurel, after all? Orange blossoms would make a sweeter coronet. And what star of destiny was ever brighter and more alluring than Vega of the Lyre? Which, being interpreted, simply meant that nothing mattered any more in this world or any other except Teddy Kent.

### III

"If I had a tail I'd lash it," groaned Ilse, casting herself on Emily's bed and hurling one of Emily's treasured volumes—a little old copy of the *Rubaiyat* Teddy had given her in high school days—across the room. The back came off and the leaves flew every which way for a Sunday. Emily was annoyed.

"Were you ever in a state that you could neither cry nor pray nor swear?" demanded Ilse.

"Sometimes," agreed Emily dryly. "But I don't take it out on books that never harmed me. I just go and bite off somebody's head."

"There wasn't anybody's head handy to bite off, but I did something that was just as effective," said Ilse, casting a malevolent glance at Perry Miller's photograph which was propped up on Emily's desk.

Emily glaned at it too, and her face Murrayfied, as Ilse expressed it. The photograph was still there but where Perry's intent and unabashed eyes had gazed out at her were now only jagged, unsightly holes.

Emily was furious. Perry had been so proud of those photographs. They were the first he had had taken in his life. "Never could afford any before," he had said frankly. He looked very handsome in them, though his pose was a bit truculent and aggressive with his wavy hair brushed back sleekly, and his firm mouth and chin showing to excellent advantage. Aunt Elizabeth had gazed at it, secretly wondering how she had ever dared make such a fine-looking young man as that eat in the kitchen. And Aunt Laura had wiped her eyes sentimentally and thought that perhaps—after all—Emily and Perry—a lawyer would be quite a thing to have in the family, coming in a good third to minister and doctor. Though, to be sure, Stovepipe Town—

Perry had rather spoiled the gift for Emily by proposing to her again. It was very hard for Perry Miller to get it into his head that anything he wanted he couldn't get. And he had always wanted Emily.

"I've got the world by the tail now," he said proudly. "Every year'll find me higher up. Why can't you make up your mind to have me, Emily?"

"Is it just a question of making up one's mind?" asked Emily satirically.

"Of course. What else?"

"Listen, Perry," said Emily decidedly. "You're a good old pal. I like you—I'll always like you. But I'm tired of this nonsense and I'm going to put a stop to it. If you ever again ask me to marry you I'll never never speak to you as long as I live. Since you are good at making up your mind make up yours which you want—my friendship or my non-existence."

"Oh, well." Perry shrugged his shoulders philosophically. He had about come to the conclusion any-

how that he might as well give up dangling after Emily
Starr and getting nothing but snubs for his pains. Ten
years was long enough to be a rejected but faithful swain.
There were other girls, after all. Perhaps he had made a
mistake. *Too* faithful and persistent. If he had wooed by
fits and starts, blowing hot and cold like Teddy Kent,
he might have had better luck. Girls were like that. But
Perry did not say this. Stovepipe Town had learned a
few things. All he said was:

"If you'd only stop looking at me in a certain way I
might get over hankering for you. Anyhow, I'd never
have got this far along if I hadn't been in love with you.
I'd just have been a hired boy somewhere or a fisher-
man at the harbour. So I'm not sorry. I haven't forgotten how you believed in me and helped me and stood
up for me to your Aunt Elizabeth. It's been—been"
—Perry's handsome face flushed suddenly and his
voice shook a little—"it's been—sweet—to dream about
you all these years. I guess I'll have to give it up now.
No use, I see. But don't take your friendship from me
too, Emily."

"Never," said Emily impulsively, putting out her
hands. "You're a brick, Perry dear. You've done wonders and I'm proud of you."

And now to find the picture he had given her ruined.
She flashed on Ilse eyes like a stormy sea.

"Ilse Burnley, how dare you do such a thing!"

"No use squizzling your eyebrows up at me like that,
beloved demon," retorted Ilse. "Hasn't no effect on me
a-tall. Couldn't endure that picture no-how. And Stovepipe Town in the background."

"What you've done is on a level with Stovepipe
Town."

"Well, he asked for it. Smirking there. 'Behold ME. I
am a Person In The Public Eye. Never had such satisfaction as boring your scissors through those conceited
orbs gave me. Two seconds more of looking at them
and I'd have flung up my head and howled. Oh, how I
hate Perry Miller! Puffed up like a poisoned pup!"

"I thought you told me you loved him," said Emily rather rudely.

"It's the same thing," said Ilse morosely. "Emily, why can't I get that creature out of my mind? It's too Victorian to say heart. I haven't any heart. I don't love him—I *do* hate him. But I can't keep from thinking about him. *That's* just a state of mind. Oh, I could yell at the moon. But the real reason I dug his eyes out was his turning Grit after having been born and raised Conservative."

"You are Conservative yourself."

"True but unimportant. I hate turncoats. I've never forgiven Henry IV for turning Catholic. Not because he was a Protestant but just because he was a turncoat. I would have been just as implacable if he had been Catholic and turned Protestant. Perry has changed his politics just for the sake of getting into partnership with Leonard Abel. There's Stovepipe Town for you. Oh, he'll be Judge Miller—and rich as wedding-cake— but—! I wish he had had a hundred eyes so that I could have bored them all out! This is one of the times I feel it would be handy to have been a bosom friend of Lucrezia Borgia."

"Who was an excellent and rather stupid woman beloved for her good works."

"Oh, I know the modern whitewashers are determined to rob history of anything that is picturesque. No matter, I shall cling to my faith in Lucrezia and William Tell. Put that picture out of my sight. *Please*, Emily."

Emily put the maltreated picture away in a drawer of her desk. Her brief anger had gone. She understood. At least she understood why the eyes had been cut out. It was harder to understand just why Ilse could care so much and so incurably for Perry Miller. And there was just a hint of pity in her heart as well— condescending pity for Ilse who cared so much for a man who didn't care for her.

"I think this will cure me," said Ilse savagely. "I

can't—I won't love a turncoat. Blind bat—congenital idiot that he is! Pah, I'm through with him. Emily, I wonder I don't hate you. Rejecting with scorn what I want so much. Ice-cold thing, did you ever really care for anything or any creature except that pen of yours?"

"Perry has never really loved me," evaded Emily. "He only imagines he does."

"Well, I'd be content if he would only just imagine he loved me. How brazen I am about it. You're the one person in the world I can have the relief of saying such things to. That's why I can't let myself hate you, after all. I daresay I'm not half as unhappy as I think myself. One never knows what may be around the next corner. After this I mean to bore Perry Miller out of my life and thoughts just as I bored his eyes out. Emily," with an abrupt change of tone and posture, "do you know I like Teddy Kent better this summer than I ever did before."

"Oh." The monosyllable was eloquent, but Ilse was deaf to all its implications.

"Yes. He's really charming. Those years in Europe have done something to him. Perhaps it's just that they've taught him to hide his selfishness better."

"Teddy Kent isn't selfish. Why do you call him selfish? Look at his devotion to his mother."

"Because she adores him. Teddy likes to be adored. That's why he's never fallen in love with any one, you know. That—and because the girls chased him so, perhaps. It was sickening in Montreal. They made such asses of themselves—waiting on him with their tongues hanging out—that I wanted to dress in male attire and swear I wasn't of their sex. No doubt it was the same in Europe. No man alive can stand six years of that without being spoiled—and contemptuous. Teddy is all right with *us*—he knows we're old pals who can see through him and will stand no nonsense. But I've seen him accepting tribute—graciously bestowing a smile—a look—a touch as a reward. Saying to every one just what he thought she'd like to hear. When I saw it I always felt I'd love to say something to him that he'd think of for years whenever he woke up at three o'clock o'night."

The sun had dropped into a bank of purple cloud behind the Delectable Mountain and a chill and shadow swept down the hill and across the dewy cloverfields to New Moon. The little room darkened and the glimpse of Blair Water through the gap in Lofty John's bush changed all at once to livid grey.

Emily's evening was spoiled. But she felt—*knew*— that Ilse was mistaken about many things. There was one comfort, too—evidently she had kept her secret well. Not even Ilse suspected it. Which was agreeable to both the Murray and the Starr.

## IV

But Emily sat long at her window looking into the black night that turned slowly to pale silver as the moon rose. So the girls had "chased" Teddy.

She wished she had not run quite so quickly when he had called from Lofty John's bush. "Oh, whistle and I'll come to you, my lad" was all very well in song. But one was not living in a Scotch ballad. And that change in Ilse's voice—that almost confidential note. Did Ilse mean—? How pretty Ilse had looked to-night. In that smart, sleeveless dress of green sprinkled with tiny golden butterflies—with the green necklace that circled her throat and fell to her hips like a long green snake— with her green, gold-buckled shoes—Ilse always wore such ravishing shoes. *Did* Ilse mean—? And if she did—?

After breakfast Aunt Laura remarked to Cousin Jimmy that she felt sure something was on the dear child's mind.

# Chapter XIV

## I

"The early bird catches—the desire of his heart," said Teddy, slipping down beside Emily on the long, silken, pale-green grasses on the bank of Blair Water.

He had come so silently that Emily had not heard him until she saw him and she could not repress a start and blush—which she hoped wildly he did not see. She had wakened early and been seized with what her clan would doubtless have considered a temperamental desire to see the sunrise and make new acquaintances with Eden. So she had stolen down New Moon stairs and through the expectant garden and Lofty John's bush to the Blair Water to meet the mystery of the dawn. It had never occurred to her that Teddy would be prowling too.

"I like to come down here at sunrise, now and then," he said. "It's about the only chance I have of being alone for a few minutes. Our evenings and afternoons are all given over to mad revelry—and Mother likes me to be with her every moment of the forenoons. She's had six such horribly lonesome years."

"I'm sorry I've intruded on your precious solitude," said Emily stiffly, possessed of a horrible fear that he might think she knew of his habit and had come purposely to meet him.

Teddy laughed.

"Don't put on New Moon airs with me, Emily Byrd Starr. You know perfectly well that finding you here is

115

the crown of the morning for me. I've always had a wild hope that it might happen. And now it has. Let's just sit here and dream together. God made this morning for us—just us two. Even talking would spoil it."

Emily agreed silently. How dear it was to sit here with Teddy on the banks of Blair Water, under the coral of the morning sky, and dream—just dream—wild, sweet, secret, unforgettable, foolish dreams. Alone with Teddy while all their world was sleeping. Oh, if this exquisite stolen moment could last! A line from some poem of Marjorie Pickthall quivered in her thought like a bar of music—

"Oh, keep the world forever at the dawn."

She said it like a prayer under her breath.

Everything was so beautiful in this magical moment before sunrise. The wild blue irises around the pond, the violet shadows in the curves of the dunes, the white, filmy mist hanging over the buttercup valley across the pond, the cloth of gold and silver that was called a field of daisies, the cool, delicious gulf breeze, the blue of far lands beyond the harbour, plumes of purple and mauve smoke going up on the still, golden air from the chimneys of Stovepipe Town where the fishermen rose early. And Teddy lying at her feet, his slim brown hands clasped behind his head. Again she felt inescapably the magnetic attraction of his personality. Felt it so strongly that she dared not meet his eyes. Yet she was admitting to herself with a secret candour which would have horrified Aunt Elizabeth that she wanted to run her fingers through his sleek black hair—feel his arms about her—press her face against his dark tender one—feel his lips on her lips—

Teddy took one of his hands from under his head and put it over hers.

For a moment of surrender she left it there. Then Ilse's words flashed into memory, searing her consciousness like a dagger of flame. "I've seen him accepting

tribute"—"graciously bestowing a touch as a reward"
—"saying to each one just what he thought she wanted
to hear." Had Teddy guessed what she had been thinking? Her thoughts had seemed so vivid to her that she
felt as if any one must *see* her thinking. Intolerable. She
sprang up abruptly, shaking off his fingers.

"I must be going home."

So blunt. Somehow, she could not make it smoother. He
must not—should not think— Teddy rose, too. A change
in his voice and look. Their marvellous moment was over.

"So must I. Mother will be missing me. She's always
up early. Poor little Mother. She hasn't changed. She
isn't proud of my success—she hates it. She thinks it
has taken me from her. The years have not made it any
easier for her. I want her to come away with me, but
she will not. I think that is partly because she cannot
bear to leave the old Tansy Patch and partly because
she can't endure seeing me shut up in my studio
working—something that would bar her out. I wonder
what made her so. I've never known her any other
way, but I think she must have been different once. It's
odd for a son to know as little of his mother's life as I
do. I don't even know what made that scar on her face.
I know next to nothing of my father—absolutely nothing of his people. She will never talk of anything in the
years before we came to Blair Water."

"Something hurt her once—hurt her so terribly she
has never got over it," said Emily.

"My father's death, perhaps?"

"No. At least, not if it were just death. There was
something else—something poisonous. Well—bye-bye."

"Going to Mrs. Chidlaw's dinner-dance to-morrow
night?"

"Yes. She is sending her car for me."

"Whew! No use after that asking you to go with me
in a one-hoss buggy—borrowed at that. Well, I must
take Ilse then. Perry to be there?"

"No. He wrote me he couldn't come—had to prepare
for his first case. It's coming up next day."

"Perry is forging ahead, isn't he? That bulldog tenacity of his never lets go of an objective once he gets his teeth into it. He'll be rich when we're still as poor as church mice. But then, we're chasing rainbow gold, aren't we?"

She would not linger—he might think she wanted to linger— "waiting with her tongue hanging out"—she turned away almost ungraciously. He had been so unregretfully ready to "take Ilse then." As if it really didn't matter much. Yet she was still conscious of his touch on her hand—it burned there yet. In that fleeting moment, in that brief caress, he had made her wholly his, as years of wifehood could never have made her Dean's. She could think of nothing else all day. She lived over and over again that moment of surrender. It seemed to her so inadequate that everything should be the same at New Moon and that Cousin Jimmy should be worrying over red spiders on his asters.

## II

A tack on the Shrewsbury road made Emily fifteen minutes late for Mrs. Chidlaw's dinner. She flung a hasty glance into the mirror before she went down and turned away satisfied. An arrow of rhinestones in her dark hair—she had hair that wore jewels well—lent the necessary note of brilliance to the new dress of silvery-green lace over a pale-blue slip that became her so well. Miss Royal had picked it for her in New York—and Aunt Elizabeth and Laura had looked askance at it. Green and blue was *such* an odd combination. And there was so little of it. But it did something to Emily when she put it on. Cousin Jimmy looked at the exquisite, shimmering young thing with stars in her eyes, in the old candlelighted kitchen and said ruefully to Aunt Laura after she had gone, "She doesn't belong to *us* in that dress."

"It made her look like an *actress*," said Aunt Elizabeth freezingly.

Emily did not feel like an actress as she ran down Mrs. Chidlaw's stairs and across the sun-room to the wide veranda where Mrs. Chidlaw had elected to hold her dinner party. She felt real, vital, happy, expectant. Teddy would be there—there would be the furtive sweetness of watching him secretly when he talked to some one else—and thought of *her*—they would dance together afterwards. Perhaps he would tell her—what she was longing to hear—

She paused for a second in the open doorway, her eyes soft and dreamy as a purple mist, looking out on the scene before her—one of those scenes which are always remembered from some subtle charm of their own.

The table was spread in the big rounded alcove at the corner of the vine-hung veranda. Beyond it tall, dark firs and Lombardies stood out against the after-sunset sky of dull rose and fading yellow. Through their stems she caught glimpses of the bay, dark and sapphire. Great masses of shadow beyond the little island of light—the gleam of pearls on Ilse's white neck. There were other guests—Professor Robins of McGill with his long, melancholy face made still longer by his odd spade-shaped beard; Lisette Chidlaw's round, cream-coloured, kissable face with its dark hair heaped high over it and her round, dark eyes; Jack Glenlake, dreamy and handsome; Annette Shaw, a sleepy, gold-and-white thing, always affecting a Mona Lisa smile; stocky little Tom Hallam with his humorous Irish face; Aylmer Vincent. Quite fat. Beginning to be bald. Still making pretty speeches to the ladies. How absurd to recall that she had once thought him Prince Charming! Solemn-looking Gus Rankin, with a vacant chair beside him, evidently for her. Elise Borland, young and chubby, showing off her lovely hands a little in the candle-light. But of all the party Emily only saw Teddy and Ilse. The rest were puppets.

They were sitting together just opposite her. Teddy sleek and well-groomed as usual, his black head close to Ilse's golden one. Ilse, a glorified shining creature in turquoise-blue taffeta, looking the queen with a foam of laces on her full bosom and rose-and-silver nosegays at her shoulder. Just as Emily looked at them Ilse lifted her eyes to Teddy's face and asked some question— some intimate, vital question, Emily felt sure, from the expression of her face. She did not recall ever having seen just that look on Ilse's face before. There was some sort of definite challenge in it. Teddy looked down and answered her. Emily knew or felt that the word "love" was in his answer. Those two looked long into each other's eyes—at least it seemed long to Emily, beholding that interchange of rapt glances. Then Ilse blushed and looked away. When had Ilse ever blushed before? And Teddy threw up his head and swept the table with eyes that seemed exultant and victorious.

Emily went out into the circle of radiance from that terrible moment of disillusion. Her heart, so gay and light a moment before, seemed cold and dead. In spite of the lights and laughter a dark, chill night seemed to be coming towards her. Everything in life seemed suddenly ugly. It was for her a dinner of bitter herbs and she never remembered anything Gus Rankin said to her. She never looked at Teddy, who seemed in wonderful spirits and was keeping up a stream of banter with Ilse, and she was chilly and unresponsive through the whole meal. Gus Rankin told all his favourite stories but, like Queen Victoria of blessed memory, Emily was not amused. Mrs. Chidlaw was provoked and repented of having sent her car for so temperamental a guest. Annoyed probably over being paired with Gus Rankin, who had been asked at the last minute to fill Perry Miller's place. And looking like an outraged duchess over it. Yet you had to be civil to her. She might put you in a book if you weren't. Remember that time she wrote the review of our play! In reality, poor Emily was thanking whatever gods there be that she was beside Gus Rankin, who never wanted or expected any one to talk.

The dance was a ghastly affair for Emily. She felt like a ghost moving among revellers she had suddenly outgrown. She danced once with Teddy and Teddy, realising that it was only her slim, silvery-green form he held, while her soul had retreated into some aloof impregnable citadel, did not ask her again. He danced several dances with Ilse and then sat out several more with her in the garden. His devotion to her was noticed and commented upon. Millicent Chidlaw asked Emily if the report that Ilse Burnley and Frederick Kent were engaged were true.

"He was always crazy about her, wasn't he?" Millicent wanted to know.

Emily, in a cool and impertinent voice, supposed so. Was Millicent watching her to see if she would flinch?

Of course he was in love with Ilse. What wonder? Ilse was so beautiful. What chance could her own moonlit charm of dark and silver have against that gold and ivory loveliness? Teddy liked *her* as a dear old pal and chum. That was all. She had been a fool *again*. Always deceiving herself. That morning by Blair Water— when she had almost let him see—perhaps he *had* seen—the thought was unbearable. Would she ever learn wisdom? Oh, yes, she had learned it to-night. No more folly. How wise and dignified and unapproachable she would be henceforth.

Wasn't there some wretched, vulgar old proverb anent locking a stable door after the horse was stolen?

And just how was she to get through the rest of the night?

# Chapter XV

## I

Emily, just home from an interminable week's visit at Uncle Oliver's, where a cousin had been getting married, heard at the post-office that Teddy Kent had gone.

"Left at an hour's notice," Mrs. Crosby told her. "Got a wire asking if he would take the vice-principalship of the College of Art in Montreal and had to go at once to see about it. Isn't that splendid? Hasn't he got on? It's really quite wonderful. Blair Water should be very proud of him, shouldn't it? Isn't it a pity his mother is so odd?"

Fortunately Mrs. Crosby never took time to await any answer to her questions. Emily knew she was turning pale and hated herself for it. She clutched her mail and hastened out of the post-office. She passed several people on the way home and never realised it. As a consequence her reputation for pride went up dangerously. But when she reached New Moon Aunt Laura handed her a letter.

"Teddy left it. He was here last night to say goodbye."

The proud Miss Starr had a narrow escape from bursting into hysterical tears on the spot. Murray in hysterics! Never had such a thing been heard of—never must be heard of. Emily gritted her teeth, took the letter silently and went to her room. The ice around her heart was melting rapidly. Oh, why had she been so cool and dignified with Teddy all that week after

Mrs. Chidlaw's dance? But she had never dreamed he would be going away so soon. And now—

She opened her letter. There was nothing in it but a clipping of some ridiculous poetry Perry had written and published in a Charlottetown paper—a paper that was not taken at New Moon. She and Teddy had laughed over it—Ilse had been too angry to laugh—and Teddy had promised to get a copy for her.

Well, he had got it.

## II

She was sitting there, looking whitely out into the soft, black, velvety night with its goblin-market of wind-tossed trees, when Ilse, who had also been away in Charlottetown, came in.

"So Teddy has gone. I see you have a letter from him, too."

Too!

"Yes," said Emily, wondering if it were a lie. Then concluded desperately she did not care whether it was a lie or not.

"He was terribly sorry to have to go so suddenly, but he had to decide at once and he couldn't decide without getting some more information about it. Teddy won't tie himself down too irrevocably to any person, no matter how tempting it is. And to be vice-principal of that college at his age is some little bouquet. Well, I'll soon have to go myself. It's been a gorgeous vacation but— Going to the dance at Derry Pond to-morrow night, Emily?"

Emily shook her head. Of what use was dancing now that Teddy was gone?

"Do you know," said Ilse pensively, "I think this summer has been rather a failure, in spite of our fun. We thought we could be children again, but we haven't been. We've only been pretending."

Pretending? Oh, if this heartache were only a pretence! And this burning shame and deep, mute hurt.

Teddy had not even cared enough to write her a line of farewell. She knew—she had known ever since the Chidlaw dance—he did not love her; but surely friendship demanded something. Even her friendship meant nothing to him. Now he had gone back to his real life and the things that mattered. And he had written Ilse. Pretend? Oh, well, she would pretend with a vengeance. There were times when the Murray pride was certainly an asset.

"I think it's as well the summer is over," she said carelessly. "I simply *must* get down to work again. I have neglected my writing shamefully the past two months."

"After all, that's all you really care about, isn't it?" said Ilse curiously. "I love my work but it doesn't possess me as yours possesses you. I'd give it up in a twinkling for—well, we're all as we're made. But is it really comfortable, Emily, to care for only one thing in life?"

"Much more comfortable than caring for too many things."

"I suppose so. Well, you ought to succeed when you lay everything on the altar of your goddess. That's the difference between us. I'm of weaker clay. There are some things I couldn't give up—some things I *won't*. And as Old Kelly advises, if I can't get what I want— well, I'll want what I can get. Isn't that common sense?"

Emily, wishing she could fool herself as easily as she could other people, went over to the window and kissed Ilse's forehead.

"We aren't children any longer—and we can't go back to childhood, Ilse. We're women—and must make the best of it. I think you'll be happy yet. I *want* you to be."

Ilse squeezed Emily's hand. "Darn common sense!" she said drearily.

If she had not been in New Moon she would probably have used the unexpurgated edition.

# Chapter XVI

## I

"Nov. 17, 19—

"There are two adjectives that are never separated in regard to a November day—'dull' and 'gloomy.' They were wedded together in the dawn of language and it is not for me to divorce them now. Accordingly, then, this day has been dull and gloomy, inside and outside, materially and spiritually.

"Yesterday wasn't so bad. There was a warm autumnal sun and Cousin Jimmy's big heap of pumpkins made a lovely pool of colour against the old grey barns, and the valley down by the brook was mellow with the late, leafless gold of juniper-trees. I walked in the afternoon through the uncanny enchantment of November woods, still haunted by loveliness, and again in the evening in the afterglow of an autumnal sunset. The evening was mild and wrapped in a great, grey, brooding stillness of windless field and waiting hill—a stillness which was yet threaded through with many little eerie, beautiful sounds which I could hear if I listened as much with my soul as my ears. Later on there was a procession of stars and I got a message from them.

"But to-day *was* dreary. And to-night virtue has gone out of me. I wrote all day but I could not write this evening. I shut myself into my room and paced it like a caged creature. ''Tis the middle of the night by the castle clock,' but there is no use in thinking of sleep. I can't sleep. The rain against the window is very dismal and the winds are marching by like armies of the dead. All the little ghostly joys of the past are haunting me—all the ghostly fears of the future.

"I keep thinking—foolishly—of the Disappointed House to-night—up there on the hill with the roar of the rainy wind about it. Somehow this is what hurts me worst to-night. Other nights it is the fact that I don't even know where Dean is this winter—or that Teddy never writes a line to me—or just that there are hours when sheer loneliness wrings the stamina out of me. In such moments I come to this old journal for comforting. It's like talking it out to a faithful friend."

## II

"Nov. 30, 19—

"I have two chrysanthemums and a rose out. The rose is a song and a dream and an enchantment all in one. The 'mums are very pretty, too, but it does not do to have them and the rose too near together. Seen by themselves they are handsome, bright blossoms, pink and yellow, and cheery, looking very well satisfied with themselves. But set the rose behind them and the change is actually amusing. They then seem like vulgar, frowsy kitchen maids beside a stately, white queen. It's not the fault of the poor 'mums that they weren't born roses, so to be fair to them I keep them by themselves and enjoy them that way.

"I wrote a *good* story to-day. I think even Mr. Carpenter would have been satisfied with it. I was happy while I was writing it. But when I finished it and came back to reality—

"Well, I'm not going to growl. Life has at least grown *livable* again. It was *not* livable through the autumn. I know Aunt Laura thought I was going into consumption. Not I. That would be too Victorian. I fought things out and conquered them and I'm a sane, *free* woman once more. Though the taste of my folly is still in my mouth at times and very bitter it is.

"Oh, I'm really getting on very well. I'm beginning to make a livable income for myself and Aunt Elizabeth reads my stories aloud o' evenings to Aunt Laura and Cousin Jimmy. I can always get through *to-day* very nicely. It's to-morrow I can't live through."

## III

"JANUARY 15, 19—

"I've been out for a moonlit snowshoe tramp. There was a nice bite of frost in the air and the night was exquisite—a frosty, starry lyric of light. Some nights are like honey—and some like wine—and some like wormwood. To-night is like wine—white wine—some clear, sparkling, fairy brew that rather goes to one's head. I am tingling all over with hope and expectation and victory over certain principalities and powers that got a grip on me last night about three o'clock.

"I have just drawn aside the curtain of my window and looked out. The garden is white and still under the moon, all ebony of shadow and silver of frosted snow. Over it all the delicate traceries where trees stand up leafless in seeming death and sorrow. But only seeming. The life-blood is at their hearts and by and by it will stir and they will clothe themselves in bridal garments of young gren leaves and pink blossoms. And over there where the biggest drift of all lies deep the Golden Ones will uplift their trumpets of the morning.

"And far beyond our garden field after field lies white and lonely in the moonlight. Lonely? I hadn't meant to write that word. It slipped in. I'm *not* lonely— I have my work and my books and the hope of spring— and I know that this calm, simple existence is a much better and happier one than the hectic life I led last summer.

"I believed that before I wrote it down. And now I don't believe it. It isn't true. This is stagnation!!

"Oh, I am—I *am*—lonely—with the loneliness of unshared thought. What is the use of denying it?

When I came in I *was* the victor—but now my banner is in the dust again."

## IV

"FEB. 20, 19—

"Something has happened to sour February's temper. Such a pevish month. The weather for the past few weeks has certainly been living up to the Murray traditions.

"A dreary snowstorm is raging and the wind is pursuing tormented wraiths over the hills. I know that out beyond the trees Blair Water is a sad, black thing in a desert of whiteness. But the great, dark, wintry night outside makes my cosy little room with its crackling fire seem cosier, and I feel must more contented with the world than I did that beautiful night in January. To-night isn't so—so *insulting*.

"To-day in *Glassford's Magazine* there was a story illustration by Teddy. I saw my own face looking out at me in the heroine. It always gives me a very ghostly sensation. And to-day it angered me as well. My face has *no right* to mean anything to him when *I* don't.

"But for all that, I cut out his picture, which was in the 'Who's Who' column, and put it in a frame and set it on my desk. I have no picture of Teddy. And to-night I took it out of the frame and laid it on the coals in the fireplace and watched it shrivel up. Just before the fire went out of it a queer little shudder went over it and Teddy seemed to wink at me—an impish, derisive wink—as if he said:

"'You *think* you've forgotten—but if you had you wouldn't have burned me. You are mine—you will always be mine—and I don't want you.'

"If a good fairy were suddenly to appear before me and offer me a wish it would be this: to have Teddy Kent come and whistle again and again in Lofty John's bush. And I would not go—not one step.

"I *can't* endure this. I *must* put him out of my life."

# Chapter XVII

## I

The Murray clan had a really terrible time in the summer that followed Emily's twenty-second birthday. Neither Teddy nor Ilse came home that summer. Ilse was touring in the West and Teddy betook himself into some northern hinterland with an Indian treaty party to make illustrations for a serial. But Emily had so many beaus that Blair Water gossip was in as bad a plight as the centipede who couldn't tell which foot came after which. So many beaus and not one of them such as the connection could approve of.

There was handsome, dashing Jack Bannister, the Derry Pond Don Juan—"a picturesque scoundrel," as Dr. Burnley called him. Certainly Jack was untrammelled by any moral code. But who knew what effect his silver tongue and good looks might have on temperamental Emily? It worried the Murrays for three weeks and then it appeared that Emily had some sense, after all. Jack Bannister faded out of the picture.

"Emily should never have even *spoken* to him," said Uncle Oliver indignantly. "Why, they say he keeps a diary and writes down all his love-affairs in it and what the girls said to him."

"Don't worry. He won't write down what *I* said to him," said Emily, when Aunt Laura reported this to her anxiously.

Harold Conway was another anxiety. A Shrewsbury man in his thirties, who looked like a poet gone to seed. With a shock of wavy dark auburn hair and brilliant brown eyes. Who "fiddled for a living."

Emily went to a concert and a play with him and the New Moon aunts had some sleepless nights. But when in Blair Water parlance Rod Dunbar "cut him out" things were even worse. The Dunbars were "nothing" when it came to religion. Rod's mother, to be sure, was a Presbyterian, but his father was a Methodist, his brother a Baptist and one sister a Christian Scientist. The other sister was a Theosophist, which was worse than all the rest because they had no idea *what* it was. In all this mixture what on earth was Rod? Certainly no match for an orthodox niece of New Moon.

"His great-uncle was a religious maniac," said Uncle Wallace gloomily. "He was kept chained in his bedroom for sixteen years. *What* has got into that girl? Is she idiot or demon?"

Yet the Dunbars were at least a respectable family; but what was to be said of Larry Dix—one of the "notorious Priest Pond Dixes"—whose father had once pastured his cows in the graveyard and whose uncle was more than suspected of having thrown a dead cat down a neighbour's well for spite? To be sure, Larry himself was doing well as a dentist and was such a deadly-serious, solemn-in-earnest young man that nothing much could be urged against him, if one could only swallow the fact that he was a Dix. Nevertheless, Aunt Elizabeth was much relieved when Emily turned him adrift.

"Such presumption," said Aunt Laura, meaning for a Dix to aspire to a Murray.

"It wasn't because of his presumption I packed him off," said Emily. "It was because of the way he made love. He made a thing ugly that should have been beautiful."

"I suppose you wouldn't have him because he didn't propose romantically," said Aunt Elizabeth contemptuously.

"No. I think my real reason was that I felt sure he

was the kind of man who would give his wife a vacuum cleaner for a Christmas present," vowed Emily.

"She will not take anything seriously," said Aunt Elizabeth in despair.

"*I* think she is bewitched," said Uncle Wallace. "She hasn't had one decent beau this summer. She's so temperamental decent fellows are scared of her."

"She's getting a terrible reputation as a flirt," mourned Aunt Ruth. "It's no wonder nobody worth while will have anything to do with her."

"Always with some fantastic love-affair on hand," snapped Uncle Wallace. The clan felt that Uncle Wallace had, with unusual felicity, hit on the very word. Emily's "love-affairs" were never the conventional, decorous things Murray love-affairs should be. They were indeed fantastic.

## II

But Emily always blessed her stars that none of the clan except Aunt Elizabeth ever knew anything about the most fantastic of them all. If they had they would have thought her temperamental with a vengeance.

It all came about in a simple, silly way. The editor of the Charlottetown *Argus*, a daily paper with some pretentions to literature, had selected from an old U.S. newspaper a certain uncopyrighted story of several chapters—*A Royal Betrothal*, by some unknown author, *Mark Greaves*, for reprinting in the special edition of *The Argus*, devoted to "boosting" the claims of Prince Edward Island as a summer resort. His staff was small and the compositors had been setting up the type for the special edition at odd moments for a month and had it all ready except the concluding chapter of *A Royal Betrothal*. This chapter had disappeared and could not be found. The editor was furious, but that did not help matters any. He could not at that late hour find another story which would exactly fill the space, nor was there time to set it up if he could. The special edition must go to press in an hour. What was to be done?

At this moment Emily wandered in. She and Mr. Wilson were good friends and she always called when in town.

"You're a godsend," said Mr. Wilson. "Will you do me a favour?" He tossed the torn and dirty chapters of *A Royal Betrothal* over to her. "For heavens' sake, get to work and write a concluding chapter to that yarn. I'll give you half an hour. They can set it up in another half-hour. And we'll have the darn thing out on time."

Emily glanced hastily over the story. As far as it went there was no hint of what "Mark Greaves" intended as a *dénouement*.

"Have you any idea how it ended?" she asked.

"No, never read it," groaned Mr. Wilson. "Just picked it for its length."

"Well, I'll do my best, though I'm not accustomed to write with flippant levity of kings and queens," agreed Emily. "This Mark Greaves, whoever he is, seems to be very much at home with royalty."

"I'll bet he never even saw one," snorted Mr. Wilson.

In the half-hour allotted to her Emily produced a quite respectable concluding chapter with a solution of the mystery which was really ingenious. Mr. Wilson snatched it with an air of relief, handed it to a compositor, and bowed Emily out with thanks.

"I wonder if any of the readers will notice where the seam comes in," reflected Emily amusedly. "And I wonder if Mark Greaves will ever see it and if so what he will think."

It did not seem in the least likely she would ever know and she dismissed the matter from her mind. Consequently when, one afternoon two weeks later, Cousin Jimmy ushered a stranger into the sitting-room where Emily was arranging roses in Aunt Elizabeth's rock-crystal goblet with its ruby base—a treasured heirloom of New Moon—Emily did not connect him with *A*

*Royal Betrothal*, though she had a distinct impression that the caller was an exceedingly irate man.

Cousin Jimmy discreetly withdrew and Aunt Laura, who had come in to place a glass dish full of strawberry preserves on the table to cool, withdrew also, wondering a little who Emily's odd-looking caller could be. Emily herself wondered. She remained standing by the table, a slim, gracious thing in her pale-green gown, shining like a star in the shadowy, old-fashioned room.

"Won't you sit down?" she questioned, with all the aloof courtesy of New Moon. But the newcomer did not move. He simply stood before her staring at her. And again Emily felt that, while he had been quite furious when he came in, he was not in the least angry now.

He must have been born, of course, because he was there—but it was incredible, she thought, he could ever have been a baby. He wore audacious clothes and a monocle, screwed into one of his eyes—eyes that seemed absurdly like little black currants with black eyebrows that made right-angled triangles above them. He had a mane of black hair reaching to his shoulders, an immensely long chin and a marble-white face. In a picture Emily thought he would have looked rather handsome and romantic. But here in the New Moon sitting-room he looked merely weird.

"Lyrical creature," he said, gazing at her.

Emily wondered if he were by any chance an escaped lunatic.

"You do not commit the crime of ugliness," he continued fervently. "This is a wonderful moment—very wonderful. 'Tis a pity we must spoil it by talking. Eyes of purple-grey, sprinkled with gold. Eyes that I have looked for all my life. Sweet eyes, in which I drowned myself eons ago."

"Who are you?" said Emily crisply, now entirely convinced that he was quite mad. He laid his hand on his heart and bowed.

"Mark Greaves—Mark D. Greaves—Mark Delage Greaves."

Mark Greaves! Emily had a confused idea that she ought to know the name. It sounded curiously familiar.

"Is it possible you do not recognise my name! Verily this is fame. Even in this remote corner of the world I should have supposed—"

"Oh," cried Emily, light suddenly breaking on her. "I—I remember now. You wrote *A Royal Betrothal*."

"The story you so unfeelingly murdered—yes."

"Oh, I'm so sorry," Emily interrupted. "Of course you would think it unpardonable. It was this way— you see—"

He stopped her by a wave of a very long, very white hand.

"No matter. No matter. It does not interest me at all now. I admit I was very angry when I came here. I am stopping at the Derry Pond Hotel of The Dunes—ah, what a name—poetry—mystery—romance—and I saw the special edition of *The Argus* this morning. I was angry—had I not a right to be?—and yet more sad than angry. My story was barbarously mutilated. A happy ending. Horrible. *My* ending was sorrowful and artistic. A happy ending can never be artistic. I hastened to the den of *The Argus*. I dissembled my anger—I discovered who was responsible. I came here—to denounce—to upbraid. I remain to worship."

Emily smiply did not know what to say. New Moon traditions held no precedent for this.

"You do not understand me. You are puzzled—your bewilderment becomes you. Again I say a wonderful moment. To come enraged—and behold divinity. To realise as soon as I saw you that you were meant for me and me alone."

Emily wished somebody would come in. This was getting nightmarish.

"It is absurd to talk so," she said shortly. "We are strangers—"

"We are *not* strangers," he interrupted. "We have

loved in some other life, of course, and our love was a violent, gorgeous thing—a love of eternity. I recognised you as soon as I entered. As soon as you have recovered from your sweet surprise you will realise this, too. When can you marry me?"

To be asked by a man to marry him five minutes after the first moment you have laid eyes on him is an experience more stimulating than pleasant. Emily was annoyed.

"Don't talk nonsense, please," she said curtly. "I am not going to marry you at any time."

"Not marry me? But you must! I have never before asked a woman to marry me. I am the famous Mark Greaves. I am rich. I have the charm and romance of my French mother and the common sense of my Scotch father. With the French side of me I feel and acknowledge your beauty and mystery. With the Scotch side of me I bow in homage to your reserve and dignity. You are ideal—adorable. Many women have loved me but I loved them not. I enter this room a free man. I go out a captive. Enchanting captivity! Adorable captor! I kneel before you in spirit."

Emily was horribly afraid he would kneel before her in the flesh. He looked quite capable of it. And suppose Aunt Elizabeth should come in.

"Please go away," she said desperately. "I'm—I'm very busy and I can't stop talking to you any longer. I'm sorry about the story—if you would let me explain—"

"I have said it does not matter about the story. Though you must learn never to write happy endings— never. I will teach you. I will teach you the beauty and artistry of sorrow and incompleteness. Ah, what a pupil you will be! What bliss to teach such a pupil! I kiss your hand."

He made a step nearer as if to seize upon it. Emily stepped backward in alarm.

"You *must* be crazy," she exclaimed.

"Do I look crazy?" demanded Mr. Greaves.

"You do," retorted Emily flatly and cruelly.

"Perhaps I do—probably I do. Crazy—intoxicated with wine of the rose. All lovers are mad. Divine madness! Oh, beautiful, unkissed lips!"

Emily drew herself up. This absurd interview must end. She was by now thoroughly angry.

"Mr. Greaves," she said—and such was the power of the Murray look that Mr. Greaves realised she meant exactly what she said. "I shan't listen to any more of this nonsense. Since you won't let me explain about the matter of the story I bid you good-afternoon."

Mr. Greaves looked gravely at her for a moment. Then he said solemnly:

"A kiss? Or a kick? Which?"

Was he speaking metaphorically? But whether or no—

"A kick," said Emily disdainfully.

Mr. Greaves suddenly seized the crystal goblet and dashed it violently against the stove.

Emily uttered a faint shriek—partly of real terror—partly of dismay. Aunt Elizabeth's treasured goblet.

"That was merely a defence reaction," said Mr. Greaves, glaring at her. "I had to do that—or kill you. Ice-maiden! Chill vestal! Cold as your northern snows! Farewell."

He did not slam the door as he went out. He merely shut it gently and irrevocably, so that Emily might realise what she had lost. When she saw that he was really out of the garden and marching indignantly down the lane as if he were crushing something beneath his feet, she permitted herself the relief of a long breath—the first she had dared to draw since his entrance.

"I suppose," she said, half hysterically, "that I ought to be thankful he did not throw the dish of strawberry preserves at me."

Aunt Elizabeth came in.

"Emily, the rock-crystal goblet! Your Grandmother Murray's goblet! And you have broken it!"

"No, really, Aunty dear, I didn't. Mr. Greaves—Mr. Mark Delage Greaves did it. He threw it at the stove."

"Threw it at the stove!" Aunt Elizabeth was staggered. "Why did he throw it at the stove?"

"Because I wouldn't marry him," said Emily.

"Marry him! Did you ever see him before?"

"Never."

Aunt Elizabeth gathered up the fragments of the crystal goblet and went out quite speechless. There was—there must be—something wrong with a girl when a man proposed marriage to her at first meeting. And hurled heirloom goblets at inoffensive stoves.

### III

But it was the affair of the Japanese prince which really gave the Murrays their bad summer.

Second-cousin Louise Murray, who had lived in Japan for twenty years, came home to Derry Pond for a visit and brought with her a young Japanese prince, the son of a friend of her husband's, who had been converted to Christianity by her efforts and wished to see something of Canada. His mere coming made a tremendous sensation in the clan and the community. But that was nothing to the next sensation when they realised that the prince had evidently and unmistakably fallen terrifically in love with Emily Byrd Starr of New Moon.

Emily liked him—was interested in him—was sorry for him in his bewildered reactions to the Presbyterian atmosphere of Derry Pond and Blair Water. Naturally a Japanese prince, even a converted one, couldn't feel exactly at home. So she talked a great deal to him—he could talk English excellently—and walked with him at moonrise in the garden—and almost every evening that slant-eyed, inscrutable face, with the black hair brushed straight back from it as smooth as satin, might be seen in the parlour of New Moon.

But it was not until he gave Emily a little frog beautifully cut out of moss agate that the Murrays took alarm. Cousin Louise sounded it first. Tearfully. *She* knew what that frog meant. Those agate frogs were heirlooms in the family of the prince. Never were they given away save as marriage and betrothal gifts. Was Emily engaged—to him? Aunt Ruth, looking as usual as if she thought every one had gone mad, came over to New Moon and made quite a scene. It annoyed Emily so much that she refused to answer any questions. She was a bit edgy to begin with over the unnecessary way her clan had heckled her all summer over suitors that were not of her choosing and whom there was not the slightest danger of her taking seriously.

"There are some things not good for you to know," she told Aunt Ruth impertinently.

And the distracted Murrays despairingly concluded that she had decided to be a Japanese princess. And if she had—well, they knew what happened when Emily made up her mind. It was something inevitable—like a visitation of God; but it was a dreadful thing. His Princeship cast no halo about him in the Murray eyes. No Murray before her would ever have dreamed of marrying any foreigner, much less a Japanese. But then of course she was temperamental.

"Always with some disreputable creature in tow," said Aunt Ruth. "But this beats everything I ever feared. A pagan—a—"

"Oh, he isn't *that*, Ruth," mourned Aunt Laura. "He is converted—Cousin Louise says she is sure he is sincere, but—"

"I tell you he's a pagan!" reiterated Aunt Ruth. "Cousin Louise could never convert anybody. Why, she's none too sound herself. And her husband is a modernist if he's *anything*. Don't tell me! A yellow pagan! Him and his agate frogs!"

She seems to have such an attraction for extraordinary men," said Aunt Elizabeth, thinking of the rock-crystal goblet.

Uncle Wallace said it was preposterous. Andrew said she might at least have picked on a white man. Cousin Louise, who felt that the clan blamed *her* for it all, pleaded tearfully that he had beautiful manners when you really knew him.

"And she might have had the Reverend James Wallace," said Aunt Elizabeth.

They lived through five weeks of this and then the prince went back to Japan. He had been summoned home by his family, Cousin Louise said—a marriage had been arranged for him with a princess of an old Samurai family. Of course he had obeyed; but he left the agate frog in Emily's possession and nobody ever knew just what he said to her one night at moonrise in the garden. Emily was a little white and strange and remote when she came in, but she smiled impishly at her aunts and Cousin Louise.

"So I'm not to be a Japanese princess after all," she said, wiping away some imaginary tears.

"Emily, I fear you've only been flirting with that poor boy," rebuked Cousin Louise. "You have made him very unhappy."

"I wasn't flirting. Our conversations were about literature and history—mostly. He will never think of me again."

"*I* know what he looked like when he read that letter," retorted Cousin Louise. "And I know the significance of agate frogs."

New Moon drew a breath of relief and thankfully settled down to routine again. Aunt Laura's old, tender eyes lost their troubled look, but Aunt Elizabeth thought sadly of the Rev. James Wallace. It had been a nerveracking summer. Blair Water whispered about that Emily Starr had been "disappointed," but predicted she would live to be thankful for it. You couldn't trust them foreigners. Not likely he was a prince at all.

# Chapter XVIII

## I

One day in the last week of October Cousin Jimmy began to plough the hill field, Emily found the lost legendary diamond of the Murrays,* and Aunt Elizabeth fell down the cellar steps and broke her leg.

Emily, in the warm amber of the afternoon, stood on the sandstone front steps of New Moon and looked about her with eyes avid for the mellow loveliness of the fading year. Most of the trees were leafless, but a little birch, still in golden array, peeped out of the young spruces—a birch *Danaë* in their shadows—and the Lombardies down the lane were like a row of great golden candles. Beyond was the sere hill field scarfed with three bright red ribbons—the "ridges" Cousin Jimmy had ploughed. Emily had been writing all day and she was tired. She went down the garden to the little vine-hung summer house—she poked dreamily about; deciding where the new tulip bulbs should be planted. Here—in this moist rich soil where Cousin Jimmy had recently pried out the mouldering old side-steps. Next spring it should be a banquet board laden with stately chalices. Emily's heel sank deeply into the moist earth and came out laden. She sauntered over to the stone bench and daintily scraped off the earth with a twig. Something fell and glittered on the grass like a dewdrop. Emily picked it up with a little cry. There in her hand was the Lost Diamond—lost over sixty years

*See *Emily of New Moon*.

before, when Great-aunt Miriam Murray had gone into the summer house.

It had been one of her childish dreams to find the Lost Diamond—she and Ilse and Teddy had hunted for it scores of times. But of late years she had not thought about it. And here it was—as bright, as beautiful, as ever. It must have been hidden in some crevice of the old side-steps and fallen to the earth when they had been torn away.

It made quite a sensation at New Moon. A few days later the Murrays had a conclave about Aunt Elizabeth's bed to decide what should be done with it. Cousin Jimmy said stoutly that finding was keeping in this case. Edward and Miriam Murray were long since dead. They had left no family. The diamond by rights was Emily's.

"We are all heirs to it," said Uncle Wallace judicially. "It cost, I've heard, a thousand dollars sixty years ago. It's a beautiful stone. The fair thing is to sell it and give Emily her mother's share."

"One shouldn't sell a family diamond," said Aunt Elizabeth firmly.

This seemed to be the general opinion at bottom. Even Uncle Wallace acknowledged the sway of *noblesse oblige*. Eventually they all agreed that the diamond should be Emily's.

"She can have it set as a little pendant for her neck," said Aunt Laura.

"It was meant for a ring," said Aunt Ruth, just for the sake of disagreeing. "And she shouldn't wear it, in any case, until she is married. A diamond as big as that is in bad taste for a young girl."

"Oh, married!" Aunt Addie gave a rather nasty little laugh. It conveyed her opinion that if Emily waited for that to wear the diamond it was just possible she might never wear it. Aunt Addie had never forgiven Emily for refusing Andrew. And here she was at twenty-three— well, nearly—with no eligible beau in sight.

"The Lost Diamond will bring you luck, Emily," said Cousin Jimmy. "I'm glad they've left it with you. It's rightly yours. But will you let me hold it sometimes, Emily,—just hold it and look into it? When I look into anything like that I—I—find myself. I'm not simple Jimmy Murray then—I'm what I would have been if I hadn't been pushed into a well. Don't say anything about it to Elizabeth, Emily, but just let me hold it and look at it once in awhile."

"My favourite gem is the diamond, when all is said and done," Emily wrote to Ilse that night. "But I love gems of all kinds—except turquoise. Them I loathe—the shallow, insipid, soulless things. The gloss of pearl, glow of ruby, tenderness of sapphire, melting violet of amethyst, moonlit glimmer of aquamarine, milk and fire of opal—I love them all."

"What about emeralds?" Ilse wrote back—a bit nastily, Emily thought, not knowing that a Shrewsbury correspondent of Ilse's wrote her now and then some unreliable gossip about Perry Miller's visits to New Moon. Perry did come to New Moon occasionally. But he had given up asking Emily to marry him and seemed wholly absorbed in his profession. Already he was regarded as a coming man and shrewd politicians were said to be biding their time until he should be old enough to "bring out" as a candidate for the Provincial House.

"Who knows? You may be 'my lady' yet," wrote Ilse. "Perry will be Sir Perry some day."

Which Emily thought was even nastier than the scratch about the emerald.

## II

At first it did not seem that the Lost Diamond had brought luck to any one at New Moon. The very evening of its finding Aunt Elizabeth broke her leg. Shawled and bonnetted for a call on a sick neighbour—bonnets had long gone out of fashion even for elderly ladies, but Aunt Elizabeth wore them still—she had started down cellar to get a jar of black currant jam for the invalid, had tripped in some way and fallen. When she was taken up it was found that her leg was broken and Aunt Elizabeth faced the fact that for the first time in her life she was to spend weeks in bed.

Of course New Moon got on without her, though she believed it couldn't. But the problem of amusing her was a more serious one than the running of New Moon. Aunt Elizabeth fretted and pined over her enforced inactivity—could not read much herself—didn't like to be read to—was sure everything was going to the dogs—was sure she was going to be lame and useless all the rest of her life—was sure Dr. Burnley was an old fool—was sure Laura would never get the apples packed properly—was sure the hired boy would cheat Cousin Jimmy.

"Would you like to hear the little story I finished today, Aunt Elizabeth?" asked Emily one evening. "It might amuse you."

"Is there any silly love-making in it?" demanded Aunt Elizabeth ungraciously.

"No love-making of any kind. It's pure comedy."

"Well, let me hear it. It may pass the time."

Emily read the story. Aunt Elizabeth made no comment whatever. But the next afternoon she said, hesitatingly, "Is there—any more—of that story you read last night?"

"No."

"Well, if there was—I wouldn't mind hearing it. It kind of took my thoughts away from myself. The folks seemed—sort of—real to me. I suppose that is why I feel as if I want to know what happens to them," concluded Aunt Elizabeth as if apologising for her weakness.

"I'll write another story about them for you," promised Emily.

When this was read Aunt Elizabeth remarked that she didn't care if she heard a third one.

"Those *Applegaths* are amusing," she said. "I've known

people like them. And that little chap, *Jerry Stowe*. What happens to him when he grows up, poor child?"

### III

Emily's idea came to her that evening as she sat idly by her window looking rather drearily out on cold meadows and hills of grey, over which a chilly, lonesome wind blew. She could hear the dry leaves blowing over the garden wall. A few great white flakes were beginning to come down.

She had had a letter from Ilse that day. Teddy's picture, *The Smiling Girl*, which had been exhibited in Montreal and had made a tremendous sensation, had been accepted by the Paris *Salon*.

"I just got back from the coast in time to see the last day of its exhibition here," wrote Ilse. "And it's you—Emily—it's you. Just that old sketch he made of you years ago completed and glorified—the one your Aunt Nancy made you so mad by keeping—remember? There you were smiling down from Teddy's canvas. The critics had a great deal to say about his colouring and technique and 'feeling' and all that sort of jargon. But one said, 'The smile on the girl's face will become as famous as Mona Lisa's.' I've seen that very smile on your face a hundred times, Emily—especially when you were seeing that unseeable thing you used to call your flash. Teddy has caught the very soul of it—not a mocking, challenging smile like Mona Lisa's—but a smile that seems to hint at some exquisitely wonderful secret you could tell if you liked—some whisper eternal—a secret that would make every one happy if they could only get you to tell it. It's only a trick, I suppose—*you* don't know that secret any more than the rest of us. But the smile suggests that you do—suggests it marvellously. Yes, your Teddy has genius—that smile proves it. What does it feel like, Emily, to realise yourself the inspiration of a genius? I'd give years of my life for such a compliment."

Emily didn't quite know what it felt like. But she did feel a certain small, futile anger with Teddy. What right had he who scorned her love and was indifferent to her friendship to paint her face—her soul—her secret vision—and hang it up for the world to gaze at? To be sure, he had told her in childhood that he meant to do it—and she had agreed then. But everything had changed since then. Everything.

Well, about this story, regarding which Aunt Elizabeth had such an Oliver Twist complex. Suppose she were to write another one—suddenly the idea came. Suppose she were to expand it into a book. Not like *A Seller of Dreams*, of course. That old glory could come back no more. But Emily had an instantaneous vision of the new book, as a whole—a witty, sparkling rill of human comedy. She ran down to Aunt Elizabeth.

"Aunty, how would you like me to write a book for you about those people in my story? Just for you—a chapter every day."

Aunt Elizabeth carefully hid the fact that she was interested.

"Oh, you can if you want to. I wouldn't mind hearing about them. But mind, you are not to put any of the neighbours in."

Emily didn't put any of the neighbours in—she didn't need to. Characters galore trooped into her consciousness, demanding a local habitation and a name. They laughed and scowled and wept and danced—and even made a little love. Aunt Elizabeth tolerated this, supposing you couldn't have a novel without some of it. Emily read a chapter every evening, and Aunt Laura and Cousin Jimmy were allowed to hear it along with Aunt Elizabeth. Cousin Jimmy was in raptures. He was sure it was the most wonderful story ever written.

"I feel young again when I'm listening to you," he said.

"Sometimes I want to laugh and sometimes I want to cry," confessed Aunt Laura. "I can't sleep for wondering what is going to happen to the *Applegaths* in the next chapter."

"It might be worse," conceded Aunt Elizabeth. "But I wish you'd cut out what you said about *Gloria Applegath's* greasy dish-towels. Mrs. Charlie Frost, of Derry Pond, will think you mean her. Her towels are always greasy."

"Chips are bound to light somewhere," said Cousin Jimmy. "*Gloria* is funny in a book, but she'd be awful to live with. Too busy saving the world. Somebody ought to tell her to read her Bible."

"I don't like *Cissy Applegath*, though," said Aunt Laura apologetically. "She has such a supercilious way of speaking."

"A shallow-pated creature," said Aunt Elizabeth.

"It's old *Jesse Applegath* I can't tolerate," said Cousin Jimmy fiercely. "A man who would kick a cat just to relieve his feelings! I'd go twenty miles to slap the old he-devil's face. But"—hopefully—"maybe he'll die before long."

"Or reform," suggested Aunt Laura mercifully.

"No, no, don't let him reform," said Cousin Jimmy anxiously. "Kill him off, if necessary, but don't reform him. I wish, though, you'd change the colour of *Peg Applegath's* eyes. I don't like green eyes—never did."

"But I can't change them. They *are* green," protested Emily.

"Well, then, *Abraham Applegath's* whiskers," pleaded Cousin Jimmy. "I like *Abraham*. He's a gay dog. Can't he help his whiskers, Emily?"

"No"—firmly—"he can't."

Why couldn't they understand? Abraham *had* whiskers—*wanted* whiskers—was determined to have whiskers. *She* couldn't change him.

"It's time we remembered that these people have no real existence," rebuked Aunt Elizabeth.

But once—Emily counted it her greatest triumph—Aunt Elizabeth laughed. She was so ashamed of it she would not even smile all the rest of the reading.

"Elizabeth thinks God doesn't like to hear us laugh,"

Cousin Jimmy whispered behind his hand to Laura. If Elizabeth had not been lying there with a broken leg Laura would have smiled. But to smile under the circumstances seemed like taking unfair advantage of her.

Cousin Jimmy went downstairs shaking his head and murmuring, "*How* does she do it? How *does* she do it! I can write poetry—but *this*. Those folks are alive!"

One of them was too much alive in Aunt Elizabeth's opinion.

"That *Nicholas Applegath* is too much like old Douglas Courcy, of Shrewsbury," she said. "I told you not to put any people we knew in it."

"Why, I never saw Douglas Courcy."

"It's him to the life. Even Jimmy noticed it. You must cut him out, Emily."

But Emily obstinately refused to "cut him out." Old *Nicholas* was one of the best characters in her book. She was very much absorbed in it by this time. The composition of it was never the ecstatic rite the creation of *A Seller of Dreams* had been, but it was very fascinating. She forgot all vexing and haunting things while she was writing it. The last chapter was finished the very day the splints were taken off Aunt Elizabeth's leg and she was carried down to the kitchen lounge.

"Well, your story has helped," she admitted. "But I'm thankful to be where I can keep my eye on things once more. What are you going to do with your book? What you are going to call it?"

"*The Moral of the Rose*."

"I don't think that is a good title at all. I don't know what it means—nobody will know."

"No matter. That is the book's name."

Aunt Elizabeth sighed.

"I don't know where you get your stubbornness from, Emily. I'm sure I don't. You never would take advice. And I know the Courcys will never speak to us again, after the book is published."

"The book hasn't any chance of being published,"

said Emily gloomily. "They'll send it back, 'damned with faint praise.'"

Aunt Elizabeth had never heard this expression before and she thought Emily had originated it and was being profane.

"Emily," she said sternly, "don't let me ever hear such a word from your lips again. I've more than suspected Ilse of such language—she's not to be judged by *our* standards. But Murrays of New Moon do *not* swear."

"It was only a quotation, Aunt Elizabeth," said Emily wearily.

She was tired—a little tired of everything. It was Christmas now and a long, dreary winter stretched before her—an empty, aimless winter. Nothing seemed worth while—not even finding a publisher for *The Moral of the Rose*.

## IV

However, she typewrote it faithfully and sent it out. It came back. She sent it out again, three times. It came back. She retyped it—the MS. was getting dog-eared—and sent it out again. At intervals all that winter and summer she sent it out, working doggedly through a list of possible publishers. I forget how many times she retyped it. It became a sort of joke—a bitter joke.

The worst of it was that the New Moon folk knew of all these rejections and their sympathy and indignation were hard to bear. Cousin Jimmy was so angry over every rejection of this masterpiece that he could not eat for a day afterwards and she gave up telling him of the journeys. Once she thought of sending it to Miss Royal and asking her if she had any influence to use. But the Murray pride would not brook the idea. Finally in the autumn when it returned from the last publisher on her list Emily did not even open the parcel. She cast it contemptuously into a compartment of her desk.

"Too sick at heart to war
With failure any more."

"That's the end of it—and of all my dreams. I'll use it up for scribbling paper. And now I'll settle down to a tepid existence of pot-boiling."

At least magazine editors were more appreciative than book publishers—as Cousin Jimmy indignantly said, they appeared to have more sense. While her book was seeking vainly for its chance her magazine clientèle grew daily. She spent long hours at her desk and enjoyed her work after a fashion. But there was a little consciousness of failure under it all. She could never get much higher on the Alpine path. The glorious city of fulfilment on its summit was not for her. Pot-boiling! That was all. Making a living in what Aunt Elizabeth thought was a shamefully easy way.

Miss Royal wrote her frankly that she was falling off.

"You're getting into a rut, Emily," she warned. "A self-satisfied rut. The admiration of Aunt Laura and Cousin Jimmy is a bad thing for you. You should be *here*—we would keep you up to the scratch."

Suppose she had gone to New York with Miss Royal when she had the chance six years ago. Would she not have been able to get her book published? Was it not the fatal Prince Edward Island postmark that condemned it—the little out-of-the-world province from which no good thing could ever come?

Perhaps! Perhaps Miss Royal had been right. But what did it matter?

No one came to Blair Water that summer. That is— Teddy Kent did not come. Ilse was in Europe again. Dean Priest seemed to have taken up his residence permanently at the Pacific Coast. Life at New Moon went on unchanged. Except that Aunt Elizabeth limped a little and Cousin Jimmy's hair turned white quite suddenly, overnight as it seemed. Now and then Emily had a quick, terrible vision that Cousin Jimmy was growing old. They were all growing old. Aunt Elizabeth was nearly seventy. And when she died New Moon went to Andrew. Already there were times when Andrew seemed to be putting on proprietary airs in his visits to New Moon. Not that he would ever live there himself, of course. But it ought to be kept in good shape against the day when it would be necessary to sell it.

"It's time those old Lombardies were cut down," said Andrew to Uncle Oliver one day. "They're getting frightfully ragged at the tops. Lombardies are so out of date now And that field with the young spruces should be drained and ploughed."

"That old orchard should be cleared out," said Uncle Oliver. "It's more like a jungle than an orchard. The trees are too old for any good anyhow. They should all be chopped down. Jimmy and Elizabeth are too old-fashioned. They don't make half the money out of this farm they should."

Emily, overhearing this, clenched her fists. To see New Moon desecrated—her old, intimate, beloved trees cut down—the spruce field where wild stawberries grew improved out of existence—the dreamy beauty of the old orchard destroyed—the little dells and slopes that kept all the ghostly joys of her past changed—altered. It was unbearable.

"If you had married Andrew New Moon would have been yours," said Aunt Elizabeth bitterly, when she found Emily crying over what they had said.

"But the changes would have come just the same," said Emily. "Andrew wouldn't have listened to me. He believes that the husband is the head of the wife."

"You will be twenty-four your next birthday," said Aunt Elizabeth. Apropos of what?

# Chapter XIX

## I

"Oct. 1, 19—

"This afternoon I sat at my window and alternately wrote at my new serial and watched a couple of dear, amusing, youngish maple-trees at the foot of the garden. They whispered secrets to each other all the afternoon. They would bend together and talk earnestly for a few moments, then spring back and look at each other, throwing up their hands comically in horror and amazement over their mutual revelations. I wonder what new scandal is afoot in Treeland."

## II

"Oct. 10, 19—

"This evening was lovely. I went up on the hill and walked about until twilight had deepened into an autumn night with a benediction of starry quietude over it. I was alone but not lonely. I was a queen in halls of fancy. I held a series of conversations with imaginary comrades and thought out so many epigrams that I was agreeably surprised at myself."

## III

"Oct. 28, 19—

"To-night I was out for one of my long walks. In a weird, purple, shadowy world, with great, cold clouds piling up above a yellow sky, hills brooding in the

151

silence of forsaken woods, ocean tumbling on a rocky shore. The whole landscape seemed

> "As those who wait
> Till judgment speak the doom of fate.

"It made me feel—horribly *alone*.

"What a creature of moods I am!

"'Fickle,' as Aunt Elizabeth says? 'Temperamental,' as Andrew says?"

## IV

"Nov. 5, 19—

"What a fit of bad temper the world has indulged in! Day before yesterday she was not unbeautiful—a dignified old dame in fitting garb of brown and ermine. Yesterday she tried to ape juvenility, putting on all the airs and graces of spring, with scarfs of blue hazes. And what a bedraggled and uncomely old hag she was, all tatters and wrinkles. She grew peevish then over her own ugliness and has raged all night and day. I awakened up in the wee sma's and heard the wind shrieking in the trees and tears of rage and spite sleeting against the pane."

## V

"Nov. 23, 19—

"This is the second day of a heavy, ceaseless autumn rain. Really, it has rained almost every day this November. We had no mail to-day. The outside world is a dismal one, with drenched and dripping trees and sodden fields. And the damp and gloom have crept into my soul and spirit and sapped out all life and energy.

"I could not read, eat, sleep, write or do anything unless I drove myself to do it and then I felt as if I were trying to do it with somebody else's hands or brain and couldn't work very well with them. I feel lustreless, dowdy and uninviting—I even bore myself.

"I shall grow mossy in this existence!

"There! I feel better for that little outburst of discontent. It has ejected something from my system. I know that into everybody's life must come some days of depression and discouragement when all things in life seem to lose savour. The sunniest day has its clouds; but one must not forget that the sun is there all the time.

"How easy it is to be a philosopher—on paper!

"(Item:—If you are out in a cold, pouring rain, does it keep you dry to remember that the sun is there just the same?)

"Well, thank heaven no two days are ever *exactly* alike!"

## VI

"There was a stormy, unrestful sunset to-night, behind the pale, blanched hills, gleaming angrily through the Lombardies and the dark fir-boughs in Lofty John's bush, that were now and again tossed suddenly and distressfully in a fitful gust of wind. I sat at my window and watched it. Below in the garden it was quite dark and I could only see dimly the dead leaves that were whirling and dancing uncannily over the flowerless paths. The poor dead leaves—yet not quite dead, it seemed. There was still enough unquiet life left in them to make them restless and forlorn. They harkened yet to every call of the wind, which cared for them no longer but only played freakishly with them and broke their rest. I felt sorry for the leaves as I watched them in the dull, weird twilight, and angry—in a petulant fashion that almost made me laugh—with the wind that would not leave them in peace. Why should they—and I—be vexed with these transient, passionate breaths of desire for a life which passed us by?

"I have not heard even from Ilse for a long time. She has forgotten me, too."

## VII

"JAN. 10, 19—

"As I came home from the post-office this evening—with three acceptances—I revelled in the winter loveliness around me. It was so very calm and still; the low sun cast such pure, pale tints of pink and heliotrope over the snow; and the great, pale-silver moon peeping over the Delectable Mountain was such a friend of mine.

"How much difference in one's outlook three acceptances make!"

## VIII

"JAN. 20, 19—

"The nights are so dreary now and there is such a brief space of grey, sunless day. I work and think all day and, when night comes down early, gloom settles on my soul. I can't describe the feeling. It is dreadful—worse than any actual pain. In so far as I can express it in words I feel a great and awful weariness—not of body or brain but of *feeling*, coupled with a haunting dread of the future—*any* future—even a happy one—nay, a happy one most of all, for in this strange mood it seems to me that to be happy would require more effort—more buoyancy than I shall possess. The fantastic shape my fear assumes is that it would be *too much trouble* to be happy—require too much energy.

"Let me be honest—in this journal if nowhere else. I know quite well what is the matter with me. This afternoon I was rummaging in my old trunk in the garret and found a packet of the letters Teddy wrote the first year he was in Montreal. I was foolish enough to sit down and read them all.

"It was a mad thing to do. I am paying for it now.

Such letters have a terrible resurrective power. I am surrounded by bitter fancies and unbidden ghosts—the little spectral joys of the past."

## IX

"FEB. 5, 19—

"Life never seems the same to me as it used to. Something is *gone*. I am not unhappy. But life seems a sort of negative affair. I enjoy it on the whole and have many beautiful moments. I have success—at least a sort of success—in growing measure and a keen appreciation of all the world and the times offer for delight and interest. But underneath it all is the haunting sense of emptiness.

"This is all because 'full knee-deep lies the winter snow' and I can't go a-prowling. Wait till a thaw comes, when I can get out to the balm of the fir-trees and the peace of the white places and the 'strength of the hills'—what a beautiful old Biblical phrase that is!—and I shall be made whole once more."

## X

"Last night I simply could not endure any longer the vaseful of dyed grasses on my mantelpiece. What if they had been there for forty years! I seized them, opened the window and strewed them over the lawn. This soothed me so that I slept like an infant. But this morning Cousin Jimmy had gathered them all up and handed them secretly back to me with a gentle warning not to let them 'blow out' again. Elizabeth would be horrified.

"I put them back in the vase. One cannot escape one's kismet."

## XI

"FEB. 22, 19—

"There was a creamy, misty sunset this evening and

then moonlight. Such moonlight. It is such a night as one might fall asleep in and dream happy dreams of gardens and songs and companionship, feeling all the while through one's sleep the splendour and radiance of white moon-world outside as one hears soft, far-away music sounding through the thoughts and words that are born of it.

"I slipped away for a solitary walk through that fairy world of glamour. I went through the orchard where the black shadows of the trees fell over the snow—I went up to the gleaming white hill with the stars over it, I lurked along fir copses dim with mystery and along still, wood aisles where the night hid from the moon-shine, I loitered across a dreamland field of ebon and ivory. I had a tryst with a friend of old days, the Wind Woman. And every breath was a lyric and every thought an ecstasy and I've come back with a soul washed white and clean in the great crystal bath of the night.

"But Aunt Elizabeth said people would think me crazy if they saw me roaming around alone at this hour of the night. And Aunt Laura made me take a drink of hot black currant decoction lest I might have taken cold. Only Cousin Jimmy partly understood.

"'You went out to escape. *I* know,' he whispered.

"'My soul has pastured with the stars
     Upon the meadowlands of space,'

I whispered in return."

## XII

"FEB. 26, 19—

"Jasper Frost has been coming out here from Shrews-bury of late. I don't think he will come any more—after our conversation of last night. He told me he loved me with a love 'that would last through eternity.' But I thought an eternity with Jasper would be rather long. Aunt Elizabeth will be a little disappointed, poor dear.

She likes Jasper and the Frosts are 'a good family.' I like him, too, but he is too prim and bandboxy.

" 'Would you like a slovenly beau?' demanded Aunt Elizabeth.

"This posed me. Because I wouldn't.

" 'Surely there's a happy medium,' I protested

" 'A girl shouldn't be too particular when she is'—I feel sure Aunt Elizabeth was going to say 'nearly twenty-four.' But she changed it to 'not *entirely* perfect herself.'

"I wish Mr. Carpenter had been alive to hear Aunt Elizabeth's italics. They were killing."

## XIII

MARCH 1, 19—

"A wonderful music of night is coming to my window from Lofty John's bush. No, *not* Lofty John's bush any more.

"Emily Byrd Starr's bush!

"I bought it to-day, with the proceeds of my latest serial. And it is mine—mine—mine. All the lovely things in it are mine—its moonlit vistas—the grace of its one big elm against the starlight—its shadowy little dells—its June-bells and ferns—its crystalline spring—its wind music sweeter than an old Cremona. No one can ever cut it down or desecrate it in any way.

"I am so happy. The wind is my comrade and the evening star my friend."

## XIV

"MARCH 23, 19—

"Is there any sound in the world sadder and weirder than the wail of the wind around the eaves and past the windows on a stormy night? It sounds as if all the broken-hearted cries of fair, unhappy women who died and were forgotten ages ago were being re-echoed in the moaning wind of to-night. All my own past pain finds a voice in it as if it were moaning a plea for re-entrance into the soul that has cast it out. There are strange sounds in that night wind clamouring there at my little window. I hear the cries of old sorrows in it—and the moans of old despairs—and the phantom songs of dead hopes. The night wind is the wandering soul of the past. It has no share in the future—and so it is mournful."

## XV

"April 10, 19—

"This morning I felt more like myself than I have for a long time. I was out for a walk over the Delectable Mountain. It was a very mild, still, misty morning with lovely pearl-grey skies and smell of spring in the air. Every turn and twist on that hill-road was an old friend to me. And everything was so young. April couldn't be old. The young spruces were so green and companionable with pearl-like beads of moisture fringing their needles.

"'You are mine,' called the sea beyond Blair Water.

"'We have a share in her,' said the hills.

"'She is my sister,' said a polly fir-tree.

"Looking at them the flash came—my old supernal moment that has come so sadly seldom these past dreary months. Will I lose it altogeter as I grow old? Will nothing but 'the light of common day' be mine then?

"But at least it came to me this morning and I felt my immortality. After all, freedom is a matter of the soul.

"'Nature never did betray the heart that loved
    her'

"She has always a gift of healing for us if we come humbly to her. Corroding memories and discontents vanished. I felt suddenly that some old gladness was yet waiting for me, just around the curve of the hill.

"The frogs are singing to-night. Why is *frog* such a funny, dear, charming, absurd word?"

## XVI

"MAY 15, 19—

"I know that when I am dead I shall sleep peaceably enough under the grasses through the summer and autumn and winter but when spring comes my heart will throb and stir in my sleep and call wistfully to all the voices calling far and wide in the world above me. Spring and morning were laughing to each other to-day and I went out to them and made a third.

"Ilse wrote to-day—a stingy little letter as far as news went—and spoke of coming home.

" 'I'm homesick,' she wrote. 'Are the wild birds still singing in the Blair Water woods and are the waves still calling beyond the dunes? I want them. And oh, to see the moon rise over the harbour as we watched it do scores of times when we were children. And I want to see you. Letters are so unsatisfactory. There are so many things I'd like to talk over with you. Do you know I felt a little *old* to-day. It was a curious sensation.'

"She never mentioned Teddy's name. But she asked, 'Is it true that Perry Miller is engaged to Judge Elmsley's daughter?'

"I don't think it is. But the mere report shows where Perry has climbed to already."

# Chapter XX

## I

On her twenty-fourth birthday Emily opened and read the letter she had written "from herself at fourteen to herself at twenty-four." It was not the amusing performance she had once expected it to be. She sat long at her window with the letter in her hand, watching the light of yellow, sinking stars over the bush that was still called Lofty John's oftener than not, from old habit. What would pop out when she opened that letter? A ghost of first youth? Of ambition? Of vanished love? Of lost friendship? Emily felt she would rather burn the letter than read it. But that would be cowardly. One must face things—even ghosts. With a sudden quick movement she cut open the envelope and took out the letter.

A whiff of old fragrance came with it. Folded in it were some dried rose-leaves—crisp brown things that crumbled to dust under her touch. Yes, she remembered that rose—Teddy had brought it to her one evening when they had been children together and he had been so proud of that first red rose that bloomed on a little house rosebush Dr. Burnley had given him—the only rose that ever did bloom on it, for that matter. His mother had resented his love for the little plant. One night it was accidentally knocked off the window-sill and broken. If Teddy thought or knew there was any connection between the two facts he never said so. Emily had kept the rose as long as possible in a little vase on her study table; but the night she had written her letter she had taken the limp, faded thing and folded it—with a kiss—between the sheets of paper. She had forgotten that it was there; and now it fell in her hand, faded, unbeautiful, like the rose-hopes of long ago, yet with some faint bitter-sweetness still about it. The whole letter seemed full of it—whether of sense or spirit she could hardly tell.

This letter was, she sternly told herself, a foolish, romantic affair. Something to be laughed at. Emily carefully laughed at some parts of it. How crude—how silly—how sentimental—how amusing! Had she really ever been young and callow enough to write such flowery, exultant nonsense? And one would have thought, too, that fourteen regarded twenty-four as verging on venerable.

"Have you written your great book?" airily asked Fourteen in conclusion. "Have you climbed to the very top of the Alpine Path? Oh, Twenty-Four, I'm envying you. It must be splendid to be *you*. Are you looking back patronisingly and pityingly to *me*? You wouldn't swing on a gate now, would you? Are you a staid old married woman with several children, living in the Disappointed House with One-You-Know-Of? Only *don't* be stodgy, I implore you, dear Twenty-Four. And do be dramatic. I love dramatic things and people. Are You Mrs. —— ——? What name will fill those blanks? Oh, dear Twenty-four, I put into this letter for you a kiss—and a handful of moonshine—and the soul of a rose—and some of the green sweetness of the old hill field—and a whiff of wild violets. I hope you are happy and famous and lovely; and I hope you haven't quite forgoten.

"Your foolish
"OLD SELF."

Emily locked the letter away.

"So much for that nonsense," she said scoffingly.

Then she sat down in her chair, and dropped her head on her desk. Little silly, dreamy, happy, ignorant

Fourteen! Always thinking that something great and wonderful and beautiful lay in the years ahead. Quite sure that the "mountain purple" could be reached Quite sure that dreams always came true. Foolish Fourteen, who yet had known how to be happy.

"I'm envying *you*," said Emily. "I wish I had never opened your letter, foolish little Fourteen. Go back to your shadowy past and don't come again—mocking me. I'm going to have a white night because of you. I'm going to lie awake all night and pity myself."

Yet already the footsteps of destiny were sounding on the stairs—though Emily thought they were only Cousin Jimmy's.

## II

He had come to bring her a letter—a thin letter—and if Emily had not been too much absorbed in herself at fourteen she might have noticed that Cousin Jimmy's eyes were as bright as a cat's and that an air of ill-concealed excitement pervaded his whole being. Moreover that, when she had thanked him absently for the letter and gone back to her desk, he remained in the shadowy hall outside, watching her slyly through the half-open door. At first he thought she was not going to open the letter—she had flung it down indifferently and sat staring at it. Cousin Jimmy went nearly mad with impatience.

But after a few minutes more of absent musing Emily roused herself with a sigh and stretched out a hand for the letter.

"If I don't miss my guess, dear little Emily, you won't sigh when you read what's in that letter," thought Cousin Jimmy exultantly.

Emily looked at the return address in the upper corner, wondering what the Wareham Publishing Company were writing to her about. The big Warehams! The oldest and most important publishing house in America. A circular of some kind, probably. Then she found herself staring incredulously at the typewritten sheet—while Cousin Jimmy performed a noiseless dance on Aunt Elizabeth's braided rug out in the hall.

"I—don't—understand," gasped Emily.

Dear Miss Starr:—

We take pleasure in advising you that our readers report favourably with regard to your story *The Moral of the Rose* and if mutually satisfactory arrangements can be made we shall be glad to add the book to our next season's lists. We shall also be interested in hearing of your plans with regard to future writing.

Very sincerely yours, etc.

"I don't—understand—" said Emily again.

Cousin Jimmy could hold himself in no longer. He made a sound between a whoop and hurrah. Emily flew across the room and dragged him in.

"Cousin Jimmy, *what* does this mean? You must know something about it—how did the House of Wareham ever get my book?"

"Have they really accepted it?" demanded Cousin Jimmy.

"Yes. And *I* never sent it to them. I wouldn't have supposed it was the least use—the *Warehams. Am* I dreaming?"

"No. I'll tell you—don't be mad now, Emily. You mind Elizabeth asked me to tidy up the garret a month ago. I was moving that old cardboard box you keep a lot of stuff in and the bottom fell out. Everthing went—so—all over the garret. I gathered 'em up—and your book manuscript was among 'em. I happened to look at a page—and then I set down—and Elizabeth came up an hour later and found me still a-sitting there on my hams reading. I'd forgot everything. My, but she was mad! The garret not half done and dinner ready. But I didn't mind what she said—I was thinking, 'If that book made me forget everything like that there's *something* in it. I'll send it somewhere.' And I didn't know anywhere to send it but to the Warehams. I'd always heard of them. And I didn't know *how* to send it—but I just stuffed it in an old cracker box and mailed it to them off-hand."

"Didn't you even send stamps for its return?" gasped Emily, horrified.

"No, never thought of it. Maybe that's why they took it. Maybe the other firms sent it back because you sent stamps."

"Hardly." Emily laughed and found herself crying.

"Emily, you ain't mad at me, are you?"

"No—no—darling—I'm only so flabbergasted, as you say yourself, that I don't know what to say or do. It's all so—the *Warehams!*"

"I've been watching the mails ever since," chuckled Cousin Jimmy. "Elizabeth has been thinking I've gone clear daft at last. If the story had come back I was going to smuggle it back to the garret—I wasn't going to let you know. But when I saw that thin envelope—I remembered you said once the thin envelopes always had good news—dear little Emily, don't cry!"

"I can't—help it—and oh, I'm sorry for what I called you, little Fourteen. You weren't silly—you were wise—you knew."

"It's gone to her head a little," said Cousin Jimmy to himself. "No wonder—after so many setbacks. But she'll soon be quite sensible again."

# Chapter XXI

## I

Teddy and Ilse were coming home for a brief ten days in July. How was it, wondered Emily, that they always came together? That couldn't be just coincidence. She dreaded the visit and wished it were over. It would be good to see Ilse again—somehow she could never feel a stranger with Ilse. No matter how long she was away, the moment she came back you found the old Ilse. But she did not want to see Teddy. Teddy who had forgotten her. Who had never written since he went away last. Teddy who was already famous, as a painter of lovely women. So famous and so successful that—Ilse wrote—he was going to give up magazine work. Emily felt a certain relief when she read that. She would no longer dread to open a magzine lest she see her own face—or soul—looking at her out of some illustration—with "Frederick Kent" scrawled in the corner, as if to say "know all men by these presents that this girl is mine." Emily resented less the pictures which looked like her whole face than the ones in which only the eyes were hers. To be able to paint her eyes like that Teddy *must* know everything that was in her soul. The thought always filled her with fury and shame—and a sense of horrible helplessness. She would not—could not—tell Teddy to stop using her as a model. She had never stooped to acknowledge to him that she had noticed any resemblance to herself in his illustrations—she *never* would stoop.

And now he was coming home—might be home any

165

time. If only she could go away—on any pretence—for a few weeks. Miss Royal was wanting her to go to New York for a visit. But it would never do to go away when Ilse was coming.

Well—Emily shook herself. What an idiot she was! Teddy was coming home, a dutiful son, to see his mother—and he would doubtless be glad enough to see old friends when their actual presence recalled them to his memory; and why should there be anything difficult about it? She must get rid of this absurd self-consciousness. She would.

She was sitting at her open window. The night outside was like a dark, heavy, perfumed flower. An expectant night—a night when things intended to happen. Very still. Only the loveliest of muted sounds—the faintest whisper of trees, the airiest sigh of wind, the half-heard, half-felt moan of the sea.

"Oh, beauty!" whispered Emily, passionately, lifting her hands to the stars. "What would I have done without you all these years?"

Beauty of night—and perfume—and mystery. Her soul was filled with it. There was, just then, room for nothing else. She bent out, lifting her face to the jewelled sky—rapt, ecstatic.

Then she heard it. A soft, silvery signal in Lofty John's bush—two higher notes and one long, low one—the old, old call that would once have sent her with flying feet to the shadows of the firs.

Emily sat as if turned to stone, her white face framed in the vines that clustered round her window. He was there—Teddy was there—in Lofty John's bush—waiting for her—calling to her as of old. Expecting her!

Almost she had sprung to her feet—almost she had run downstairs where he was waiting for her. But—

Was he only trying to see if he still had the old power over her?

He had gone away two years ago without even a written word of farewell. Would the Murray pride condone that? Would the Murray pride run to meet the man who had held her of so little account? The Murray pride would not. Emily's young face took on lines of stubborn determination in the dim light. She would not go. Let him call as he might. "Whistle and I'll come to you, my lad," indeed! No more of that for Emily Byrd Starr. Teddy Kent need not imagine that he could come and go as went the years and find her meekly waiting to answer his lordly signal.

Again the call came—twice. He was there—so close to her. In a moment if she liked, she could be beside him—her hands in his—his eyes looking into hers—perhaps—

He had gone away without saying good-bye to her!

Emily rose deliberately and lighted her lamp. She sat down at her desk near the window, took up her pen and fell to writing—or a semblance of writing. Steadily she wrote—next day she found sheets covered with aimless repetitions of old poems learned in schooldays—and as she wrote she listened. Would the call come again? Once more? It did not. When she was quite sure it was not coming again she put out her light and lay down on her bed with her face in the pillow. Pride was quite satisfied. She had shown him she was not to be whistled off and on. Oh, how thankful she felt that she had been firm enough not to go. For which reason, no doubt, her pillow was wet with savage tears.

## II

He came next night—with Ilse—in his new car. And there was handshaking and giety and laughter—oh, a great deal of laughter. Ilse was looking radiant in a big yellow hat trimmed with crimson roses. One of those preposterous hats only Ilse could get away with. How unlike the neglected, almost ragged Ilse of olden days. Yet just as lovable as ever. Nobody could help loving Ilse. Teddy was charming, too—with just the right amount of mingled interest and detachment an old resident coming back to childhood's home would naturally feel. Interested in everything and everybody. Oh, yes, indeed, hugely! Ilse tells me you're bringing out a book. Capital. What's it about? Must get a copy. Blair Water quite unchanged. Delightful to come back to a place where time seems to stand still.

Emily almost thought she must have dreamed the whistle in Lofty John's bush.

But she went for a drive to Priest Pond with him and Ilse—and made quite a sensation, for cars were still great novelties thereabouts. And they had a merry, delightful time—then and for the few remaining days of their visit. Ilse had meant to stay three weeks but found she could stay only five days. And Teddy, who seemed to be master of his own time, decided to stay no longer, too. And they both came over to say good-bye to Emily and all went for a farewell moonlit spin—and laughed a great deal—and Ilse, with a hug, declared it was just like old times and Teddy agreed.

"If only Perry had been round," he amended. "I'm sorry not to have seen old Perry. They tell me he is getting on like a house afire."

Perry had gone to the Coast on business for his firm. Emily bragged a little about him and his success. Teddy Kent need not suppose he was the only one who was arriving.

"Are his manners any better than they used to be?" asked Ilse.

"His manners are good enough for us simple Prince Edward Islanders," said Emily, nastily.

"Oh, well, I admit I never saw him pick his teeth in public," conceded Ilse. "Do you know"—with a sly, sidelong glance at Teddy which Emily instantly noticed—"once I fancied myself quite in love with Perry Miller."

"Lucky Perry!" said Teddy with what seemed a quiet smile of satisfied understanding.

Ilse did not kiss Emily good-bye, but she shook hands very cordially as did Teddy. Emily was thanking her stars, in genuine earnest this time, that she had not gone to Teddy when he whistled—if he ever had whistled. They drove gaily off down the lane. But when a few moments later Emily turned to go into New Moon there were flying footsteps behind her and she was enveloped in a silken embrace.

"Emily darling, good-bye. I love you as much as ever—but everything is so horribly changed—and we can never find the Islands of Enchantment again. I wish I hadn't come home at all—but say you love me and always will. I couldn't bear it if you didn't."

"Of course I'll always love you, Ilse."

They kissed lingeringly—almost sadly—among the faint, cold, sweet perfumes of night. Ilse went down the lane to where Teddy was purring and scintillating for her—or his car was—and Emily went into New Moon where her two old aunts and Cousin Jimmy were waiting for her.

"I wonder if Ilse and Teddy will ever be married," said Aunt Laura.

"It's time Ilse was settling down," said Aunt Elizabeth.

"Poor Ilse," said Cousin Jimmy inexplicably.

### III

One late, lovely autumn day in November Emily walked home from the Blair Water post-office with a letter from Ilse and a parcel. She was athrill with an intoxication of excitement that easily passed for happiness. The whole day had been a strangely unreasonably delightful one of ripe sunshine on the sere hills, faint, grape-like bloom on the far-away woods and a soft, blue sky with little wisps of grey cloud like cast-off veils. Emily had wakened in the morning from a dream of Teddy—the dear, friendly Teddy of the old days— and all day she had been haunted by an odd sense of his nearness. It seemed as if his footstep sounded at her side and as if she might come upon him suddenly when she rounded a spruce-fringed curve in the red road or went down into some sunny hollow where the ferns were thick and golden—find him smiling at her with no shadow of change between them, the years of exile and alienation forgotten. She had not really thought much about him for a long while. The summer and autumn had been busy—she was hard at work on a new story—Ilse's letters had been few and scrappy. Why this sudden, irrational sense of his nearness? When she got Ilse's fat letter she was quite sure there was some news of Teddy in it.

But it was the little parcel that was responsible for her excitement. It was stamped with the sign manual of the House of Wareham and Emily knew what it must hold. Her book—her *Moral of the Rose*.

She hurried home by the cross-lots road—the little old road over which the vagabond wandered and the lover went to his lady and children to joy and tired men home—the road that linked up eventually with the pasture field by the Blair Water and the Yesterday Road. Once in the grey-boughed solitude of the Yesterday Road Emily sat down in a bay of brown bracken and opened her parcel.

There lay her book. *Her* book, spleet-new from the publishers. It was a proud, wonderful, thrilling moment. The crest of the Alpine Path at last? Emily lifted her shining eyes to the deep blue November sky and saw peak after peak of sunlit azure still towering beyond. Always new heights of aspiration. One could never reach the top really. But what a moment when one reached a plateau and outlook like this! What a reward for the long years of toil and endeavour and disappointment and discouragement.

But oh, for her unborn *Seller of Dreams*!

## IV

The excitement at New Moon that afternoon almost equalled Emily's own. Cousin Jimmy gave up unblushingly his plan of finishing the ploughing of the hill field to sit at home and gloat over the book. Aunt Laura cried—of course—and Aunt Elizabeth looked indifferent, merely remarking in a tone of surprise that it was bound like a real book. Evidently Aunt Elizabeth had been expecting paper covers. But she made some rather foolish mistakes in her quilt patches that afternoon and she did not once ask Jimmy why he wasn't ploughing. And when some callers dropped in later on *The Moral of the Rose* was mysteriously on the parlour table, though it had been up on Emily's desk when Aunt Elizabeth saw the automobile drive into the yard. Aunt Elizabeth never mentioned it and neither of the callers noticed it. When they went away Aunt Elizabeth said witheringly that John Angus had less sense than ever he had and that for her part, if *she* were Cousin Margaret, she would *not* wear clothes twenty years too young for her.

"An old ewe tricked out like a lamb," said Aunt Elizabeth contemptuously.

If they had done what was expected of them in regard to *The Moral of the Rose* Aunt Elizabeth would probably have said that John Angus had always been a jovial, good-natured sort of creature and that it was really wonderful how Cousin Margaret had held her own.

### V

In all the excitement Emily had—not exactly forgotten Ilse's letter, but wanted to wait until things had settled down a little before reading it. At twilight she went to her room and sat down in the fading light. The wind had changed at sunset and the evening was cold and edged. What Jimmy called a "skiff" of snow had fallen suddenly whitening the world and the withered, unlovely garden. But the storm-cloud had passed and the sky was clear and yellow over the white hills and dark firs. The odd perfume that Ilse always affected floated out of her letter when it was opened. Emily had always vaguely disliked it. But then her taste differed from Ilse's in the matter of perfumes as in so many others. Ilse liked the exotic, oriental, provocative odours.

To the day of her death Emily will never catch a whiff of that perfume without turning cold and sick.

"Exactly one thousand times have I planned to write to you," wrote Ilse, "but when one is revolving rapidly on the wheel of things there doesn't seem to be an opportunity for anything one really wants to do. All these months I've been so rushed that I've felt precisely like a cat just one jump ahead of a dog. If I stopped for a breath it would catch me.

"But the spirit moves me to utter a few yowls to-night. I've something to tell you. And your darling letter came to-day—so I will write to-night, and let the dog eat me if he will.

"I'm glad you're keeping well and good-humoured. There are times I envy you fiercely, Emily—your New Moon quiet and peace and leisure—your intense absorption and satisfaction in your work—your singleness of purpose. 'If thine eye be single thy whole body shall be full of light.' That's either in the Bible or Shakespeare, but wherever it is, it is true. I remember you told me once you envied me my opportunities of travel. Emily, old dear, rushing about from one place to another isn't travelling. If you were like your foolish Ilse, chasing a score of butterfly projects and ambitions you wouldn't be so happy. You always remind me—always did remind me, even in our old chummy days—of somebody's line—'her soul was like a star and dwelt apart.'

"Well, when one can't get the thing one really wants, one can't help chasing after anything that *might* make a decent substitute. I know you've always thought me an unmitigated donkey because I cared so much about Perry Miller. I knew you never quite understood. You couldn't. You never really cared a hoot about any he-creature, did you, Emily? So you thought me an idiot. I daresay I was. But I'm going to be sensible in future. I'm going to marry Teddy Kent.

"There—it's out!"

# VI

Emily laid down—or dropped—the letter for a moment. She did not feel either pain or surprise—one does not feel either, I am told, when a bullet strikes the heart. It seemed to her that she had always known this was coming—always. At least, since the night of Mrs. Chidlaw's dinner-dance. And yet, now that it had really happened, it seemed to her that she was suffering everything of death but its merciful dying. In the dim, twilit mirror before her she saw her own face. Had Emily-in-the-glass ever looked like that before? But her room was just the same. After a few moments— or years—Emily picked up the letter and read on.

"I'm not in love with Teddy, of course. But he's just got to be a habit with me. I can't do without him—and I either have to do without him or marry him. He won't stand my hesitation any longer. Besides, he's going to be very famous. I shall enjoy being the wife of a famous man. Also, he will have the simoleons, too. Not that I'm altogether mercenary, Emily. I said 'No' to a millionaire last week. A nice fellow, too—but with a face like a good-natured weasel's, if there can be such a thing. And he *cried* when I told him I wouldn't marry him. Oh, it was ghastly.

"Yes, it's mostly ambition, I grant you. And a certain odd kind of weariness and impatience with my life as it has been these last few years. Everything seems squeezed dry. But I'm really fond of Teddy—always was. He's nice and companionable and our taste in jokes is exactly the same. And he never bores me. I have no use for people who bore me. Of course he's too good-looking for a man—he'll aways be a target for the headhunters. But since I don't care *too* much for him I shan't be tortured by jealousy. In life's morning march when my bosom was young I could have fried in boiling oil anyone—except you—at whom Perry Miller cast a sheep's eye.

"I've thought for years and known for weeks that this was coming some day. But I've been staving Teddy off—I wouldn't let him say the words that would really bind us. I don't know whether I'd ever have scraped up the courage to let him say them, but destiny took a hand. We were out for a spin two weeks ago one evening and a most unseasonable and malignant thunderstorm came up. We had a dreadful time getting back—there was no place on that bare, lonely hill-road we could stop—the rain fell in torrents, the thunder crashed, the lightning flashed. It was unendurable and we didn't endure it. We just tore through it and cussed. Then it cleared off as suddenly as it had begun—and my nerves went to pieces—fancy! I *have* nerves now—and I began to cry like a frightened, foolish baby. And Teddy's arms were about me and he was saying I *must* marry him—and let him take care of me. I suppose I said I would because it's quite clear he thinks we are engaged. He has given me a blue Chow pup and a sapphire ring—a sapphire he picked up in Europe somewhere—an historic jewel for which a murder was once committed, I believe.

"I think it will be rather nice to be taken care of. Properly. I never was, you know. Dad had no use for me until you found out the truth about Mother—what a witch you were! And after that he adored and spoiled me. But he didn't take any more real care of me than before.

"We are to be married next June. Dad will be pleased, I fancy. Teddy was always the white-haired boy with him. Besides, I think he was beginning to be a little scared I was never going to hook a husband. Dad plumes himself on being a radical but at heart he out-Victorians the Victorians.

"And of course you must be my bridesmaid. Oh, Emily dear, how I wish I could see you to-night—talk with you—one of our old-time spiels—walk with you over the Delectable Mountain and along the ferny, frosted woodside, hang about that old garden by the sea where red poppies blow—all our old familiar places. I wish—I think I really do wish—I was ragged bare-

footed, wild Ilse Burnley again. Life is pleasant still—
oh, I don't say it isn't. Very pleasant—in spots—like the
curate's immortal egg. But the 'first fine careless rapture'
—the thrush may recapture it but we never. Emily, old
pal, would you turn the clock back if you could?"

## VII

Emily read the letter over three times. Then she sat
for a very long time at her window, looking blindly out
on the blanched, dim world lying under the terrible
mockery of a sky full of stars. The wind around the
eaves was full of ghostly voices. Bits here and there in
Ilse's letter turned and twisted and vanished in her
consciousness like little venomous snakes, each with a
mortal sting.

"Your singleness of purpose"—"you never cared for
any one"—"of course you must be my bridesmaid"
—"I'm really very fond of Teddy"—"my hesitation."

*Could* any girl really "hesitate" over accepting Teddy
Kent? Emily heard a little note of bitter laughter. Was it
something in herself that laughed—or that vanishing
spectre of Teddy that had haunted her all day—or an
old smothered persistent hope that laughed before it
died at last?

And at that very moment probably Ilse and Teddy
were together.

"If I had gone—that night—last summer—when he
called—would it have made any difference?" was the
question that asked itself over and over again madden-
ingly.

"I wish I could hate Ilse. It would make it easier,"
she thought drearily. "If she loved Teddy I think I *could*
hate her. Somehow it isn't so dreadful when she doesn't.
It ought to be *more* dreadful. It's very strange that I can
bear the thought of his loving her when I couldn't bear
the thought of her loving him."

A great weariness suddenly possessed her. For the
first time in her life death seemed a friend. It was very

late when she finally went to bed. Towards morning she slept a little. But awakened stupidly at dawn. What was it she had heard?

She remembered.

She got up and dressed—as she must get up and dress every morning to come for endless years.

"Well," she said aloud to Emily-in-the-glass. "I've spilled my cup of life's wine on the ground—somehow. And she will give me no more. So I must go thirsty. Would—*would* it have been different if I had gone to him that night he called. If I only knew!" She thought she could see Dean's ironical, compassionate eyes.

Suddenly she laughed.

"In plain English—as Ilse would say—what a devilish mess I've made of things!"

# Chapter XXII

## I

Life, of course, went on in spite of its dreadfulness. The routine of existence doesn't stop because one is miserable. There were even some moments that were not altogether bad. Emily again measured her strength with pain and again conquered. With the Murray pride and the Starr reserve at her elbow she wrote Ilse a letter of good wishes with which nobody could have found fault. If that were only all she had to do! If only people wouldn't keep on talking to her about Ilse and Teddy.

The engagement was announced in the Montreal papers and then in the Island ones.

"Yes, they're engaged and heaven help every one concerned," said Dr. Burnley. But he could not hide his satisfaction in it.

"Thought at one time *you* and Teddy were going to make a match of it," he said jovially to Emily—who smiled gallantly and said something about the unexpected always happening.

"Anyhow we'll have a wedding that *is* a wedding," declared the doctor. "We haven't had a wedding in the clan for God knows how long. I thought they'd forgotten how. I'll show 'em. Ilse writes me you're to be bridesmaid. And I'll be wanting you to oversee things generally. Can't trust a wedding to a housekeeper."

"Anything I can do, of course," said Emily automatically. Nobody should suspect what she felt—not if she died for it. She would even be bridesmaid.

177

If it had not been for that prospect ahead she thought she could have got through the winter not unhappily. For *The Moral of the Rose* was a success from the start. The first edition exhausted in ten days—three large editions in two weeks—five in eight weeks. Exaggerated reports of the pecuniary returns were circulated everywhere. For the first time Uncle Wallace looked at her with respect and Aunt Addie wished secretly that Andrew hadn't been consoled quite so soon. Old Cousin Charlotte, of Derry Pond, heard of the many editions and opined that Emily must be very busy if she had to put all the books together and sew them herself. The Shrewsbury people were furious because they imagined they were in the book. Every family believed *it* was the Applegaths.

"You were right not to come to New York," wrote Miss Royal. "You could never have written *The Moral of the Rose* here. Wild roses won't grow in city streets. And your story is like a wild rose, dear, all sweetness and unexpectedness with sly little thorns of wit and satire. It has power, delicacy, understanding. It's not just story-telling. There's some magicry in it. Emily Byrd Starr, where do you get your uncanny understanding of human nature—you infant?"

Dean wrote too—"good creative work, Emily. Your characters are natural and human and delightful. And I like the glowing spirit of youth that pervades the book."

## II

"I had hoped to learn something from the reviews, but they are all too contradictory," said Emily. "What one reviewer pronounces the book's greatest merit another condemns as its worst fault. Listen to these— 'Miss Starr never succeeds in making her characters convincing' and 'One fancies that some of the author's characters must have been copied from real life. They are so absolutely true to nature that they could hardly be the work of imagination.' "

"I told you people would recognise old Douglas Courcy," interjected Aunt Elizabeth.

" 'A very tiresome book'—'a very delightful book' —'very undistinguished fiction' and 'on every page the work of the finished artist is apparent'—'a book of cheap and weak romanticism' and 'a classic quality in the book'—'a unique story of a rare order of literary workmanship' and 'a silly, worthless, colourless and desultory story'—'an ephemeral sort of affair' and 'a book destined to live.' What *is* one to believe?"

"I would just believe only the favourable ones," said Aunt Laura.

Emily sighed.

"My tendency is just the other way. I can't help believing the unfavourable ones are true and that the favourable ones were written by morons. But I don't really mind much what they say about the *book*. It's only when they criticise my heroine that I'm hurt and furious. I saw red over these reviews of darling *Peggy*. 'A girl of extraordinary stupidity'—'the heroine has too marked a self-consciousness of her mission.' "

"I *did* think she was a bit of a flirt," conceded Cousin Jimmy.

" 'A thin, sweetish heroine'—'the heroine is something of a bore'—'queer but altogether too queer.' "

"I told you she shouldn't have had green eyes," groaned Cousin Jimmy. "A heroine should always have blue eyes."

"Oh, but listen to this," cried Emily gaily—" '*Peg Applegath* is simply irresistible'—'Peg is a remarkably vivid personality'—'a fascinating heroine'—'*Peg* is too delightful not to be credited while we are under her spell'—'one of the immortal girls of literature.' What about green eyes now, Cousin Jimmy?"

Cousin Jimmy shook his head. He was not convinced.

"Here's a review for you," twinkled Emily. " 'A psychological problem with roots that stretch far into subliminal depths which would give the book weight and value if it were grappled with sincerely.' "

"I know the meaning of all those words by themselves except two, but put together they don't make any sense," protested Cousin Jimmy ruefully.

" 'Beneath the elusiveness and atmospheric charm is a wonderful firmness of character delineation.' "

"I don't quite get that either," confessed Cousin Jimmy, "but it sounds kind of favourable."

" 'A conventional and commonplace book.' "

"What does 'conventional' mean?" asked Aunt Elizabeth, who would not have been posed by transubstantiation or Gnosticism.

" 'Beautifully written and full of sparkling humour. Miss Starr is a real artist in literature.' "

"Oh, now, *there's* a reviewer with some sense," purred Cousin Jimmy.

" 'The general impression left by the book is that it might be much worse.' "

"*That* reviewer was trying to be smart, I suppose," said Aunt Elizabeth, apparently quite oblivious of the fact that she had said the very same thing herself.

" 'This book lacks spontaneity. It is saccharine and melodramatic, mawkish and naïve.' "

"I know I fell into the well," said Cousin Jimmy pitifully. "Is that why I can't make head or tail out of that?"

"Here's one you can understand—perhaps. 'Miss Starr must have invented the *Applegath* orchard as well as her green-eyed heroine. There are no orchards in Prince Edward Island. They are killed by the harsh, salt winds that blow across that narrow sandy strip.' "

"Read that again please, Emily."

Emily complied. Cousin Jimmy scratched his head, then shook it. "Do they let that kind run loose over there?"

" 'The story is a charming one, charmingly told. The characters are skilfully depicted, the dialogue deftly handled, the descriptive passages surprisingly effective. The quiet humour is simply delightful.' "

"I hope this will not make you vain, Emily," said Aunt Elizabeth warningly.

"If it does, here's the antidote. " 'This feeble, pretentious and sentimental story—if story it can be called—is full of banalities and trivialities. A mass of disconnected episodes and scraps of conversation, intermingled with long periods of reflection and self-examination.' "

"I wonder if the creature who wrote that knew the meaning of the words himself," said Aunt Laura.

" 'The scene of this story is laid in Prince Edward Island, a detached portion of land off the coast of Newfoundland.' "

"Don't Yankees *ever* study geography?" snorted exasperated Cousin Jimmy.

" 'A story that will not corrupt its readers.' "

"*There's* a real compliment now," said Aunt Elizabeth.

Cousin Jimmy looked doubtful. It sounded all right but—of course dear little Emily's book couldn't corrupt any one but—

" 'To review a book of this kind is like attempting to dissect a butterfly's wing or strip a rose of its petals to discover the secret of its fragrance.' "

"Too highfalutin," sniffed Aunt Elizabeth.

" 'Honeyed sentimentality which the author evidently supposes is poetic fancy.' "

"Wouldn't I like to smack his gob," said Cousin Jimmy feelingly.

" 'Harmless and easy reading.' "

"I don't know why, but I don't quite like the sound of that," commented Aunt Laura.

" 'This story will keep a kindly smile upon your lips and in your heart as well.' "

"Come now, that's English. I can understand *that*," beamed Cousin Jimmy.

" 'We began but found it impossible to finish this crude and tiresome book.' "

"Well, all *I* can say," said Cousin Jimmy indignantly,

"is that the oftener I read *The Moral of the Rose* the better I like it. Why, I was reading it for the fourth time yesterday and I was so interested I clean forgot all about dinner."

Emily smiled. It was better to have won her standing with the New Moon folks than with the world. What mattered it what any reviewer said when Aunt Elizabeth remarked with an air of uttering the final judgment:

"Well, I never could have believed that a pack of lies could sound as much like the real truth as that book does."

# Chapter XXIII

## I

Emily, coming home one January night from an evening call, decided to use the cross-lots road that skirted the Tansy Patch. It had been a winter almost without snow and the ground under her feet was bare and hard. She seemed the only living creature abroad in the night and she walked slowly, savouring the fine, grim, eerie charm of flowerless meadows and silent woods, of the moon breaking suddenly out of black clouds over the lowlands of pointed firs; and trying, more or less successfully, not to think of the letter that had come from Ilse that day—one of Ilse's gay, incoherent letters, where one fact stood out barely. The wedding day was set—the fifteenth of June.

"I want you to wear harebell blue gauze over ivory taffeta for your bridesmaid dress, darling. How your black silk hair will shine over it!

"My bridal robe is going to be of ivory velvet and old Great-aunt Edith in Scotland is sending me out her veil of rose-point and Great-aunt Theresa in the same historic land is sending me a train of silver oriental embroidery that her husband once brought home from Constantinople. I'll veil it with tulle. Won't I be a dazzling creature? I don't think the dear old souls knew I existed till Dad wrote them about my 'forthcoming nuptials.' Dad is far more excited over everything than I am.

"Teddy and I are going to spend our honeymoon in old inns in out-of-the-way European corners—places

183

where nobody else wants to go—Vallambroso and so on. That line of Milton's always intrigued me—'thick as autumnal leaves that strew the brooks in Vallambroso.' When you take it away from its horrible context it is a picture of sheer delight.

"I'll be home in May for my last preparations and Teddy will come the first of June to spend a little while with his mother. How *is* she taking it, Emily? Have you any idea? I can't get anything out of Teddy, so I suppose she doesn't like it. She always hated me, I know. But then she seemed to hate every one—with a special venom for you. I won't be particularly fortunate in my mother-in-law. I'll always have an eerie feeling that she's secretly heaping maledictions on my head. However, Teddy is nice enough to make up for her. He really is. I'd no idea how nice he could be and I'm growing fonder of him every day. Honestly. When I look at him and realise how handsome and charming he is I can't understand why I'm not madly in love with him. But it's really much more comfortable not to be. If I were I'd be heartbroken every time we quarrelled. We're always quarrelling—you know me of old. We always will. We'll spoil every wonderful moment with a quarrel. But life won't be dull."

Emily shivered. Her own life was looking very bleak and starved just then. Oh, how—nice—it would be when the wedding was over—the wedding where *she* should be bride—yes, *should*—and was to be bridesmaid—and people done talking of it. "Harebell blue over ivory taffeta!" Sackcloth and ashes, rather.

## II

"Emily. Emily Starr."

Emily almost jumped. She had not seen Mrs. Kent in the gloom until they were face to face—at the little side path that led up to the Tansy Patch. She was standing there, bareheaded in the chill night, with outstretched hand.

"Emily, I want to have a talk with you. I saw you go past here at sunset and I've been watching for you ever since. Come up to the house."

Emily would much rather have refused. Yet she turned and silently climbed the steep, root-ribbed path, with Mrs. Kent flitting before her like a little dead leaf borne along by the wind. Through the ragged old garden where nothing ever grew but tansy, and into the little house that was as shabby as it had always been. People said Teddy Kent might fix up his mother's house a bit if he were making all the money folks said he was. But Emily knew that Mrs. Kent would not let him—would not have anything changed.

She looked around the little place curiously. She had not been in it for many years—not since the long-ago days when she and Ilse and Teddy had been children there. It seemed quite unchanged. As of yore, the house seemed to be afraid of laughter. Some one always seemed to be praying in it. It had an atmosphere of prayer. And the old willow to the west was still tap-tapping on the window with ghostly finger-tips. On the mantel was a recent photograph of Teddy—a good one. He seemed on the point of speaking—of saying something triumphant—exultant.

"Emily, I've found the rainbow gold. Fame—and love."

She turned her back on it and sat down. Mrs. Kent sat opposite—a faded, shrinking little figure with the long scar slanting palely across her bitter mouth and lined face—the face that must have been very pretty once. She was looking intently, searchingly at Emily; but, as Emily instantly realised, the old smouldering hatred had gone out of her eyes—her tired eyes that must once have been young and eager and laughter-lit. She leaned forward and touched Emily's arm with her slim, claw-like fingers.

"You know that Teddy is going to marry Ilse Burnley," she said.

"Yes."

"What do you feel about it?"

Emily moved impatiently.

"What do my feelings matter, Mrs. Kent? Teddy loves Ilse. She is a beautiful, brilliant, warm-hearted girl. I am sure they will be very happy."

"Do *you* still love him?"

Emily wondered why she did not feel resentment. But Mrs. Kent was not to be judged by ordinary rules. And here was a fine chance to save her face by a cool little lie—just a few indifferent words. "Not any longer, Mrs. Kent. Oh, I know I once imagined I did—imagining things like that is one of my weaknesses unfortunately. But I find I don't care at all."

Why couldn't she say them? Well, she couldn't that was all. She could never, in any words, deny her love for Teddy. It was so much a part of herself that it had a divine right to truth. And was there not, too, a secret relief in feeling that here at least was one person with whom she could be herself—before whom she need not pretend or hide?

"I don't think you have any right to ask that question, Mrs. Kent. But—I do."

Mrs. Kent laughed silently.

"I used to hate you. I don't hate you any longer. We are one now, you and I. We love him. And he has forgotten us—he cares nothing for us—he has gone to *her*."

"He does care for you, Mrs. Kent. He always did. Surely you can understand that there is more than one kind of love. And I hope—you are not going to hate Ilse because Teddy loves her."

"No, I don't hate her. She is more beautiful than you, but there is no mystery about her. She will never possess him wholly as you would have. It's quite different. But I want to know this—are you unhappy because of this?"

"No. Only for a few minutes now and then. Generally I am too much interested in my work to brood morbidly on what can't be mine."

Mrs. Kent had listened thirstily. "Yes—yes—exactly. I thought so. The Murrays are so sensible. Some day— some day—you'll be glad this has happened—glad that Teddy didn't care for you. Don't you think you will?"

"Perhaps."

"Oh, I am sure of it. It's so much better for you. Oh, you don't know the suffering and wretchedness you will be spared. It's madness to love anything too much. God *is* jealous. If you married Teddy he would break your heart—they always do. It is best—you will live to feel it was best."

Tap—tap—tap went he old willow.

"Need we talk of this any more, Mrs. Kent?"

"Do you remember that night I found you and Teddy in the graveyard?" asked Mrs. Kent, apparently deaf to Emily's question.

"Yes." Emily found herself remembering it very vividly—that strange wonderful night when Teddy had saved her from mad Mr. Morrison and said such sweet, unforgettable things to her.

"Oh, how I hated you that night!" exclaimed Mrs. Kent. "But I shouldn't have said those things to you. All my life I've been saying things I shouldn't. Once I said a terrible thing—such a terrible thing. I've never been able to get the echo of it out of my ears. And do you remember what *you* said to *me*? That was why I let Teddy go away from me. It was *your* doing. If he hadn't gone you mightn't have lost him. Are you sorry you spoke so?"

"No. If anything I said helped to clear the way for him I'm glad—glad."

"You would do it over again?"

"I would."

"And don't you hate Ilse bitterly? She has taken what you wanted. You *must* hate her."

"I do not. I love Ilse dearly as I always did. She has taken nothing from me that was ever mine."

"I don't understand it—I don't understand it," half whispered Mrs. Kent. "*My* love isn't like that. Perhaps that is why it has always made me so unhappy. No, I don't hate you any longer. But oh, I did hate you. I knew Teddy cared more for you than he did for me. Didn't you and he talk about me—criticise me?"

"Never."

"I thought you did. People were always doing that—always."

Suddenly Mrs. Kent struck her tiny thin hands together violently.

"Why didn't you tell me you didn't love him any longer? Why didn't you—even if it was a lie? That was what I wanted to hear. I could have believed you. The Murrays never lie."

"Oh, what does it matter?" cried tortured Emily again.

"My love means nothing to him now. He is Ilse's. You need not be jealous of me any longer, Mrs. Kent."

"I'm not—I'm not—it isn't that." Mrs. Kent looked at her very oddly. "Oh, if I only dared—but no—but no, it's too late. It would be no use now. I don't think I know what I'm saying. Only—Emily—will you come to see me sometimes? It's lonely here—very lonely—so much worse now when he belongs to Ilse. His picture came last Wednesday—no, Thursday. There is so little to distinguish the days here. I put it up there, but it makes things worse. He was thinking of her in it—can't you tell by his eyes he was thinking of the woman he loves? I am of no importance to him now. I am of no importance to anybody."

"If I come to see you—you mustn't talk of him—or of them," said Emily, pityingly.

"I won't. Oh, I won't. Though that won't prevent us from thinking of them, will it? You'll sit there—and I'll sit here—and we'll talk of the weather and think of *him*. How amusing! But—when you've really forgotten him—when you really don't care any more—you'll tell me, won't you."

Emily nodded and rose to go. She could not endure

this any longer. "And if there is ever anything I can do for you, Mrs. Kent—"

"I want rest—rest," said Mrs. Kent, laughing wildly. "Can you find that for me? Don't you know I'm a ghost, Emily? I died years ago. I walk in the dark."

As the door closed behind her Emily heard Mrs. Kent beginning to cry terribly. With a sigh of relief she turned to the crisp open spaces of the wind and the night, the shadows and the frosty moon. Ah, one could breathe here.

# Chapter XXIV

## I

Ilse came in May—a gay laughing Ilse. Almost *too* gay and laughing, Emily thought. Ilse had always been a merry, irresponsible creature; but not quite so unceasingly as now. She never had a serious mood, apparently. She made a jest of everything, even her marriage. Aunt Elizabeth and Aunt Laura were quite shocked at her. A girl who was so soon to assume the responsibilities of wedded life should be more thoughtful and sober. Ilse told Emily they were mid-Victorian screams. She chatted ceaselessly when she and Emily were together, but never *talked* to her, despite the desire expressed in her letters for old-time spiels. Perhaps she was not quite all to blame for this. Emily, in spite of her determination to be exactly the same as of yore, could not help a certain restraint and reserve, born of her secret pain and her fierce determination to hide it. Ilse felt the restraint, though wholly unsuspicious of the cause. Emily was just naturally growing a little bit New Moonish, that was all, living there alone with those dear old antediluvians.

"When Teddy and I come back and set up house in Montreal you must spend every winter with us, darling. New Moon is a dear place in summer, but in winter you must be absolutely buried alive."

Emily made no promises. She did not see herself as a guest in Teddy's home. Every night she told herself she could not possibly endure to-morrow. But when to-morrow came it was livable. It was even possible to talk dress and details calmly with Ilse. The harebell blue dress became a reality and Emily tried it on two nights before Teddy was expected home. The wedding was only two weeks away now.

"You look like a dream in it, Emily," said Ilse, stretched out on Emily's bed with the grace and abandon of a cat—Teddy's sapphire blotting her finger darkly. "You'll make all my velvet and lace gorgeousness look obvious and crude. Did I tell you Teddy is bringing Lorne Halsey with him for best man? I'm positively thrilled— the great Halsey. His mother has been so ill he didn't think he could come. But the obliging old lady has suddenly recovered and he's actually coming. His new book is a wow. Everybody in Montreal was raving over it and he's the most interesting and improbable creature. Wouldn't it be wonderful if you and he were to fall in love with each other, Emily?"

"Don't go matchmaking for me, Ilse," said Emily with a faint smile, as she took off the harebell dress. "I feel in my bones that I shall achieve old-maidenhood, which is an entirely different thing from having old-maidenhood thrust upon you."

"To be sure, he looks like a gargoyle," said Ilse meditatively. "If it hadn't been for that I think I might have married him myself. I'm almost sure I could have. His way of making love was to ask me my opinion about things. That was agreeable. But I had a hunch that if we were married he would stop asking for my opinion. That would *not* be agreeable. Besides, nobody could ever tell what he really thought. He might be looking as though he adored you and thinking he saw crow's-feet around your eyes. By the way, isn't Teddy the most beautiful thing?"

"He was always a nice-looking boy."

"'A nice-looking boy,'" mimicked Ilse. "Emily Starr, if you ever do marry I hope your husband will chain you in the dog-kennel. I'll be calling you Aunt Emily in a minute. Why, there's nobody in Montreal who can hold a candle to him. It's his looks I love really—not him. Sometimes he bores me—really. Although I was so sure he wouldn't. He never did before we were engaged. I have a premonition that some day I'll throw the teapot at him. Isn't it a pity we can't have two husbands? One to look at and one to talk to. But Teddy and I will be by way of being a stunning couple, won't we, honey? He so dark—I so fair. Ideal. I've always wished I was 'a dark ladye'—like you—but when I said so to Teddy he just laughed and quoted the old verse,

> " 'If the bards of old the truth have told
>     The sirens had raven hair.
> But over the earth since art had birth,
>     They paint the angels fair.'

That's the nearest Teddy will ever get to calling *me* an angel. Luckily. For when all's said and done, Emily, I'd rather—are you sure the door is shut so that Aunt Laura won't drop dead?—I'd *much* rather be a siren than an angel. Wouldn't you?"

"Let's check up the invitations now and make sure we haven't left anybody out," was Emily's response to this riot of words.

"Isn't it terrible to belong to a clan like ours?" said Ilse peevishly. "There's such a ghastly lot of old frumps and bores that have to be among those present. I hope some day I'll get where there are no relations. I wish the whole damn affair was over. You're sure you addressed a bid to Perry, aren't you?"

"Yes."

"I wonder if he'll come? I hope he will. What a goose I was ever to fancy I cared so much for him! I used to hope—all sorts of things, in spite of the fact I knew he was crazy about you. But I never hoped after Mrs. Chidlaw's dinner-dance. Do you remember it, Emily?"

Yes, Emily remembered *that*.

"Till then I'd always hoped a *little*—that some day when he realised he couldn't have you—I'd catch his heart on the rebound—wasn't that the Victorian phrase?

I thought he'd be at the Chidlaws'—and I knew he had been invited. And I asked Teddy if Perry were coming. Teddy looked right into my eyes meaningly and said, 'Perry will not be here. He's working on the case he has to appear in to-morrow. Perry's goal is ambition. He has no time for love.'

"I knew he was trying to warn me—and I knew it was no use to go on hoping—anything. So I gave up definitely. Well, it's turned out all right. Isn't it charming how things do turn out so beautifully? Makes one quite believe in an overruling Providence. Isn't it nice to be able to blame everything on God?"

Emily hardly heard Ilse as she mechanically hung up the blue dress in her closet and slipped into a little green sport suit. So *that* was what Teddy had said to Ilse that night years ago when she knew he had uttered the word "love." And she had been so chilly to him because of it. Well, not likely it mattered. No doubt he had only been warning Ilse because he wanted to turn her maiden thoughts from Perry and concentrate them on himself. She felt relieved when Ilse finally went home. Ilse's light, continual chatter rather got on her nerves—though she was ashamed to admit it. But then her nerves were on edge under this long-drawn-out torture. Two weeks more of it—and then, thank God, at least peace.

## II

She went up to the Tansy Patch in the dusk to take back a book Mrs. Kent had lent her the night before. The visit must be made before Teddy came home. She had been up to the Tansy Patch several times since that first evening and an odd sort of friendship had sprung up between her and Mrs. Kent. They lent each other books and talked of everything except the one thing that mattered most to them. The book Emily was returning was on old copy of *The South African Farm*. Emily had expressed a wish to read it and Mrs. Kent

had gone upstairs and presently came down with it—
her white face a little whiter and the scar buring redly
across it as always when she was deeply moved.

"Here is the book you want," she said. "I had it in a
box upstairs."

Emily finished reading the book before she went to
sleep. She was not sleeping well now and the nights
were long. The book had a musty, unaired odour—
evidently the box Mrs. Kent spoke of had not been
opened for a long time. And in it Emily found a thin
letter, unstamped, addressed to Mrs. David Kent.

The curious thing about the letter was that it was,
apparently, unopened. Well, letters often resealed themselves like that, if placed under pressure, when the flap
had pulled open untorn in the first opening. Not likely
it was of much significance. But of course she would
mention it when she took the book back.

"Did you know there was a letter in this book, Mrs.
Kent?"

"A letter. Did you say a letter?"

"Yes. Addressed to you."

Emily held the letter out to Mrs. Kent, whose face
became ghastly as she looked at the handwriting.

"You found that—in that book?" she whispered. "In
that book that hasn't been opened for over twenty-five
years? Do you know—who wrote this letter? My—
husband wrote it—and I have never read it—never
known of it."

Emily felt herself in the presence of some tragedy—
the secret torture of Mrs. Kent's life, perhaps.

"I will go away—so that you can read it alone," she
said gently and went out, leaving Mrs. Kent standing
in the shadowy little room, holding the letter in her
hand—as one might hold a snake.

### III

"I sent for you to-night because there is something I
must tell you," said Mrs. Kent.

She was sitting, a tiny erect, determined creature in the armchair by the window in the harsh light of a cold sunset. It was June but it was cold. The sky was hard and autumnal. Emily, walking up the cross-lots path had shivered and wished herself at home. But Mrs. Kent's note had been urgent—almost peremptory. Why in the world did she want her! Surely, it could not be anything in connection with Teddy. And yet what else could make Mrs. Kent send for her in this fashion?

The moment she saw Mrs. Kent she was conscious of a curious change in her—a change hard to define. She was as frail, as pitiful as ever. There seemed even a certain defiant light in her eyes. But for the first time since she had known Mrs. Kent Emily did not feel that she was in the presence of an unhappy woman. There was peace here—a strange, sorrowful, long-unknown peace. The tortured soul was—at last—off the rack.

"I have been dead—and in hell—but now I am alive again," said Mrs. Kent. "It's you who have done this— you found the letter. And so there is something I must tell you. It will make you hate me. And I shall be sorry for that now. But it must be told."

Emily felt a sudden distaste for hearing whatever it was Mrs. Kent had to tell. It had—must have—something to do with Teddy. And she did not want to hear anything—*anything*—about Teddy now—Teddy who would be Ilse's husband in two weeks.

"Don't you think—perhaps—it would be better not to tell me?"

"It must be told. I have committed a wrong and I must confess it. I cannot undo it—I suppose it is too late to undo it—but it must be told. But there are other things that must be told first. Things I've never spoken of—things that have been torturing me until I've screamed out loud at night sometimes with the anguish of them. Oh, you will never forgive me—but I think you will be a little sorry for me."

"I've always felt sorry for you, Mrs. Kent."

"I think you did—yes, I think you did. But you

couldn't realise it all. Emily, I wasn't like this when I was a girl. I was—like other people then. And I was pretty—indeed I was. When David Kent came and made me love him I was pretty. And he loved me—*then*—and he always loved me. He says so in this letter."

She plucked it from the bosom of her dress and kissed it almost savagely.

"I can't let you see it, Emily. No eyes but mine must ever see it. But I'll tell you what is in it. Oh, you can't know—you can't understand how much I loved him, Emily. You think you love Teddy. But you don't—you *can't* love him as I loved his father."

Emily had a different opinion on this point, but she did not say so.

"He married me and took me home to Malton where his people lived. We were so happy at first—too happy. I told you God was jealous. And his people did not like me—not from the first. They thought David had married beneath him—that I wasn't good enough for him. They were always trying to come between us. Oh, I knew; I knew what they were after. His mother hated me. She never called me Aileen—only 'you' and 'David's wife.' I hated her because she was always watching me—never said anything—never did anything. Just *watched* me. I was never one of them. I never seemed able to understand their jokes. They were always laughing over something—me, half the time, I thought. They would write letters to David and never mention me. Some of them were always freezingly polite to me and some of them were always giving me digs. Once one of his sisters sent me a book on etiquette. Something was always hurting me—and I couldn't strike back—I couldn't hurt what was hurting me. David took their part—he had secrets with them he kept from me. But in spite of it all I was happy—till I dropped the lamp and my dress caught fire and scarred my face like this. After that I couldn't believe David could keep on loving me. I was so ugly. My nerves got raw and I couldn't help quarrelling with him over every trifle. But he was patient. He forgave me again and again. Only I was so afraid he couldn't love me with that scar. I knew I was going to have a baby, but I kept putting off telling him. I was afraid he would love it more than he did me. And then—I did a terrible thing. I hate to tell you of it. David had a dog—he loved it so much that I hated it. I—I poisoned it. I don't know what possessed me. I never used to be like that—not till I was burned. Perhaps it was because the baby was coming."

Mrs. Kent stopped and changed suddenly from a woman quivering with unveiled feeling to a prim Victorian.

"I shouldn't talk about such matters to a young girl," she said anxiously.

"I have known for some years that babies do not come in Dr. Burnley's black bag," assured Emily gravely.

"Well"—Mrs. Kent underwent another transformation into passionate Aileen Kent again—"David found out what I had done. Oh,—oh, his face! We had a dreadful quarrel. It was just before he went out to Winnipeg on a business trip. I—I was so furious over what he said that I screamed out—oh, Emily—that I hoped I would never see his face again. I never did. God took me at my word. He died of pneumonia in Winnipeg. I never knew he was ill till the word of his death came. And the nurse was a girl he had once thought something of and who loved him. *She* waited on him and tended him while I was at home hating him. That is what I have thought I could never forgive God for. She packed up his things and sent them home—that book among them. He must have bought it in Winnipeg. I never opened it—I never could bear to touch it. He must have written that letter when he was near death and put it in the book for me—and perhaps died before he could tell her it was there. Maybe she knew and wouldn't tell me. And it has been there all these years, Emily—all these years when I've been believing David died angry with me—unforgiving me.

I've dreamed of him night after night—always with his face turned away from me. Oh, twenty-seven years of that, Emily—twenty-seven years. Think of it. Haven't I atoned! And last night I opened and read his letter, Emily—just a few lines scribbled with a pencil—his poor hand could hardly hold it. He called me Dear Little Wife and said I must forgive him—*I forgive him*—for being so harsh and angry that last day—and he forgave me for what I had done—and said I mustn't worry over it nor over what I said about not seeing his face again—he knew I didn't mean it—that he understood things better at the last—and he had always loved me dearly and always would—and—something more I can't tell anybody—too dear, too wonderful. Oh, Emily, can you imagine what this means to me—to know he didn't die angry with me—that he died loving me and thinking tenderly of me? But I didn't know it then. And I—I don't think I've ever been quite right since. I know all his people thought me crazy. When Teddy was born I came up here away from them all. So that they couldn't lure him away from me. I wouldn't take a cent from them. I had David's insurance—we could just live on that. Teddy was all I had—and *you* came—and I knew you would take him from me. I knew he loved you—always. Oh, yes he did. When he went away I used to write him of all your flirtations. And two years ago—you remember he had to go to Montreal so suddenly—and you were away—he couldn't wait to say good-bye. But he wrote you a letter."

Emily gave a little choked cry of denial.

"Oh, he did. I saw it lying on his table when he had gone out. I steamed the flap open and read it. I burned the letter, Emily—but I can tell you what was in it. Could I ever forget! He told you he had meant to tell you how much he loved you before he went—and if you could care a little for him to write and tell him so. But if you couldn't not to write at all. Oh, how I hated you. I burned the letter and sealed up a copy of some poetry verses that were in it. And he mailed it never knowing the difference. I was never sorry—never, not even when he wrote me he was going to marry Ilse. But last night—when you brought me that letter—and forgiveness—and peace—oh, I felt I had done an awful thing. I've ruined your life—and perhaps Teddy's. Can you ever forgive me, Emily?"

## IV

Emily, amid all the whirl of emotions roused by Mrs. Kent's tale, was keenly conscious of only one thing. Bitterness—humiliation—shame had vanished from her being. Teddy *had* loved her. The sweetness of the revelation blotted out, for the time at least, all other feelings. Anger—resentment—could find no place in her soul. She felt like a new creature. And there was sincerity in heart and tone as she said slowly:

"I do—I do. I understand."

Mrs. Kent suddenly wrung her hands.

"Emily—is it too late? Is it too late? They're not married yet—I know he doesn't love her as he loved you. If you told him—if I told him—"

"No, no, no," cried Emily passionately. "It *is* too late. He must never know—you must never tell him. He loves Ilse now. I am sure of that—and telling him this would do no good and much evil. Promise me—dear Mrs. Kent, if you feel you owe me anything promise me, you'll never tell him."

"But you—you will be unhappy—"

"I will not be unhappy—not now. You don't know what a difference this has made. The sting has gone out of everything. I am going to have a happy, busy, useful life and regret for old dreams will have no place in it. The wound will heal now."

"It was—a terrible thing for me to do," whispered Mrs. Kent. "I see that—at last."

"I suppose it was. But I'm not thinking of that. Only that I've got my self-respect back."

"The Murray pride," whispered Mrs. Kent, staring at

her. "After all, Emily Starr, I believe pride is a stronger passion with you than love."

"Perhaps," said Emily smiling.

### V

She was in such a tumult of feeling when she reached home that she did a thing she was always ashamed of. Perry Miller was waiting in the New Moon garden for her. She had not seen him for a long time and at any other hour would have been glad to see him. Perry's friendship, now that he had finally given up all hope of anything else, was a very pleasant part of her life. He had developed in the last few years—he was manly, humorous, much less boastful. He had even acquired certain fundamental rules of social etiquette and learned not to have too many hands and feet. He was too busy to come often to New Moon, but Emily always enjoyed his visits when he did come—except to-night. She wanted to be alone—to think things over—classify her emotions—revel in her restored sense of self-respect. To pace up and down among the silken poppy-ladies of the garden and talk with Perry was an almost impossible thing. She was in a frenzy of impatience to be rid of him. And Perry did not sense this at all. He had not seen her for a long while—and there were many things to talk over—Ilse's wedding in especial. He kept on asking questions about it until Emily really didn't know what she was saying. Perry was a bit squiffy over the fact that *he* had not been asked to be groomsman. He thought he had a right to be—the old chum of both.

"I never thought Teddy would turn me down cold like that," he growled. "I suppose he feels himself too big to have Stovepipe Town for groomsman."

Then Emily did her dreadful thing—before she realised what she was saying, in her impatient annoyance with Perry for casting such aspersions on Teddy the words leaped out quite involuntarily.

"You goose! It wasn't Teddy at all. Do you think Ilse

would have you as groomsman—when she hoped for years you would be the groom?"

The moment she had spoken she stood aghast, sick with shame and remorse. What had she done? Betrayed friendship—violated confidence—a shameful, unpardonable thing. Could *she*, Emily Byrd Starr of New Moon have done *this*?

Perry was standing by the dial staring at her dumfounded.

"Emily, you don't mean that. Ilse never thought of me that way, did she?"

Emily miserably realised that the spoken word could not be recalled and that the mess she had made of things couldn't be mended by any fibs.

"She did—at one time. Of course she got over it long ago."

"*Me!* Why, Emily she always seemed to despise me—always ragging me about something—I never could please her—you remember."

"Oh, I remember," said Emily wearily. "She thought so much of you, she hated to see you fall below her standard. If she hadn't liked you—do you suppose she would have cared what grammar you used or what etiquette you smashed? I should never have told you this, Perry. I shall be ashamed of it all my life. You must never let her suspect you know."

"Of course not. Anyhow, she's forgotten it long ago."

"Oh—yes. But you can understand why it wouldn't be especially agreeable for her to have you as best man at her wedding. I hated to have you think Teddy such a snob. And now, you won't mind, will you, Perry, if I ask you to go? I'm very tired—and I've so much to do the next two weeks."

"You ought to be in bed, that's a fact," agreed Perry. "I'm a beast to be keeping you up. But when I come here it seems so much like old times I never want to go. What a set of shavers we were! And now Ilse and Teddy are going to be married. We're getting on a bit."

"Next thing you'll be a staid old married man yourself, Perry," said Emily, trying to smile. "I've been hearing things."

"Not on your life! I've given up that idea for good. Not that I'm pining after you yet in particular—only nobody has any flavour after you. I've tried. I'm doomed to die a bachelor. They tell me it's an easy death. But I've got a few ambitions by the tail and I'm not kicking about life. Bye-bye, dear. I'll see you at the wedding. It's in the afternoon, isn't it?"

"Yes." Emily wondered she could speak so calmly of it. "Three o'clock—then supper—and a motor drive to Shrewsbury to catch the evening boat. Perry, Perry, I wish I hadn't told you that about Ilse. It was mean—mean—as we used to say in school—I never thought I could do such a thing."

"Now, don't go worrying over that. I'm as tickled as a dog with two tails to think Ilse ever thought that much of me, at any time. Don't you think I've sense enough to know what a compliment it was? And don't you think I understand what bricks you two girls always were to me and how much I owe you for letting me be your friend? I've never had any illusions about Stovepipe Town or the real difference between us. I wasn't such a fool as not to understand *that*. I've climbed a bit—I mean to climb higher—but you and Ilse were *born* to it. And you never let me feel the difference as some girls did. I shan't forget Rhoda Stuart's dirty little slurs. So you don't think I'd be such a cur now as to go strutting because I've found out Ilse once had a bit of a fancy for me—or that I'd ever let her think I knew? I've left that much of Stovepipe Town behind, anyhow—even if I still have to think what fork I'll pick up first. Emily—*do* you remember the night your Aunt Ruth caught me kissing you?"*

"I should think I do."

"The only time I ever did kiss you," said Perry nonsentimentally. "And *it* wasn't much of a shot, was

*See *Emily Climbs*.

it? When I think of the old lady standing there in her nightgown with the candle!"

Perry went off laughing and Emily went to her room.

"Emily-in-the-glass," she said almost gaily, "I can look you squarely in the eyes again. I'm not ashamed any longer. He *did* love me."

She stood there smiling for a little space. And then the smile faded.

"Oh, if I had only got that letter!" she whispered piteously.

# Chapter XXV

## I

Only two weeks till the wedding. Emily found out how long two weeks can be, in spite of the fact that every waking moment was crowded with doings, domestic and social. The affair was much talked of everywhere. Emily set her teeth and went through with it. Ilse was here—there—everywhere. Doing nothing—saying much.

"About as composed as a flea," growled Dr. Burnley.

"Ilse has got to be such a restless creature," complained Aunt Elizabeth. "She seems to be frightened people wouldn't know she was alive if she sat still a moment."

"I've got forty-nine remedies for seasickness," said Ilse. "If Aunt Kate Mitchell gets here I'll have fifty. Isn't it delightful to have thoughtful relatives, Emily?"

They were alone in Ilse's room. It was the evening Teddy was expected. Ilse had tried on half a dozen different dresses and tossed them aside scornfully.

"Emily, *what* will I wear? Decide for me."

"Not I. Besides—what difference does it make what you put on?"

"True—too true. Teddy never notices what I have on. I like a man who *does* notice and tells me of it. I like a man who likes me better in silk than in gingham."

Emily looked out of the window into a tangled garden where the moonlight was an untroubled silver sea bearing softly on its breast a fleet of poppies. "I meant that Teddy—won't think of your dress—only of *you.*"

204

"Emily, why do you persist in talking as if you thought Teddy and I were madly in love with each other? Is it that Victorian complex of yours?"

"For heaven's sake, shut up about things Victorian!" Emily exclaimed with unusual, un-Murraylike violence. "I'm tired of it. You call every nice, simple, natural emotion Victorian. The whole world to-day seems to be steeped in a scorn for things Victorian. Do they know what they're talking of? But I like sane, decent things— if *that* is Victorian."

"Emily, Emily, do you suppose Aunt Elizabeth would think it either a sane or a decent thing to be madly in love?"

Both girls laughed and the sudden tension relaxed.

"You're not off, Emily?"

"Of course I am. Do you think I'd play gooseberry at such a time as this?"

"There you go again. Do *you* think I want to be shut up alone a whole evening with undiluted Teddy? We'll have a scene every few minutes over something. Of course scenes are lovely. They brighten up life so. I've just got to have a scene once a week. You know I always did enjoy a good fight. Remember how you and I used to scrap? You haven't been a bit of good at a row lately. Even Teddy is only half-hearted in a set-to. Perry, now—*he* could fight. Think what gorgeous rows Perry and I would have had. Our quarrels would have been splendid. Nothing petty—or *quarrelsome*—about them. And how we would have loved each other between them! Oh-hone-a-rie!"

"Are you hankering after Perry Miller yet?" demanded Emily fiercely.

"No, dear infant. And neither am I crazy about Teddy. After all, ours is only second-hand love on both sides, you know. Cold soup warmed over. Don't worry. I'll be good for him. I'll keep him up to the notch in everything much better than if I thought him a little lower than the angels. It doesn't do to think a man is perfection because *he* naturally thinks so, too, and when he finds some one who agrees with him he is inclined to rest on his oars. It riles me up a bit when every one seems to think I'm so amazingly lucky to 'get' Teddy for a husband. Comes Aunt Ida Mitchell— 'You are getting a perfectly wonderful husband, Ilse' —comes Bridget Mooney from Stovepipe Town scrubbing the floor—'Gosh but you're gettin' a swell man, Miss'—'Sisters under their skins,' you perceive. Teddy is well enough—especially since he found out he isn't the only man in the world. He has learned sense somewhere. I'd like to know what girl taught it to him. Oh, there was one. He told me something about the affair—not much but enough. She used to snub him terribly—and then after she had led him on to think she cared she turned him down cold. Never even answered the letter in which he told her he loved her. I hate that girl, Emily—isn't it odd?"

"Don't hate her," said Emily, wearily. "Perhaps she didn't know what she was doing."

"I hate her for using Teddy like that. Though it did him heaps of good. Why do I hate her, Emily? Employ your renowned skill in psychological analysis and expound to me that mystery."

"You hate her—because—to borrow a certain crude expression we've often heard—you're 'taking her leavings.'"

"You demon! I suppose it's so. How ugly some things are when you ferret them out! I've been flattering myself that it was a noble hatred because she made Teddy suffer. After all, the Victorians were right in covering lots of things up. Ugly things should be hidden. Now, go home if you must and I'll try to look like some one about to receive a blessing."

## II

Lorne Halsey came with Teddy—the great Halsey whom Emily liked very much in spite of his gargoyleishness. A comical looking fellow with vital, mocking eyes, who seemed to look upon everything in general and Frederick Kent's wedding in particular as a huge joke. Somehow, this attitude made things a little easier for Emily. She was very brilliant and gay in the evenings they all spent together. She was terribly afraid of silence in Teddy's presence. "Never be silent with the person you love and distrust," Mr. Carpenter had said once. "Silence betrays."

Teddy was very friendly, but his gaze always omitted Emily. Once, when they all walked in the old, overgrown, willow-bordered lawn of the Burnley place, Ilse stumbled on the happy idea of picking out your favourite star.

"Mine is Sirius. Lorne?"

"Antares of the Scorpion—the red star of the south," said Halsey.

"Bellatrix of Orion," said Emily quickly. She had never thought about Bellatrix before, but she dared not hesitate a moment before Teddy.

"I have no especial favourite—there is only one star I hate. Vega of the Lyre," said Teddy quietly. His voice was charged with a significance which instantly made every one uncomfortable though neither Halsey nor Ilse knew why. No more was said about stars. But Emily watched alone till they faded out one by one in the dawn.

### III

Three nights before the wedding day Blair Water and Derry Pond were much scandalised because Ilse Burnley had been seen driving with Perry Miller in his new runabout at some ungodly hour. Ilse coolly admitted it when Emily reproached her.

"Of course I did. I had had such a dull, bored evening with Teddy. We began it well with a quarrel over my blue Chow. Teddy said I cared more for it than I did for him. I said of course I did. It infuriated him, though he didn't believe it. Teddy, manlike, really believes I'm dying about him.

"'A dog that never chased a cat in its life,' he sneered.

"Then we both sulked the rest of the evening. He went home at eleven without kissing me. I resolved I'd do something foolish and beautiful for the last time, so I sneaked down the lane for a lovely, lonely walk down to the dunes. Perry came along in his car and I just changed my mind and went for a little moonlit spin with him. I wasn't married *yet*. Don't be after looking at me so. We only stayed out till one and we were really very good and proper. I only wondered once—just what would happen if I suddenly said, 'Perry, darling, *you're* the only man I've ever really cared a hang for. Why can't *we* get married?' I wonder if when I'm eighty I'll wish I'd said it."

"You told me you had quite got over caring for Perry."

"But did you believe me? Emily, thank God you're not a Burnley."

Emily reflected bitterly that it was not much better being a Murray. If it had not been for her Murray pride she would have gone to Teddy the night he called her—and she would have been to-morrow's bride—not Ilse.

To-morrow. It was to-morrow—the morrow when she would have to stand near Teddy and hear him vowing likelong devotion to another woman. All was in readiness. The wedding supper that pleased even Dr. Burnley, who had decreed that there should be "a good, old-fashioned wedding-super—none of your modern dabs of this and that. The bride and groom mayn't want much maybe, but the rest of us still have stomachs. And this is the first wedding for years. We've been getting pretty much like heaven in one respect anyhow—neither marrying nor giving in marriage. I want to spread. And tell Laura for heaven's sake not to yowl at the wedding."

So Aunts Elizabeth and Laura saw to it that for the first time in twenty years the Burnley house had a thorough cleaning from top to bottom. Dr. Burnley thanked God forcibly several times that he would only have to go through this once, but nobody paid any attention to him. Elizabeth and Laura had new satin dresses made. It was such a long time since they had had any excuse for new satin dresses.

Aunt Elizabeth made the wedding-cakes and saw to the hams and chickens. Laura made creams and jellies and salads and Emily carried them over to the Burnley place, wondering at times if she wouldn't soon wake up—before—before—

"I'll be glad when all this fuss is over," growled Cousin Jimmy. "Emily's working herself to death—look at the eyes of her!"

## IV

"Stay with me to-night, Emily," entreated Ilse. "I swear I won't talk you to death and I won't cry either. Though I admit if I could just be snuffed out to-night like a candle I wouldn't mind. Jean Askew was Milly Hyslop's bridesmaid and she spent the night before her wedding with her and they both cried all night. Fancy such an orgy of tears. Milly cried because she was going to be married—and I suppose Jean must have been crying because she wasn't. Thank heaven, Emily, you and I were never the miauling kind. We'll be more likely to fight than cry, won't we? I wonder if Mrs. Kent will come to-morrow? I don't suppose so. Teddy says she never mentions his marriage. Though he says she seems oddly changed—gentler—calmer—more like other women. Emily, do you realise that by this time to-morrow I'll be Ilse Kent?"

Yes, Emily realised *that*.

They said nothing more. But two hours later when wakeful Emily had supposed the motionless Ilse was

sound asleep Ilse suddenly sat up in bed and grabbed
Emily's hand in the darkness.

"Emily—if one could only go to sleep unmarried—
and wake up married—how nice it would be."

## V

It was dawn—the dawn of Ilse wedding-day. Ilse was
sleeping when Emily slipped out of bed and went to the
window. Dawn. A cluster of dark pines in a trance of
calm down by the Blair Water. The air tremulous with
elfin music; the wind winnowing the dunes; dancing
amber waves on the harbour; the eastern sky abloom; the
lighthouse at the harbour pearl-white against the ethereal sky; beyond all the blue field of the sea with its foam
blossoms and behind that golden haze that swathed the
hill of the Tansy Patch, Teddy—wakeful—waiting— wel-
coming the day that gave him his heart's desire. Emily's
soul was washed empty of every wish or hope or desire
except that the day were over.

"It is," she thought, "comforting when a thing becomes irrevocable."

"Emily—Emily."

Emily turned from the window.

"It's a lovely day, Ilse. The sun will shine on you.
Ilse—what is the matter? Ilse—you're crying!"

"I can't—help it," sniffled Ilse. "It seems to be the
proper, inescapable caper after all. I beg Milly's par-
don. But—I'm so beastly afraid. It's an infernal sensation. Do you think it would do any good if I threw
myself on the floor and screamed?"

"What are you afraid of?" said Emily, a little impatiently.

"Oh,"—Ilse sprang defiantly out of bed—"afraid I'll
stick my tongue out at the minister. What else?"

## VI

What a morning! It always seemed a sort of nightmare recollection to Emily. Guests of the clan came

early—Emily welcomed them until she felt that the smile must be frozen on her face. There were endless wedding-gifts to unwrap and arrange. Ilse, before she dressed came to look over them indifferently.

"Who sent in that afternoon tea set?" she asked.

"Perry," said Emily. She had helped him choose it. A dainty service in a quaint old-fashioned rose design. A card with Perry's black forcible handwriting. "To Ilse with the best wishes of her old friend Perry."

Ilse deliberately picked up piece after piece and dashed it in fragments on the floor before the transfixed Emily could stop her.

"*Ilse!* Have you gone crazy?"

"There! What a glorious smash! Sweep up the fragments, Emily. That was just as good as screaming on the floor. Better. I can go through with it now."

Emily disposed of the fragments just in time—Mrs. Clarinda Mitchell came billowing in, pale-blue muslin and a cherry-hued scarf. A sonsy, smiling, good-hearted cousin-by-marriage. Interested in everything. Who gave this?—Who had sent that?

"She'll be *such* a sweet bride, I'm sure," gushed Mrs. Clarinda. "And Teddy Kent is *such* a splendid fellow. It's really an ideal marriage, isn't it? One of those you read about! I love weddings like this. I thank my stars I didn't lose my interest in youthful things when I lost my youth. I've lots of sentiment in me yet—and I'm not afraid to show it. And *did* Ilse's wedding stockings really cost fourteen dollars?"

Aunt Isabella Hyslop, *née* Mitchell, was gloomy. Offended because her costly present of cut sherbet glasses had been placed beside Cousin Annabel's funny set of old-fashioned crocheted doilies. Inclined to take a dark view of things.

"I hope everything will go off well. But I've got an uneasy feeling that trouble is coming—a presentiment, so to speak. Do you believe in signs? A big black cat ran right across the road in front of us down in the hollow. And right on that tree as we turned in at the lane was the fragment of an old election poster, 'Blue Ruin,' in black letters three inches long staring us in the face."

"That might mean bad luck for you, but hardly for Ilse."

Aunt Isabella shook her head. She would *not* be comforted.

"They say the wedding dress is like nothing ever seen on Prince Edward Island. *Do* you think such extravagance proper, Miss Starr?"

"The expensive part of it was a present from Ilse's old great-aunts in Scotland, Mrs. Mitchell. And most of us are married only once."

Whereupon Emily remembered that Aunt Isabella had been married three times and wondered if there wasn't something in black cat magic.

Aunt Isabella swept coldly off, and later on was heard to say that "that Starr girl is really intolerable since she got a book published. Thinks herself at liberty to insult any one."

Emily, before she had time to thank the Fates for her freedom, fell into the clutches of more Mitchell relatives. This aunt did not approve of another aunt's gift of a pair of ornate Bohemian glass vases.

"Bessie Jane never had much sense. A foolish choice. The children will be sure to unhook the prisms and lose them."

"What children?"

"Why, the children they will have, of course."

"Miss Starr will put that in a book, Matilda," warned her husband, chuckling. Then he chuckled again and whispered to Emily:

"Why aren't *you* the bride to-day? How come Ilse cut you out, hey?"

## VII

Emily was thankful when she was summoned upstairs to help Ilse dress. Though even here aunts and cousins kept bobbing in and out, saying distracting things.

"Emily, do you remember the day of our first summer together when we fought over the honour of playing bride in one of our dramatic stunts? Well, I feel as if I were just playing bride. This isn't real."

Emily felt, too, as if it were not real. But soon—soon now—it would be all over and she could be blessedly alone. And Ilse when dressed was such an exquisite bride that she justified all the fuss of the wedding. How Teddy *must* love her!

"Doesn't she look just like a queen?" whispered Aunt Laura adoringly.

Emily having slipped into her own harebell blue kissed the flushed maiden face under the rose-point cap and pearls of its bridal veil.

"Ilse dear, don't think me hopelessly Victorian if I say I hope you'll be happy 'ever after.'"

Ilse squeezed her hand, but laughed a little too loudly.

"I hope it isn't Queen Victoria Aunt Laura thinks I resemble," she whispered. "And I have the most horrible suspicion that Aunt Janie Milburn is praying for me. Her face betrayed her when she came in to kiss me. It always makes me furious to suspect that people are praying for me. Now, Emily, do me one last favour. Herd everybody out of this room—everybody. I want to be alone, absolutely alone, for a few minutes."

Somehow Emily managed it. The aunts and cousins fluttered downstairs. Dr. Burnley was waiting impatiently in the hall.

"Won't you soon be ready? Teddy and Halsey are waiting for the signal to go down into the drawing-room."

"Ilse wants a few minutes alone. Oh, Aunt Ida, I'm so glad you got here"—to a stout lady who was coming pantingly up the stairs. "We were afraid something had happened to prevent you."

"Something did," gasped Aunt Ida—who was really

a second-cousin. In spite of her breathlessness Aunt Ida was happy. She always liked to be the first to tell a piece of news—especially unpleasant news. "And the doctor couldn't come at all—I had to get a taxi. That poor Perry Miller—you know him, don't you? Such a clever young chap—was killed in a motor collision about an hour ago."

Emily stifled a shriek, with a frantic glance at Ilse's door. It was slightly ajar. Dr. Burnley was saying:

"Perry Miller killed! Good God, how horrible!"

"Well, as good as killed. He must be dead by this time—he was unconscious when they dragged him out of the wreck. They took him to the Charlottetown hospital and 'phoned for Bill, who dashed right off, of course. It's a mercy Ilse isn't marrying a doctor. Have I time to take off my things before the ceremony?"

Emily, crushing her anguish over Perry, showed Aunt Ida to the spare room and returned to Dr. Burnley.

"Don't let Ilse know about this," he cautioned needlessly. "It would spoil her wedding—she and Perry were old cronies. And hadn't you better hurry up a little? It's past the time."

Emily, with more of a nightmare feeling than ever, went down the hall and knocked on Ilse's door. There was no answer. She opened the door. On the floor in a forlorn heap lay the bridal veil and the priceless bouquet of orchids which must have cost Teddy more than any Murray or Burnley bride had ever paid before for her whole trousseau, but Ilse was nowhere to be seen. A window was open, the one over the kitchen stoop.

"What's the matter?" exclaimed Dr. Burnley impatiently, coming up behind Emily. "Where's Ilse?"

"She's—gone," said Emily stupidly.

"Gone—gone where?"

"To Perry Miller." Emily knew it quite well. Ilse had heard Aunt Ida and—

"Damn!" said Dr. Burnley.

## VIII

In a few moments the house was a scene of consternation and flabbergasted wedding guests, all exclaiming and asking questions. Dr. Burnley lost his head and turned himself loose, running through his whole repertoire of profanity, regardless of women-folks.

Even Aunt Elizabeth was paralysed. There was no precedent to go by. Juliet Murray, to be sure, had eloped. But she had got married. No clan bride had ever done anything like *this*. Emily alone retained some power of rational thought and action. It was she who found out from young Rob Mitchell how Ilse had gone. He had been parking his car in the barnyard when—

"I saw her spring out of that window with her train wrapped around her shoulders. She slid down the roof and jumped to the ground like a cat—tore out to the lane, jumped in Ken Mitchell's runabout and was off like the devil was after her. I thought she must have gone crazy."

"She has—in a way. Rob, you must go after her. Wait—I'll get Dr. Burnley to go with you. I must stay here to see to things. Oh, be as quick as you can. It's only fourteen miles to Charlottetown. You can go and come in an hour. You *must* bring her back—I'll tell the guests to wait—"

"You'll not make much out of this mess, Emily," prophesied Rob.

## IX

Even an hour like that passed. But Dr. Burnley and Rob returned alone. Ilse would not come—that was all there was to it. Perry Miller was not killed—was not even seriously injured—but Ilse would not come. She told her father that she was going to marry Perry Miller and nobody else.

The doctor was the centre of a little group of dismayed and tearful women in the upper hall. Aunt Elizabeth, Aunt Laura, Aunt Ruth, Emily.

"I suppose if her mother had lived this wouldn't have happened," said the doctor dazedly. "I never dreamed she cared for Miller. I wish somebody had wrung Ida Mitchell's neck in time. Oh, cry—cry—yes, cry"—fiercely to poor Aunt Laura. "What good will yelping do? What a devil of a mess! Somebody's got to tell Kent—I suppose I must. And those distracted fools down there have to be fed. That's what half of them came for, anyway. Emily, you seem to be the only creature left in the world with a grain of sense. See to things, there's a good girl."

Emily was not of an hysterical temperament, but for the second time in her life she was feeling that the only thing she could do would be to scream as loud and long as possible. Things had got to the point where only screaming would clear the air. But she got the guests marshalled to the tables. Excitement calmed down somewhat when they found they were not to be cheated out of everything. But the wedding-feast was hardly a success.

Even those who were hungry had an uneasy feeling that it wasn't the thing to eat heartily under such circumstances. Nobody enjoyed it except old Uncle Tom Mitchell, who frankly went to weddings for the spread and didn't care whether there was a ceremony or not. Brides might come and brides might go but a square meal was a feed. So he ate steadily away, only pausing now and then to shake his head solemnly and ask, "What air the women coming to?"

Cousin Isabella was set up on presentiments for life, but nobody listened to her. Most of the guests were afraid to speak, for fear of saying the wrong thing. Uncle Oliver reflected that he had seen many funeral repasts that were more cheerful. The waitresses were hurried and flurried and made ludicrous mistakes. Mrs. Derwent, the young and pretty wife of the new minister, looked to be on the point of tears—nay, actually had tears in her eyes. Perhaps she had been building on the prospective wedding fee. Perhaps its loss meant no new hat for her. Emily, glancing at her as she passed a jelly, wanted to laugh—a desire as hysterical as her wish to scream. But no desire at all showed itself on her cold white face. Shrewsbury people said she was as disdainful and indifferent as always. Could *anything* really make that girl *feel*?

And under it all she was keenly conscious of only one question. "Where was Teddy? What was he feeling—thinking—doing?" She hated Ilse for hurting him—shaming him. She did not see how *anything* could go on after *this*. It was one of those events which *must* stop time.

X

"What a day!" sobbed Aunt Laura as they walked home in the dusk. "What a disgrace! What a scandal!"

"Allan Burnley has only himself to blame," said Aunt Elizabeth. "He has let Ilse do absolutely as she pleases all her life. She was never taught any self-control. All her life she had done exactly as she wanted to do whenever the whim took her. No sense of responsibility whatever."

"But if she loved Perry Miller," pleaded Laura.

"Why did she promise to marry Teddy Kent then? And treat him like this? No, you need make no excuses for Ilse. Fancy a Burnley going to Stovepipe Town for a husband!"

"Some one will have to see about sending the presents back," moaned Laura. "I locked the door of the room where they were. One never knows—at such a time—"

Emily found herself alone in her room at last—too dazed, stricken, exhausted, to feel much of anything. A huge, round, striped ball unrolled itself on her bed and opened wide pink jaws.

"Daff," said Emily wearily, "you're the only thing in the world that stays put."

She had a nasty sleepless night with a brief dawn slumber. From which she wakened to a new world where everything had to be readjusted. And she felt too tired to care for readjustment.

# Chapter XXVI

## I

Ilse did not look as if she wanted excuses made for her when, two days later, she walked unannounced into Emily's room. She looked rosy, audacious, triumphant.

Emily stared at her.

"Well, I suppose the earthquake is over. What is left standing?"

"Ilse! How could you!"

Ilse pulled a notebook out of her handbag and pretended to consult it.

"I wrote down a list of the things you'd say. That was the first one. You've said it. The next is, 'Aren't you ashamed of yourself?' I'm not, you know," added Ilse impudently.

"I know you're not. That's why I don't ask it."

"I'm not ashamed—and I'm not sorry. I'm only a litle bit sorry that I'm *not* sorry. And I'm shamelessly happy. But I suppose I spoiled the party. No doubt the old meows are having the time of their lives. They've got their craws full for once."

"How do you suppose Teddy is feeling?" asked Emily sternly.

"Is he feeling any worse than Dean did? There's an old proverb about glass houses."

Emily crimsoned.

"I know—I used Dean badly—but I didn't—"

"Jilt him at the altar! True. But I didn't think about Teddy at all when I heard Aunt Ida say Perry was

218

killed. I was quite mad. My one thought was to see Perry once before he died. I *had* to. And I found when I got there that, as Mark Twain said, the report of his death was greatly exaggerated. He wasn't even badly hurt—was sitting up in bed, his face all bruised and bandaged—looking like the devil. Want to hear what happened, Emily?"

Ilse dropped on the floor at Emily's feet—and looked coaxingly up into Emily's face.

"Honey, what's the use of disapproving a thing that was foreordained? That won't alter anything. I got a glimpse of Aunt Laura in the sitting-room as I sneaked upstairs. She was looking like something that had been left out overnight. But you have a streak in you that isn't Murray. *You* should understand. Don't waste your sympathy on Teddy. He doesn't love me—I've always known it. It's only his conceit that will suffer. Here—give him his sapphire for me, will you?' Ilse saw something in Emily's face she didn't like. "It can go to join Dean's emerald."

"Teddy left for Montreal the day after—after—"

"After the wedding that wasn't," finished Ilse. "Did you see him, Emily?"

"No."

"Well, if he'd go and shoot big game in Africa for awhile he'd get over it very quickly. Emily, I'm going to marry Perry—next year. It's all settled. I fell on his neck and kissed him as soon as I saw him. I let go my train and it streamed magnificently over the floor. I knew the nurse thought I had just got out of Dr. Percy's private asylum. But I turned her out of the room. And I told Perry I loved him and that I would never, never mary Teddy Kent no matter what happened—and then he asked me if I'd marry *him*—or I told him he must marry me—or neither of us asked—we just understood. I honestly don't remember which—and I don't care. Emily, if I were dead and Perry came and looked at me I'd live again. Of course I know he's always been after you— but he's going to love me as he never loved you. We were made for each other."

"Perry was never really in love with me," said Emily. "He liked me tremendously, that was all. He didn't know the difference—then." She looked down into Ilse's radiant face—and all her old, old love for this perverse, adorable friend rushed to eyes and lips.

"Dearest, I hope you'll be happy—always."

"How blessedly Victorian that sounds!" said Ilse contentedly. "Oh, I can be quiet now, Emily. For weeks I've been afraid that if I let myself be quiet for a moment I'd *bolt*. And I don't even mind if Aunt Janie is praying for me. I believe I rather hope she is."

"What does your father say?"

"Oh, Dad." Ilse shrugged her shoulders. "He's still in the clutches of his old ancestral temper. Won't speak to me. But he'll come round. He's really as much to blame as I am for what I've done. You know I've never asked any one in my life if I could do a thing. I just did it. Father never prevented me. At first because he hated me—then because he wanted to make up for hating me."

"I think you'll have to ask Perry sometimes if you can do things."

"I won't mind *that*. You'll be surprised to see what a dutiful wife I'll make. Of course I'm going right away— back to work. And in a year's time people will have forgotten—and Perry and I will be married quietly somewhere. No more rose-point veils and oriental trains and clan weddings for me. Lord, what an escape! Ten minutes later I'd have been married to Teddy. Think what a scandal there'd have been then when Aunt Ida arrived. Because I'd have gone just the same, you know."

## II

That summer was a hard time for Emily. The very anguish of her suffering had filled life and now that it was over she realised its emptiness. Then, too, to go anywhere meant martyrdom. Every one talking about the wedding, asking, wondering, surmising. But at last the wild gossip and clatter over Ilse's kididoes had finally died away and people found something else to talk about. Emily was left alone.

Alone? Ay, that was it. Always alone. Love—friendship gone forever. Nothing left but ambition. Emily settled herself resolutely down to work. Life ran again in its old accustomed grooves. Year after year the seasons walked by her door. Violet-sprinkled valleys of spring— blossom-script of summer—minstrel-firs of autumn—pale fires of the Milky Way on winter nights—soft, new-mooned skies of April—gnomish beauty of dark Lombardies against a moonrise—deep of sea calling to deep of wind—lonely yellow leaves falling in October dusks— woven moonlight in the orchard. Oh, there was beauty in life still—always would be. Immortal, indestructible beauty beyond all the stain and blur of mortal passion. She had some very glorious hours of inspiration and achievement. But mere beauty which had once satisfied her soul could not wholly satisfy it now. New Moon was unchanged, undisturbed by the changes that came elsewhere. Mrs. Kent had gone to live with Teddy. The old Tansy Patch was sold to some Halifax man for a summer home. Perry went to Montreal one autumn and brought Ilse back with him. They were living happily in Charlottetown, where Emily often visited them, astutely evading the matrimonial traps Ilse was always setting for her. It was becoming an accepted thing in the clan that Emily would not marry.

"Another old maid at New Moon," as Uncle Wallace said gracefully.

"And to think of all the men she might have had," said Aunt Elizabeth bitterly. "My Wallace—Aylmer Vincent—Andrew—"

"But if she didn't—love—them," faltered Aunt Laura.

"Laura, you need not be indelicate."

Old Kelly, who still went his rounds—"and will till

the crack of doom," declared Ilse—had quite given up teasing Emily about getting married, though he occasionally made regretful, cryptic allusions to "toad ointment." There was none of his significant nods and winks. Instead, he always gravely asked her what book she did be working on now, and drove off shaking his spiky grey head. "What do the men be thinking of, anyway? Get up, my nag, get up."

Some men were still thinking of Emily, it appeared. Andrew, now a brisk young widower, would have come at the beck of a finger Emily never lifted. Graham Mitchell, of Shrewsbury, unmistakably had intentions. Emily wouldn't have him because he had a slight cast in one eye. At least, that was what the Murrays supposed. They could think of no other reason for her refusal of so good a match. Shrewsbury people declared that he figured in her next novel and that she had only been "leading him on" to "get material." A reputed Klondike "millionaire" pursued her for a winter, but disappeared as briefly in the spring.

"Since she has published those books she thinks no one good enough for her," said Blair Water folks.

Aunt Elizabeth did not regret the Klondike man—he was only a Derry Pond Butterworth, to begin with, and what were the Butterworths? Aunt Elizabeth always contrived to give the impression that Butterworths did not exist. They might imagine they did, but the Murrays knew better. But she did not see why Emily could not take Mooresby, of the firm of Mooresby and Parker, Charlottetown. Emily's explanation that Mr. Mooresby could never live down the fact that he had once had his picture in the papers as a Perkins' Food Baby struck Aunt Elizabeth as very inadequate. But Aunt Elizabeth at last admitted that she could not understand the younger generation.

### III

Of Teddy Emily never heard, save from occasional items in newspapers which represented him as advancing steadily in his career. He was beginning to have an international reputation as a portrait painter. The old days of magazine illustrations were gone and Emily was never now confronted with her own face—or her own smile—or her own eyes—looking out at her from some casual page.

One winter Mrs. Kent died. Before her death she sent Emily a brief note—the only word Emily had ever had from her.

"I am dying. When I am dead, Emily, tell Teddy about the letter. I've tried to tell him, but I couldn't. I couldn't tell my son I had done *that*. Tell him for me."

Emily smiled sadly as she put the letter away. It was too late to tell Teddy. He had long since ceased to care for her. And she—she would love him forever. And even though he knew it not, surely such love would hover around him all his life like an invisible benediction, not understood but dimly felt, guarding him from ill and keeping from him all things of harm and evil.

## IV

That same winter it was bruited abroad that Jim Butterworth of Derry Pond, had bought or was about to buy the Disappointed House. He meant, so rumour said, to haul it away, rebuild and enlarge it; and doubtless when this was done he would install therein as mistress a certain buxom, thrifty damsel of Derry Pond known as "Geordie Bridge's Mabel." Emily heard the report with anguish. She slipped out that evening in the chill spring dusk and went up the dim overgrown path over the spruce hill to the front gate of the little house like an unquiet ghost. Surely it couldn't be true that Dean had sold it. The house belonged to the hill. One couldn't imagine the hill without it.

Once Emily had got Aunt Laura to see about bringing her own belongings from it—all but the gazing-ball. She could not bear to see that. It must be still hanging there, reflecting in its silver gloom by the dim light that fell through the slits of the shutters, the living-room just as it was when she and Dean had parted. Rumour said Dean had taken nothing from it. All he had put in it was still there.

The little house must be very cold. It was so long since there was a fire in it. How neglected—how lonely—how heartbroken it looked. No light in the window—grass growing thickly over the paths—rank weeds crowding around the long-unopened door.

Emily stretched out her arms as if she wanted to put them around the house. Daff rubbed against her ankles and purred pleadingly. He did not like damp, chilly prowls—the fireside at New Moon was better for a pussy not so young as he once was. Emily lifted the old cat and set him on the crumbling gatepost.

"Daff," she said, "there is an old fireplace in that house—with the ashes of a dead fire in it—a fireplace where pussies should bask and children dream. And that will never happen now, Daff, for Mabel Geordie doesn't like open fireplaces—dirty, dusty things—a Quebec heater is so much warmer and more economical. Don't you wish—or do you!—Daff, that you and I had been more sensible creatures, alive to the superior advantages of Quebec heaters!"

# Chapter XXVII

## I

It came clearly and suddenly on the air of a June evening. And old, old call—two higher notes and one long and soft and low. Emily Starr, dreaming at her window, heard it and stood up, her face suddenly gone white. Dreaming still—she must be! Teddy Kent was thousands of miles away, in the Orient—so much she knew from an item in a Montreal paper. Yes, she had dreamed it—imagined it.

It came again. And Emily *knew* that Teddy was there, waiting for her in Lofty John's bush—calling to her across the years. She went down slowly—out—across the garden. Of course Teddy was there—under the firs. It seemed the most natural thing in the world that he should come to her there, in that old-world garden where the three Lombardies still kept guard. Nothing was wanting to bridge the years. There was no gulf. He put out his hands and drew her to him, with no conventional greeting. And spoke as if there were no years—no memories—between them.

"Don't tell me you can't love me—you can—you must—why, Emily"—his eyes had met the moonlit brilliance of hers for a moment—"you *do*."

## II

"It's dreadful what little things lead people to mis-understand each other," said Emily some minutes—or hours—later.

225

"I've been trying all my life to tell you I love you," said Teddy. "Do you remember that evening long ago in the To-morrow Road after we left high school? Just as I was trying to scare up my courage to ask you if you'd wait for me you said night air was bad for you and went in. I thought it a poor excuse for getting rid of me—I knew you didn't care a hoot about night air. That set me back for years. When I heard about you and Aylmer Vincent—Mother wrote you were engaged it was a nasty shock. For the first time it occurred to me that you really didn't belong to me, after all. And that winter you were ill—I was nearly wild. Away there in France where I couldn't see you. And people writing that Dean Priest was always with you and would probably marry you if you recovered. Then came the word that you *were* going to marry him. I won't talk of that. But when you—*you*—saved me from going to my death on the *Flavian* I knew you *did* belong to me, once and for all, whether *you* knew it or not. Then I tried again that morning by Blair Water—and again you snubbed me mercilessly. Shaking off my touch as if my hand were a snake. And you never answered my letter. Emily, *why* didn't you? You say you've always cared—"

"I never got the letter.'

"Never got it? But I mailed it—"

"Yes, I know. I must tell you—she said I was to tell you—" She told him briefly.

"My *mother*? Did *that*?"

"You mustn't judge her harshly, Teddy. You know she wasn't like other women. Her quarrel with your father—did you know—"

"Yes, she told me all about that—when she came to me in Montreal. But *this*—Emily—"

"Let us just forget it—and forgive. She was so warped and unhappy she didn't know what she was doing. And I—I—was too proud—too proud to go when you called me that last time. I *wanted* to go—but I thought you were only amusing yourself—"

"I gave up hope then—finally. It had fooled me too

often. I saw you at your window, shining, as it seemed to me, with an icy radiance like some cold, wintry star—I knew you heard me—it was the first time you had failed to answer our old call. There seemed nothing to do but forget you—if I could. I never succeeded, but I thought I did—except when I looked at Vega of the Lyre. And I was lonely. Ilse was a good pal. Besides, I think I thought I could talk to her about you—keep a little corner in your life as the husband of some one you loved. I knew Ilse didn't care much for me—I was only the consolation prize. But I thought we could jog along very well together and help each other keep away the fearful lonesomeness of the world. And then"—Teddy laughed at himself—"when she 'left me at the altar' according to the very formula of Bertha M. Clay I was furious. She had made such a fool of me—me, who fancied I was beginning to cut quite a figure in the world. My word, how I hated women for awhile! And I was hurt, too. I had got very fond of Ilse—I really did love her—in a way."

"In a way." Emily felt no jealousy of that.

### III

"I don't know as I'd take Ilse' leavings," remarked Aunt Elizabeth.

Emily flashed on Aunt Elizabeth one of her old starry looks.

"Ilse's leavings. Why, Teddy has always belonged to me and I to him. Heart, soul and body," said Emily.

Aunt Elizabeth shuddered. One ought to feel these things—perhaps—but it was indecent to say them.

"Always sly," was Aunt Ruth's comment.

"She'd better marry him right off before she changes her mind *again*," said Aunt Addie.

"I suppose she won't wipe *his* kisses off," said Uncle Wallace.

Yet, on the whole, the clan were pleased. Much pleased. After all the anxieties over Emily's love-affairs, to see her "settled" so respectably with a "boy" well known to them, who had, so far as they knew at least, no bad habits and no disgraceful antecedents. And who was doing pretty well in the business of picture-painting. They would not exactly say so, but Old Kelly said it for them.

"Ah, now, that's something like," said Old Kelly approvingly.

## IV

Dean wrote a little while before the quiet bridal at New Moon. A fat letter with an enclosure—a deed to the Disappointed House and all it contained.

"I want you to take this, Star, as my wedding gift. That house must not be disappointed again. I want it to live at last. You and Teddy can make use of it as a summer home. And some day I will come to see you in it. I claim my old corner in your house of friendship now and then."

"How very—dear—of Dean. And I am so glad—he is not hurt any longer."

She was standing where To-morrow Road opened out on the Blair Water valley. Behind her she heard Teddy's eager footsteps coming to *her*. Before her on the dark hill, against the sunset, was the little beloved grey house that was to be disappointed no longer.

## About the Author

L. M. MONTOGOMERY's fascinating accounts of the lives and romances of Anne, Emily, and other well-loved characters have achieved long-lasting popularity the world over. Born in 1874 in Prince Edward Island, Canada, Lucy Maud showed an early flair for storytelling. She soon began to have her writing published in papers and magazines, and when she died in Toronto in 1942 she had written more than twenty novels and a large number of short stories. Most of her books are set in Prince Edward Island, which she loved very much and wrote of most beautifully. *Anne of Green Gables*, her most popular work, has been translated into thirty-six languages, made into a film twice, and has had continuing success as a stage play. Lucy Maud Montgomery's early home in Cavendish, P.E.I., where she is buried, is a much-visited historic site.

# TEENAGERS FACE LIFE AND LOVE

Choose books filled with fun and adventure, discovery and disenchantment, failure and conquest, triumph and tragedy, life and love.

| | | | |
|---|---|---|---|
| ☐ | 23370 | **EMILY'S QUEST OF THE NEW MOON** <br> Lucy Maud Montgomery | $2.95 |
| ☐ | 22605 | **NOTES FOR ANOTHER LIFE** <br> Sue Ellen Bridgers | $2.25 |
| ☐ | 22742 | **ON THE ROPES**   Otto Salassi | $1.95 |
| ☐ | 22512 | **SUMMER BEGINS**   Sandy Asher | $1.95 |
| ☐ | 22540 | **THE GIRL WHO WANTED A BOY** <br> Paul Zindel | $2.25 |
| ☐ | 20908 | **DADDY LONG LEGS**   Jean Webster | $1.95 |
| ☐ | 20910 | **IN OUR HOUSE SCOTT IS MY BROTHER** <br> C. S. Adler | $1.95 |
| ☐ | 23618 | **HIGH AND OUTSIDE**   Linnea A. Due | $2.25 |
| ☐ | 20868 | **HAUNTED**   Judith St. George | $1.95 |
| ☐ | 20646 | **THE LATE GREAT ME**   Sandra Scoppettone | $2.25 |
| ☐ | 23447 | **HOME BEFORE DARK**   Sue Ellen Bridgers | $1.95 |
| ☐ | 13671 | **ALL TOGETHER NOW**   Sue Ellen Bridgers | $1.95 |
| ☐ | 20871 | **THE GIRLS OF HUNTINGTON HOUSE** | $2.25 |
| ☐ | 23680 | **CHLORIS AND THE WEIRDOS**   Kin Platt | $2.25 |
| ☐ | 23004 | **GENTLEHANDS**   M. E. Kerr | $2.25 |
| ☐ | 20474 | **WHERE THE RED FERN GROWS** <br> Wilson Rawls | $2.50 |
| ☐ | 20170 | **CONFESSIONS OF A TEENAGE BABOON** <br> Paul Zindel | $2.25 |
| ☐ | 14687 | **SUMMER OF MY GERMAN SOLDIER** <br> Bette Greene | $2.25 |

**Prices and availability subject to change without notice.**

Buy them at your bookstore or use this handy coupon for ordering:

# Life, Love and Adventure from the Teenagers View

*Here are books of life, love, adventure, mystery, and suspense for every teenager's interest.*

| | | | |
|---|---|---|---|
| ☐ | 23562 | **THE FIRST OFFICIAL MONEY-MAKING BOOK FOR ALL AGES** Anita Malnig | $2.50 |
| ☐ | 23214 | **UNDER PLUM LAKE** Lionel Davidson | $2.25 |
| ☐ | 23350 | **SLIM DOWN CAMP** Stephen Manes | $2.25 |
| ☐ | 20909 | **TERM PAPER** A. Rinaldi | $2.25 |
| ☐ | 23080 | **INCREDIBLE JOURNEY** S. Burnford | $2.25 |
| ☐ | 23624 | **NEVER CRY WOLF** F. Mowat | $2.95 |
| ☐ | 20444 | **ROLL OF THUNDER HEAR MY CRY** M. Taylor | $2.25 |
| ☐ | 22790 | **SHANE** J. Schaefer | $2.25 |
| ☐ | 23736 | **WHEN THE LEGENDS DIE** H. Borland | $1.95 |
| ☐ | 20918 | **ALL IN GOOD TIME** Edward Ormondroyd | $1.95 |

**Prices and availability subject to change without notice.**